Seven For A Secret

(Never To Be Told)

By Clive Woodall

First Impression

Published by Ziji Publishing 2005

Ziji Publishing
60 Elgin Crescent, London W11 2JJ, England.
020 7727 6066

Distributed by Duckworth
First Floor, 90-93 Cowcross Street,
London EC1M 6BF
Tel: 020 7490 7300 Fax: 020 7490 0080
email: info@duckworth-publishers.co.uk

ISBN 0-7156-3394-5 (Adult)
ISBN 0-7156-3413-5 (Child)

F

1738069

Set in 11/16.5pt Italian Garamond
Printed and bound by CPD Ltd., Wales.

For my beautiful wife, Trish – my whole world.

Chapter One

'We are the sons and daughters of the dark.
We are the children of the night.
We call upon the ghosts of the fallen:
Resurrect yourselves. Rise up, and live again.
Lead us, Dark Lords. Show us your power.
Support us with your strength, that we may carry out your will.
For we are your sons and daughters of the dark.
Your children of the night.'

The chant filled each branch of Cra Wyd. It resonated through the treetops, and chilled the heart of every creature scurrying and scuttling in the blackness below. It could not be called a song. The voices were uniformly raucous and harsh. The caws and rasps held no music. No melody. Just passionate belief. The monotone was hypnotic, and each repetition increased its power.

No, it could not be called a song. Songs were for daylight. Sung in joy. In celebration. This chant was meant for the night. Sung by black throats, through black beaks. Black eyes blazed to its dark message. Black feathers ruffled in guilty pleasure, as black deeds from a time long past were brought back to life in the hearts and minds of the black choir. Evil deeds, best forgotten, best left alone, to rot along with their perpetrators. But tonight they were no longer forgotten corpses, pale skeletons, dry and dusty feathers. Tonight they were alive.

Cra Wyd was too insubstantial to be considered a forest. It was a copse of maybe a hundred trees. A deciduous wood was rare in this pine–covered region. Its nakedness gave clear indication of the season, as if the wind whistling through its bare branches weren't proof enough. March was coming in like a lion. Roaring and raving. Ripping at any presumptuous early shoots. Not yet, it said. Spring can wait a while. I hold sway for now.

And yet the trees had been partially clothed in the last few weeks. Nests adorned many of the bare boughs. Huge, untidy structures, made of twigs and debris. Here and there something silvery glinted in the pale sunshine: a discarded wrapping, ring pull or bottle cap. Treasure to be hoarded and admired. Loot from Man's dustbins and rubbish tips. Precious amid the drab brown. And tempting, too, to greedy eyes of neighbours, and passers by. Something to be fought for. A rookery was always a place for fights. Squabbles were constant, noise was incessant. And Cra Wyd was the largest of its kind in the whole of Birddom.

The recovery of the corvidae had been slow. Hunted and persecuted. Forced to hide. For years there had been little time for breeding. Individual survival was the prime objective. But Time moves on. The hunters grew weary of vigilance against an enemy without power. Dedication wavered, then broke, and evil began slowly, inexorably, to grow once more. It was a gradual process. Rebuilding something that is broken takes time. Even now it was but a pinprick; the bite of a flea compared to its former might.

But all over Birddom, not just in this harsh corner of its northern-most climes, the corvidae were on the rise. Harsh lessons had been learnt, and the watchword was secrecy. All was covert. All hidden. Midnight meetings. A most unnatural hour for birds, save for owls. Darkness was a cloak which covered and concealed. As yet, Birddom was unaware of its peril.

*

'I thought that we were going to see Tomar.' Olivia voiced her protest in the face of her brother's selfishness.

'I get bored visiting him, if the truth be told,' Merion replied.

The young female robin bridled at such a hurtful remark. 'But we owe him our lives,' she argued passionately, 'as does every bird in Birddom.'

'Then let them visit him!' Merion snapped petulantly. 'Oh, I'm sorry, sis. But you must know how I feel. I love that old owl as much as you do, but he tells the same stories over and over, and I know them by heart already.'

Olivia's eyes sparkled with anger. 'Those stories are our history. They define who we are. They are the tales of our father and our mother, never forget that.'

'But they are the past, and that is where Tomar lives. I for one am more concerned about the future.'

Merion's beak closed defiantly upon this pronouncement, and his sister realised the futility of further argument.

'Well, I'm going anyway, though I don't know what I shall say to Tomar. Shall I tell him that you are ill?'

'Tell him what you like. No, wait. Don't tell him that I'm ill, tell him that I'm busy.'

'I would never be so cruel,' Olivia said, sadly. 'He is the leader of the Council of the Owls, the highest in the land. And I will always be grateful that he was never too busy for us!'

'He might be the leader of the Council now. But for how much longer? His day is nearly done. He can barely flap his wings. He is fed and cared for like an invalid, and without this support he would have been dead two or three years ago. You know I speak the truth.'

Olivia's wingtips drooped with weary resignation, but she tried once more to reach her brother. 'Tomar is old, and his body may be failing. But his wisdom endures, and it is that wisdom that leads us still. On the right path and on the straight way.'

'Is he still right? Others, equally wise, are openly expressing their doubts. The bargain with the insects, for instance. Oh, it was a necessity at the time of the Great Battle. We needed their help to defeat the corvidae, and a treaty, agreeing that no bird would in future take any insect for food, was Tomar's only option. As Mother has told us often enough, we would not have won without their aid. But why do we need to adhere to it any longer?

'Enforcement causes great hardship and unrest, especially amongst the incomers. They do not understand the need of so unnatural an abstinence. And neither do I. Insects are prolific. The whole world seethes with them. They are on every leaf. Every rock. And yet we go hungry.' Merion paused to stare at his sister, daring her to contradict him. When he received only silence as a reply, he went on. 'Do we have their gratitude? Do we have their friendship? Don't they still infest our nests? Still sting and bite us? Still live upon our bodies, gorging on our very blood? I think that this is a hard price to pay for a pledge made in a time of dire need.'

'So you would go back on Tomar's word? Make nought of all that he believed in, and fought for?'

'For the sake of a juicy, wriggling caterpillar filling my belly, yes I would!'

Olivia looked shocked. 'Then you are not the brother that I have known and loved all these years.'

Merion flinched, then flicked his beak skywards in a gesture of dismissal. 'Times change. We all change with them. You go your way, sis, and I will go mine.'

'My way is with Tomar, and with Portia, our mother!' Olivia exclaimed, tears in her eyes.

'And my way is with the future,' was Merion's cold reply.

'Merion's words have some justice,' said Tomar, considering Olivia's story with typical stoicism. 'There have been consequences in our pact with the insects that I could and perhaps should have foreseen. Their sheer weight of numbers now that they are unchecked has been felt on a wider stage than our own. Man has become angry and that is never to be desired, because his anger is unfocused and reactionary. And Birddom has begun to feel its force.

'I never envisaged the impact that our deal with the insects could have upon his world. Man has no tolerance for infestation. He has an irrational fear of insects, wholly disproportionate to their size. And he reacts with unchecked violence. He seeks to protect himself with nets – vast structures raised in our flight-paths, as well as those of the insects. Many of our flock have died as a result, and that weighs heavily upon my heart. The spraying too is indiscriminate and lethal. Maybe Merion is right. I have unleashed a monster upon our people. Perhaps, in the name of good, I have in fact done great ill.'

'No, Tomar. I will not stand by and let it be said that you chose wrong.'

Portia's voice was strong and sure, and she stood wing-to-wing with her daughter, facing the old owl from a branch opposite his perch. Tomar smiled at the distant memory of another robin who had stood on that very same spot, and had argued just as vehemently in Tomar's moments of self-doubt. The old owl flapped his great wings, as if to shake off his growing sense of despondency.

'Thank you, my friend,' he replied. 'It was the only choice to be made. It was our one chance, and it gave us both victory and a lasting peace. But this is a different age. And Birddom's enemy has changed. Whilst the corvidae no longer pose a threat, nor probably ever will again, we face peril from a different quarter, and one that may spell our extinction as certainly as the magpies, had they been victorious.'

'Will the Council meet again soon?' Olivia asked.

'At dawn on the day following the next full moon,' Tomar replied, and there was a note of trepidation in his voice.

'Why does that worry you so?'

Portia's question was perceptive, and Tomar thought for a while, trying to coalesce his vague misgivings into something tangible. But it was like trying to make a nest out of mist.

'I don't know, my dear. It's just a feeling that is all. I can't explain it. But it's as if the Council is changing too. Moving forward in a direction that I am not sure that I can follow. Maybe I'm just too old. A relic of the past, as Merion says.'

'The day that you are too old is the day that Birddom is lost!' was Portia's grave reply.

Tomar's fears were fully justified. The Council of the Owls was changing. In the early years following the war with the magpies, and the arrival of the incomers, the Council had been a productive force for good, and had led Birddom in a prolonged period of peace and happiness. But, as Nature intends, the make-up of the Council had altered, as successive generations of owls had replaced fallen members. There was a much younger emphasis to the twelve now, with Tomar quite isolated in age and experience from the rest. He was still much revered, of course, and it was the care and support of those same Council members that kept him alive. But that reverence and love could not altogether mask a swell of dissatisfaction with the maintenance of the status quo in Birddom. Change is a natural process, and many of the owls desired change. Especially since Man's anger had been provoked, and Birddom had become a dangerous place once more.

The next meeting would be a crucial one, for that same danger had been brought home to the Council of the Owls itself by the death of one of its members. Quake, a tawny owl of middle years, had flown into a newly-erected net near his home, and the injury to his wing had left him easy prey to a family of hungry foxes. Sorrow was widespread at the news of Quake's passing, but Tomar felt it particularly keenly. Quake had been a staunch supporter, a traditionalist who had stood four-square with his Great Owl in the face of any opposition. His trust in Tomar had been complete, his loyalty undoubted. Now he was gone, and would be replaced. And therein lay Tomar's vague unquiet. There was really only one candidate for the vacant perch on the Council.

Engar was the obvious choice. A fine specimen of a barn owl, he was similar in many ways to Cerival, Tomar's mentor when he first joined the Council all those years ago. And Engar would bring a lot to the Council: fresh ideas, vociferously expressed, and a power that had seemed to be lacking of late. He would be a leader, not a follower.

Tomar was not worried about being usurped as Great Owl. Not for a while anyway. But he was not sure about Engar, and he simply couldn't put a feather on the reason why. There was something hidden, some essence of deception, but nothing that Tomar could grasp hold of. He would have to vote for Engar to join the Council. He could give no justification not to do so. But he didn't altogether trust him. Still, maybe it would be better to have Engar on the inside, where he could keep an eye on him. And maybe the younger owl would prove Tomar's doubts to be unjust. The old owl knew only that he would be happy with that outcome. But for now the unease persisted.

Engar was deep in thought, preening himself absent-mindedly under each wing, as he perched high in the oak. He sat facing inwards on one of a ring of trees made sacred in Birddom. Its lofty position dominated the countryside for miles around, and had made it the ideal initial site for the Council, when it had first met all those years ago. Engar's knowledge of the history of the Council of the Owls was sketchy at best. He had no interest in the past. Other owls could waste their time learning and passing on the ancient tales. They were irrelevant to a modern owl. They were stories of a different time, a different reality. His gaze swept across the ring, imagining, as he did so, owls on every perch, vying for their moment in the spotlight. All so much empty rhetoric and self-importance. He despised them. Tomar most of all.

Engar could barely think of the old owl who clung on so determinedly to the leadership of the Council without anger welling up inside of him. Tomar represented honour and justice, tradition and goodness. Engar spat, as if trying to clear an irritating feather from the back of his throat. Tomar had to go! That is why he had come here. To look around his enemy's domain. To view the lie of the land and prepare himself. Not out of respect or awe, but as a tactic. This would be a long war, and the first battles would be fought here. Battles of words and ideas. But first he had to be on the inside, chosen and accepted as one of them, but all the while working like slow poison. Killing from within, and causing the maximum amount of pain as it did so.

Merion was a bundle of nervous excitement as he sat waiting. So much so that he began to sing to himself to calm his nerves, chirruping away for several bars until he registered the tune and stopped himself. It was a song that Tomar had taught him, and he didn't want to think about the old owl.

'Better stop singing, then,' the robin said out loud, to the surrounding leaves and branches. And it was true. What could he sing that he hadn't learnt first-wing from the beak of the Great Owl? He owed Tomar everything. The owl had saved his life, and had devoted years of patience and understanding to Merion and his sister. But he was so old, and entrenched in the past. Engar had said that the future waits for no owl. Engar had a vision of a new Birddom, free of the strictures of tradition and law. A Birddom where one could do what one wanted to do, say what one wanted to say, eat...

Merion looked down guiltily at the glistening husk of the beetle on the branch between his feet. The black carapace and gossamer wings were all that remained of the insect. This was not the first time that the robin had betrayed his old friend. He had feasted on flesh for some months now. Engar had said that the law was meaningless and unenforceable. Who was to know, after all? And wasn't it a law against Nature?

The Council had been plain wrong to have enforced such a law, and Tomar had had no right to have made the bargain on behalf of Birddom in the first place. He hadn't even been Great Owl at the time, had he? Engar had said that birds should be free to eat whatever pleased them, not bound by antiquated rules handed down by an institution past its usefulness. Well, he would make some changes, he had promised. When he joined the Council he would see that they tore up the rule book, and made new laws that were relevant to the lives of a modern bird. When Engar was Great Owl, things would be different, and a new order would prevail. As the robin sat waiting for an audience with his idol, the irony of Engar's vision for the future was entirely lost to him.

*

The gathering was greater than ever before, and an air of expectancy hung over the rookery. Every branch was weighed down by black bodies, yet Cra Wyd was unnaturally silent. No squabbles broke out, even when more birds arrived to join the throng. Space was found, and they were accommodated. This was no time for petty rivalry or jealousy. It was too important a moment. And still the corvidae waited. For 'he' was coming. The stillness of the rookery was eerie and menacing. It was as if the whole place were holding its breath. Waiting.

And then, suddenly, he was among them, and crow and rook, magpie and jay gazed in awe and reverence. But not one dared draw nearer. He seemed almost surrounded by a force field of his own, a protective shield that repelled such intimacy.

The massed ranks of the corvidae simply sat and stared. And waited. The moment called for a fanfare of crowing and cawing, but instead he began to speak, quietly.

'I have lived for a very long time. Lived to see our rise as a power in the land. A rise that gave us the chance to puff out our chest feathers with pride. A rise that shook the whole of Birddom, and made us great. A nation to be feared. But I lived to see our fall also. A fall made inevitable by the weakness of our leader. Slyekin didn't want glory for the corvidae. He wanted it for himself. He cared nothing for your fathers, who fought to fulfil his mad schemes. He cared nothing for your fathers, who died honourably, protecting a flawed ideal. Slyekin thought that he was immortal. He was not. And now his bones rot in the ground, tainting the very soil that holds them, dishonouring those brethren who died for his sake.'

An angry hiss of exhalation greeted the slight pause. In that moment, he knew he had them. Not that there had been any doubt. The crowd were ravenous for what he had to offer. They would snatch it from his beak, like a hungry chick, and swallow it whole. It was the same everywhere that he went, across the length and breadth of Birddom.

He began again, 'Many deemed wise in Birddom think that I am dead. But, as you see...'

This time his speech was halted by a roar of approval, and the branches of the rookery shook with the noise of cheering birds. Traska waited until they had quietened before continuing, 'I am very much alive. As we are very much alive – a nation, a brethren who will rise again. But this time to glory. And ultimate victory!'

Chapter Two

Tomar sat on his perch in the ring of oaks and looked about him, sensing the mood of the Council. Engar had used his time well in the preceding weeks, and had obviously built up strong support amongst the younger members. It was as Tomar had predicted. The Council of the Owls was split: five owls for Engar, and five against.

Tradition decreed that the appointment of a new member needed a unanimous vote. But Engar's supporters spoke out vociferously about the need to change, to modernise the Council. They derided that tradition, and said that it had no place today. That the will of the majority should prevail. This was the message being reinforced by every speaker on Engar's side, and Tomar had no doubt that it originated from the barn owl himself. Engar had engineered the confrontation in order to force Tomar into a corner. As Great Owl, his was now the casting vote, if he chose to capitulate to this new idea of Council democracy. The aged leader of Birddom shook his head sorrowfully, then called for silence.

'My friends,' he said. 'Times have indeed changed. But then, when did they not? And, in that spirit, I too call for a change. A change in our procedures that I think will not be unwelcome to some here, to whom tradition means little. For tradition has always held that an electee to the Council has no voice until he or she is chosen. I ask you to agree to alter that edict here and now. I want to hear Engar speak to us. I want to know why he believes we should choose him to become a member of the Council of the Owls.'

No one demurred, and a hush descended over the clearing as they waited for Engar to speak. The barn owl took his time. He knew that he had to choose his words carefully. Tomar's change of tactic had surprised him. And so he sat still in the centre of the circle and composed himself. Then, aware that all around him feathers were being ruffled with expectancy and impatience, he began.

'I thank the Great Owl for giving me this unique opportunity to speak to the Council. I deem it a great honour that you should want to hear my words.'

His eyes at this point traversed the treetops, receiving several approving nods from his supporters. He could not, however, meet Tomar's eye, and instead looked down at his claws, cleared his throat and continued.

'I have nothing but admiration for the work of the Council in the past. Its mighty deeds are legendary throughout Birddom, and all of its members, past and present, are duly revered. Indeed, without this Council, there would be no Birddom, only the utter blackness conceived by Slyekin. Without the Council, the world would have been lost to us. But we prevailed. We defeated the enemy and ensured a future for the land. And it is to that future that I look today. Not to the past. A future where all birds are equal, and power is devolved to all. Do not think that I seek to undermine the Council. I do not. I want only to make it more democratic, less aloof from the common bird. I have so many ideas. So many radical proposals that I believe will serve Birddom well, and give it a brighter future. If I am chosen. If I am given the chance to serve.'

The challenge to Tomar was unmistakable. A gauntlet had been thrown down. And all eyes looked towards the Great Owl as he considered his reply.

'I seem to be in a unique position in this new, would-be democracy of ours. I now seem to have a power allowed to none of my predecessors for I see that the power of decision-making for the Council is with me alone. And, while I decide, I ask you all to reflect for a moment whether this outcome is what you truly desire. Whether this change will benefit Birddom, or weaken it.'

The old owl paused. He preened his wing-feathers for a few seconds before looking up, and fixing Engar with his calm gaze.

'Engar has spoken with passion and enthusiasm for his new way. And maybe he is right. Maybe the Council is outdated and irrelevant, although it has served Birddom well for generations. Maybe its absolute authority for creating the laws of the land is undemocratic, although its decisions in the past have been for the good of every bird. What I do know is that Birddom is at peace and that, faced with no common enemy to unite us, we are in danger of confrontation and conflict amongst ourselves. This will damage the Council and Birddom. So I propose that Engar join as a member of the Council of the Owls. I cast my vote on his behalf.'

The spring-tight tension that had built in the clearing evaporated in an instant, and relief showed in many faces around the ring. Engar's own face wore a look of enormous satisfaction. He took off from his lowly position in the centre of the ring, and took his place on the vacant oak, ready to address the Council. But, as he opened his beak to speak, Tomar forestalled him.

'Welcome, Engar,' said the Great Owl. 'Welcome to the Council of the Owls. May you serve Birddom well.'

'That weak, decrepit old fool. You should have seen how he caved in when faced with the inevitable. They wanted me. They all wanted me!'

Engar strutted before his guest, eager for further approbation.

'Don't underestimate Tomar,' came the dry reply. 'That owl has more about him than you'll ever understand, may he rot. And I don't like this meek acceptance. I don't like it at all. You can be sure that Tomar's got something under his wing.'

'Rubbish!' exclaimed Engar. 'He's past it, that's all. He's finished. Washed up. I'm the power on the Council now. It won't be long before they make me Great Owl.'

'So far as I understand it, you've barely been allowed to open your beak yet, my impatient friend. So let's take it one step at a time, shall we? We must stick to our plan. I don't want you to do anything to alienate Tomar for now. Play your part. Suggest changes, but not too many. Be circumspect, Engar. Your day will come.'

Owl and magpie looked at each other, as if sealing some pact. The body of a greenfinch lay between them, and they took turns in feeding.

'Engar, where are you? Can I come and see you?' The high-pitched, sweet voice of the young robin carried clearly on the air.

Traska looked up regretfully from his bloody meal. 'Merion mustn't see me here. I ought to hide. Mind me well, Engar, and do as I say. You will be the Great Owl, but only when I decide that the time is right. Now answer that young robin. I am sure that he is eager to hear your news.'

And, with that, the ancient magpie hopped away into the undergrowth, calling softly as he disappeared, 'Toss that finch in here. I might as well eat while I listen. Oh, what a delicious irony, that Kirrick's offspring is now on the side of darkness!'

Merion flew into view scant seconds after Traska had hidden himself. Engar spotted the robin, and hooted a greeting.

'Ah, there you are. Welcome, Merion, my young friend. Come

down. Come down and join me.'

The robin flitted down through the tree until he reached a branch facing the barn owl. 'Engar,' he cheeped expectantly. 'What news from the Council?'

'Oh, everything went much as I expected,' replied Engar.

Merion clapped his wings in delight. 'So they voted for you? You're a member of the Council of the Owls now?'

'Did you ever doubt it?' Engar asked pointedly.

The robin stammered an immediate apology. 'I'm sorry, Engar. I didn't mean any disrespect. I always knew that you would win a place on the Council. Birddom needs your new way of thinking. You will be a great success.'

Engar smiled, as if the flattery was his due, and puffed out his chest feathers, savouring the moment. 'My personal success means nothing to me. I am only glad that I will be able to serve Birddom. I really believe that I can make a difference. The Council was tired, and going nowhere. But now that I have won a majority we can make some real changes. Oh, I know that it will take time. But I'm in no hurry. I respect the traditions of the Council, and I admire the old guard for what they have done in the past, Tomar especially.'

'I'm glad to hear it,' Merion said. 'For that old owl means a lot to me, even though I get exasperated by his old-fashioned values.'

'He means a lot to all of us,' Engar lied, and Traska, well hidden, fought to suppress a chuckle at the barn owl's blatant mendacity.

'Mother, why are you so troubled?'

'I am afraid, Olivia my dear. I had thought that we had put the darkness behind us when we defeated the magpies. But evil arose once more when Traska returned and kidnapped Merion and yourself. Then

Traska was vanquished, and the light returned to Birddom. But now I fear that a shadow is again among us. I can't see where the threat is coming from, although I agree with Tomar. I do not trust that owl, Engar. Don't ask me to explain why. I'm not sure that I could. But he seems false, albeit that he is a fine specimen of a bird.'

'A fair face hiding a foul heart?' Olivia replied.

Portia nodded. 'Yes, he may have the body of an owl. But I fear that he has the heart of a magpie!'

'I know, Mother. I've tried to explain that to Merion, but he simply won't listen. He is besotted with Engar's ideas. His visions about the new Birddom. I am so frightened that we may have lost him for good.' Olivia's eyes filled with tears at the thought of a world without her brother's strength and friendship.

'Now don't distress yourself so,' Portia said, consolingly. 'I know my son. He is a good robin, like his father. He is eager to learn. He wants to change the world. That is understandable. But above all he knows the difference between wrong and right. Have faith in your brother, Olivia. He will never betray us. In the end he will realise the truth about Engar. But he won't accept it from us. So, for now, we must keep our own counsel, and trust that Kirrick's blood will win through. Then you will get your brother back. And I will have my son.'

Tomar brooded for several days following the Council of the Owls' portentous meeting. He had returned immediately to Tanglewood, and had scarcely strayed more than a few wing-flaps from his nest since then. The food-store provided by his young helpers had hardly been touched. Tomar was thinking. And his thoughts were sombre. He had never felt so alone. Nor so isolated. His physical infirmity was extremely irksome to him. He was a prisoner of his own body. How he longed to see friendly faces. To seek wise counsel from those that he could trust. But Storne, Darreal and Kraken, his triumvirate of staunch allies in the Great Battle, were too far away. If only he could talk to them. Explain his fears about Engar. Seek their advice.

For Tomar was extremely worried. Not for himself. But for the very future of Birddom. A Birddom led by what? A council? A single owl? Every bird? And facing what? War with the insects? That prospect was too terrible to imagine. But it could be the consequence of any relaxation of the strictures that he, Tomar, had imposed upon his flock. The insects would inevitably see it as a betrayal. What else would they do? Accept being eaten? No. The old owl knew all too well that they would react angrily to being made a food-source once again. And the enormity of their numbers churned the fear in Tomar's stomach. Nothing could withstand the backlash of their rage. The depredations of the corvidae would seem like pin-pricks in comparison. Birddom would be utterly obliterated.

Tomar let his mind drift back to those times of hope – oh, how long ago they now seemed – when the sun was blotted out by the hordes of small birds fleeing danger in Wingland, and bringing the promise of a continuing future for Birddom. Once the initial joy had passed, Tomar had faced the huge task of reinforcing his pact with the insects amongst the incomers. It was not the welcome that they had expected, and certainly not the idyll that they had been promised by Portia, when she had attempted, without success, to lure them away from their homeland. Only the enormity of the danger from which they had fled prevented any incomer from turning tail and flying back whence they came.

To some it meant a major change of lifestyle, adapting to a totally new diet. For specialised feeders, such as the flycatchers and the wagtails, it was a hard time, and they would not have survived without the help and encouragement of other, more omnivorous species, who showed and shared their food-sources with their beleaguered cousins. During this time of transition, it was Tomar's will alone that kept the pact from breaking. The unique regard in which he was held by the whole of Birddom, and the fact that huge and powerful birds, such as eagles and falcons, were also deferring to the Council's pronouncements, meant that it was grudgingly accepted by the foreigners that Tomar's word was law.

Of course, in the intervening years, that law had been broken. But these were invariably isolated cases, which, when discovered, were dealt with amongst the incomers themselves, without recourse to the judgement and mercy of the Council of the Owls. And this internal rule of law proved harsh but effective. Summary execution was the norm for any bird found transgressing for the sake of live food in its belly. Tomar regretted the severity of the punishment meted out, but knew better than to interfere. His pact was being upheld, and Birddom was a safer place because of it.

Chapter Three

A mild Spring gave way to a sweltering June, which caused a proliferation of insect life never before witnessed in Birddom. Mayflies were in abundance, yellow jackets buzzed everywhere, hornets droned, and house flies invaded every human home in numbers that could not be tolerated.

Man reacted with savagery to this escalation. Insects had been a worrying nuisance, dealt with in limited fashion. Now they were the enemy, and Man had a huge arsenal at his fingertips. Indeed, in a war in which he was outnumbered by billions, Man was fortunate that he was the only active aggressor. For, as Tomar had envisaged in his own worst nightmares, nothing could have withstood a co-ordinated attack by such a multitude as could have been mustered by even a single species of insect. But, as it was, Man waged war on a one-to-one basis, and each individual insect was defenceless against his range of weaponry. Nets proliferated, until no part of Birddom, within a two mile radius of any human conurbation, was unprotected. They totally enclosed towns and villages, hamlets and farmland, but the fine mesh required to keep the insect nation at bay meant that Man began to live in a permanent twilight. That same mesh had detrimental consequences as well. For it prevented the natural interaction between insect and crops. Natural pollination was impossible, and the expense incurred in artificially reproducing this activity meant that food prices soared.

The netting had serious consequences for birds across the length and breadth of Birddom as well. Apart from the danger of becoming entangled in the fine mesh, birds everywhere were denied yet another food source, as seed, grain and fruit were protected and thus prohibited. Man was, however, not content merely to stay inside his nets. Spraying became a commonplace activity, with a vast fleet of small aircraft hurriedly constructed for the purpose. From dawn until dusk, insecticide rained down upon the land, in such concentrations that thousands of birds were inadvertently made victims. Man did not desire this, but neither did he care overmuch. His was a single-minded war, and if there were unplanned casualties, so be it.

Then Man unleashed another terror into Birddom. For his paranoia was such that he chose to blame his domesticated animals, pets and livestock, for the rise in the number of insects infesting his world. The livestock, vital as a food source, were dipped and treated. Pets were simply thrown out to fend for themselves in the wild. So now Birddom faced the additional threat of thousands of canine and feline predators, made desperate by the abrupt termination of their erstwhile cosy existence, roaming the land, intent on survival.

Birddom pulled together in the face of these awesome threats. Food was rationed and shared scrupulously among the population. Wild berries became a luxury, taken only sparingly, and many birds were forced to supplement their diet with grasses and weeds. The population shifted, too. Under attack mainly in open areas, and especially around stretches of water, where spraying was at its most intense, birds were forced to uproot, and relocate to strange habitats. In a matter of weeks, woodlands overflowed with exotic species, such as reed warblers, grey and yellow wagtails, and even kingfishers. Again and again it was only the strength of community that saved individuals and whole species from extermination. Natural evolution was replaced by the more immediate adage, "Adapt or die!" The woodlands offered the best protection from overhead spraying, and the best hiding places from the threat of predators. In these dark days, not only birds of a feather flocked together!

Kopa was a chaffinch of unusual intelligence. His species were generally viewed as chatterers. They were gregarious, certainly, and often gathered in large flocks for a good gossip. But Kopa was a bit of a loner and a thinker, too. An incomer from Wingland, he had quickly adapted to his new home, and had made great efforts to learn the language of Birddom, not only his own, but the dialectic variations peculiar to the brambling and his near-cousin, the siskin. For Kopa had travelled much since coming to Birddom. And had learnt much, too. Things that troubled him, and made him fearful.

It was from Kopa that Tomar first heard of the rumours about the corvids. Initially, the Great Owl dismissed them from his mind. He had other, more pressing business. Man was the enemy now. The corvids were a thing of the past. The spectre of black and white paled into insignificance compared to Man's all-encompassing fury. But there was a tiny place in Tomar's heart which quailed a little at the news that the magpies might return to challenge for supremacy in Birddom.

'I'm too old,' he told himself. 'I have no strength left for *that* fight, on top of everything that threatens us now. Dear Creator, let it only be a rumour.'

But Kopa would not let it rest at that. He had been disappointed by Tomar's response. The ancient owl was revered throughout the land as the wisest bird in Birddom, but Kopa thought sadly that he could detect the effects of age on that great mind. In fact, Tomar had taken his warning very seriously, but Kopa had the impatience of youth, and mistook Tomar's external calmness for indifference. So the young chaffinch decided that he would collect more evidence about the activities of the corvidae, so that next time he would not be ignored.

But where to begin? He could scarcely go gallivanting across the land in the present threatening climate. Traversing open stretches of land could prove swiftly fatal. However, Kopa could not just sit on his tail and do nothing. He decided to follow the only safe route. Along the spine of Birddom ran an almost unbroken covering of woodland, from south to north. He would take that direction and visit his northern cousins, using their nests as a base from which to explore that inhospitable part of Birddom. Tiny though he was by comparison, he would become the hunter, with the corvidae as his prey. He would verify the threat that they once again posed, and would return to Tomar, armed with knowledge to which the old owl would have to listen.

In earlier and even darker times, Kirrick had followed a similar path north, in one of his three epic flights. On that occasion he had been doing Tomar's bidding, seeking aid from the eagles. The old owl was in ignorance of Kopa's own journey, but he would surely have approved. The chaffinch himself had heard of Kirrick's exploits, of course. The robin remained one of Birddom's greatest heroes. And so it was that, proud to be replicating one of Kirrick's heroic journeys, Kopa flew north.

With single-minded strength and unity of purpose, the Council of the Owls had striven mightily over the last few months to control and minimise the damage inflicted upon Birddom by Man's backlash against the insects. Engar had forced himself very much to the fore in this. He had a flair for organisation, and was already seen as very much an owl of action. His self-confidence deceived many of his fellow Council members into believing that, in the face of this current crisis, Engar was the bird who was really in charge. He played his cards very cleverly, his own words during discussions often reflecting the generally-accepted wisdom of the moment. He was particularly adept at rewording Tomar's ideas as his own, embellishing them with promises of valour and success, which were improbable at best, under the circumstances. But it was what the other owls wanted to hear, bravado in the face of an insurmountable enemy. And Tomar had to concede that Engar's strategy was effective. He had galvanised Birddom into an effective machine for survival and self-preservation. Under his direction, every bird looked out for the needs of his neighbour, making personal sacrifices for the good of all. It was egalitarian and utopian, exactly as Engar had preached when he was trying to gain admittance to the Council. And it worked. But still Tomar held on to the mistrust that he felt towards the barn owl.

His misgivings were given fresh substance when Engar spoke out against him at the next Council meeting.

'I am tired of listening to an owl whose time has clearly been and gone,' the barn owl cried. 'Tomar has been a great servant of this Council for many years, but recent events have shown that there is a need for someone younger and stronger to bear the weight of the burdens of leadership. I issue a challenge to Tomar's right to continue as Great Owl and leader of this Council. And I will tell you why.

'Birddom has never been a more dangerous place in which to make a nest. For what does the future hold for our young? A choice – and what a choice! – of being torn apart by a roving pack of savage animals, or dying a slower, but equally excruciating death from an invisible and deadly enemy from above. And for those who survive? Food is scarcer than ever before, and every bird huddles hungry and dispirited in his home, often too weak to venture out and forage for what little there is.

But there *is* food! In abundance, and there for the taking. We cannot challenge Man. But we can help him. By doing what comes naturally. By doing what birds are supposed to do: eat insects!

'If we can lessen their vast numbers we can guarantee our own survival. For not only will we have access to a food source that has for so long been stupidly denied to us, but also Man will surely scale down his atrocities against us, once the insect population is reduced to a more natural level. We can all benefit, by changing one simple law. It was necessary once, but now it is outdated and threatens our very survival. This is why I am challenging Tomar. Because he made the deal with the insects that means that our young now go hungry. If Tomar is allowed to remain as Great Owl – if we persist in this foolhardy pact – then Birddom dies!'

Pandemonium reigned for several minutes, as every voice was raised at the same time. All of the owls were eager to voice their opinions. Most wanted to be heard supporting Engar. They could feel his power growing, and wanted to be a part of his rise to glory. One or two owls spoke out in support of Tomar, concerned that events might swiftly spiral out of control without the Great Owl's ability to rationalise and reflect calmly on any issue. Only a solitary owl remained silent throughout the uproar. Tomar blinked unhappily at the sight before him. Owls at each others' throats, verbally if not physically. What good were they, as leaders of the land, if they wasted their efforts squabbling and fighting amongst themselves? Tomar despaired for the future of the Council.

It was left to Engar to bring order back to the proceedings. In a loud, clear voice he called for silence, and was rewarded by a gradual reduction of the hubbub.

'Thank you, my friends. I see that there is still a passion within the

Council. A passion to do the right thing for the whole of Birddom. But we need to decide. Right here and now. Vacillation is for the weak. And the Council needs to be strong today. Strong enough to overcome sentiment. Strong enough to make the difficult choices. But they are the right choices, my friends. The ones that need to be made. Let us vote now.'

'I think that it is still my privilege to lead the Council of the Owls,' Tomar interjected firmly. 'And my privilege also to call for any vote. I shall do so. But first I should like to counsel this gathering, maybe for the last time, against a hasty decision that might bring long years of regret. Engar believes that Man will be influenced by our actions if we break our sacred pact with the insects, and take them once more for food. He will not. Man does not think about us at all. His hatred, overwhelming as it is, is directed elsewhere. He will seek nothing less than the total eradication of all insect life, irrespective of the catastrophe that will befall his world as a result.

'How many insects can we eat? Even if we gorge our bellies daily for a hundred years, we can only make a pinprick in their vast numbers. Their multitudinousness is their great strength, and our great peril. For, if we break our pact, they will turn against us. Then we will face two terrible enemies: Man and insects. And then Birddom will indeed die!'

'The insects will not attack us. Have they attacked Man, in the face of his murderous actions against them?'

'They have no pact with Man,' replied Tomar, simply. 'They do not trust Man. But they trust us, and I for one am loath to break that trust.'

Three or four owls murmured an uneasy agreement with Tomar's point of view, but were swiftly silenced in the face of Engar's glare.

'You said that you would call for a vote. Do so now, old bird!'

Eleven pairs of huge eyes fixed upon Tomar's face. The old tawny owl gave an almost imperceptible shrug, and then began the formal process of decision-making by vote – the age-old method by which the Council of the Owls held sway as rulers and law-makers in Birddom. He called for each owl to take his or her place in the Council ring. But before he could proceed any further, Engar interrupted him once more.

'We must vote on the Great Owl's position first,' he shouted across the clearing.

'It is against precedent. The usual process is to deal with the order of business, ahead of personal vendettas.'

'What could be more important to the business of this Council than its faith in its own leader? How can any other business be conducted by someone in whom the majority has no confidence?'

Tomar felt a tiny thrill of hope spark within his chest. Engar might just be over-reaching, in his desire for absolute power.

'So be it,' he answered stoically. 'Let the first vote be taken. The choice before the Council is a simple one. Do I, your Great Owl, retain your confidence as an owl capable of leading this Council, and Birddom as a whole? Or do you wish to choose another? I will ask each of you in turn, beak to beak and eye to eye, as is our tradition. And I will not hold it against any owl here if he votes against me with a clear conscience.'

Tomar flew down to the ground in the centre of the clearing, and spoke with authority, for all to hear.

'I do not feel that it is yet time for me to relinquish my position as Great Owl. I believe that I can still be of service to this land of ours. As such, and as is my right, I cast my vote in my own favour. So now it is up to you. Remember the rules of our Council in such circumstances. We have always abided by the rule of eleven against one when voting to change a leader. Remember also that the time for speeches and grand-standing are over. I call first upon Engar.'

The barn owl's face was a mask of fury as he flapped down and alighted, facing his adversary.

'Engar. Newest of our Council. How do you vote?'

'I vote to replace Tomar as our Great Owl with someone younger and more able to lead Birddom into the future.'

It was as Tomar had hoped. Engar had taken the bait. He simply hadn't been able to resist sniping at his opponent, when face-to-face. Tomar cut him short, reminding him that the election of a successor was a separate issue, and not one usually undertaken before the whole Council had decided upon the incumbent's removal. Engar was forced to swallow the rebuke in silence. He returned swiftly to his place in the circle.

Tomar called upon Creer next, and the long-eared owl dutifully left his perch and joined Tomar in the centre of the ring. Next to Engar, Creer was the most recent addition to the Council, and Tomar had little doubt as to where his loyalties lay. He had been among the most vociferous in support of Engar.

Creer looked around the circle slowly, and announced clearly to his audience of peers, 'I too vote to replace Tomar as Great Owl!'

'Thank you,' the old owl muttered, too quietly for the rest of the gathering to hear, and Creer looked suitably abashed in the face of such dignity.

Pellar followed, then Steele and Cerca. They all voted against the Great Owl. The flame of hope inside Tomar's frail frame flickered with each body blow to his pride. And so it went on. Meldra came next, unable to look Tomar in the eye. She had served on the Council for all but one of the post-war years, having been chosen as replacement for Caitlin, who had chosen retirement and the quiet life, once law and order had been fully restored and Birddom, with its influx of new life, was whole once more. She, more than any other owl there, had seen

Tomar at work, striving with all of his might for the good of Birddom.

'I am sorry, Tomar,' she muttered, shame-facedly, and then said, more clearly,

'I cast my vote against the Great Owl.'

The next two owls, Wensus and Janvar, barn owls both, voted with their own kind.

Engar looked triumphant, sure now that Tomar stood alone. 'Eight against one!' he said in his head, over and over again. 'Tomar is finished, and I will be Great Owl!'

'I call upon Lostri,' Tomar intoned, matter-of-factly, trying not to betray his interior turmoil. His stomach churned with nerves, and he felt sick. But he lifted his eyes to meet those of his friend, as the only other tawny owl on the Council landed on the springy grass in front of him.

Unlike so many of the others, Lostri met Tomar's gaze with an even appraisal of his own. He essayed a sketch of a smile, but his words, when they came, dashed the last of Tomar's hopes.

'I greet you, Tomar. I love you, my dear friend. But I believe that Engar's way is the right one. The Council is more important than any individual. I vote against you as Great Owl.'

Tomar matched Lostri's brief smile with one of his own. 'You have not voted with your heart, my friend, but with your mind. And I respect your decision.'

Lostri lingered for a moment, on the point of embracing the old, defeated owl who still stood so resolute in the face of such indignity. Then he too turned from Tomar, and flapped away back to his branch. Engar could not resist clapping his wing-tips together in delight.

'Nine against one. Nine against one!' he repeated silently.

Only two owls, Faron and Calipha, remained to save Tomar from ignominious defeat, and Birddom from catastrophe. But the old owl now held out little hope. He had pinned his faith on Lostri, of all the Council members. But he could not blame his friend. Alone among the owls, Lostri had weighed the pros and cons of the argument rationally, and had made his choice in what he believed were the best interests of Birddom. The best that Tomar could now hope for was that one of the two remaining owls would do the same, but do so in his favour.

Chapter Four

Kopa was taking a considerable risk travelling alone over such a long distance. But he felt driven by the need to prove himself, and his own kind, worthy of a place in Birddom. As an incomer, he was keenly aware that, although their influx had been been desirable in helping to repopulate the land, they owed a debt of gratitude to Tomar and the Council of the Owls. Kopa was eager to repay at least part of that debt, by helping to ensure the future of the land that he had grown to love as his own. Birddom was a beautiful place, and the little chaffinch knew that he would even give his life in its service, if need be.

Kopa travelled cautiously and, of necessity, slowly. He could not risk long periods of open flight, which would have hastened his journey considerably. The skies were not safe, thanks to Man's blazing anger. The cover provided by the tree-tops offered the chaffinch adequate protection from the deadly 'rain' of insecticide. But he had little chance to stretch his wings, flitting from tree to tree, and branch to branch. These constant short bursts of flight were exhausting, and used up a great deal of the little bird's energy. As he travelled north, Kopa took what meals he could, mindful all the while of the food shortages everywhere. He also took shelter, and gathered news, from all manner of small birds along the route.

It was fortunate that the young chaffinch was skilled in language, as he shared nests and perches with wren and blue tit, linnet and nuthatch, as well as every variety of finch. It was as well also that Kopa was a skilled interrogator. For he was able to gain information about the pockets of corvidae scattered across the land, without attracting too much attention, or raising too many fears. He would often spend the best part of a day chatting amiably to a willing, friendly goldfinch, hearing his and his entire family's whole life story, but, at the same time, picking up a nugget or two of precious news about goings-on at the local rookery. Few birds now lived in fear of the corvids, although everyone was cautious, and avoided them as much as they could. But, as outcasts, they inevitably attracted attention and curiosity, especially as time lessened the memory of their atrocities.

Kopa learnt that the rooks and crows were becoming more organised, coming together as large resident groupings, where before they had been utterly scattered in the aftermath of the Great Battle, living isolated and in hiding. Now they formed large social groups, their numbers increasing at a rapid rate since the winter.

More worryingly, they would hold gatherings, when several rookeries would meet and talk long into the night. Few small birds had the courage to eavesdrop on such large and threatening flocks of their erstwhile enemies. So most of what Kopa was told was based upon speculation and rumour. But it disturbed him greatly nonetheless. He heard stories of raucous celebrations, with dark recitations of evil deeds, glorying once again in former acts of violence and mayhem. It seemed to Kopa, as he travelled and learnt more, that there was an emerging pattern to what he was being told. Everywhere he went, and doubtless all across the length and breadth of Birddom, if stories were to be believed, the corvidae were on the rise. Growing stronger. And more dangerous.

Engar had never seen Traska so angry, and he quailed before the wrath of his mentor.

'You fool! Your arrogance has been your undoing. I told you to wait. I told you that the time wasn't right for you to challenge Tomar. But would you listen? Oh no, you knew better, didn't you? You've put our cause back by months, you idiot!'

Engar bridled at the scorn in Traska's words. 'But we won, Traska. Tomar is finished.'

'Oh, finished is he? Tell me, Engar. Who is Great Owl and leader of the Council?'

'It's just a matter of time,' Engar replied, defensively. 'He was only saved by a single vote. The entire Council are with me, not him. He is crippled and powerless now.'

'Your head for counting is a little suspect. The entire Council was not with you, Engar. You lost the vote. A vote it was crucial that we won.'

'It was only one owl. One stupid owl. Calipha can be persuaded to see the error of her ways. She will vote with us next time.'

'Next time. Next time,' Traska repeated, mocking his protégé. 'You've given Tomar breathing space. And, more dangerously, thinking space. The next Council meeting won't be held any time soon, you can be sure of that. Tomar will spend his time trying to shore up his power base. He still has friends and admirers on the Council, and don't you forget it. No. We will have to force his wing, and much earlier than I had intended, thanks to your vanity.'

'How will we do that?' Engar asked, in a hurt voice.

'We will have to encourage disobedience of his damn-fool law. But it'll need to be carefully planned. We will need widespread support. Not that I foresee any problems, a hungry bird is a susceptible bird. And every bird in Birddom is hungry. But now you must listen to me once more, and do exactly as I say. You must curb your self-importance, and sublimate your own desire for power to the greater cause. Do you understand?'

'Of course. I will do whatever you say.'

'Good. Finally I seem to have got through to you. The first thing that we will need to do is to enlist support. I think, my friend, that it is high-time that your little friend Merion proved his loyalty.'

Tomar had not felt so weary since the aftermath of the Great Battle, long years ago now. It was as if he had taken a physical beating, and was bruised and bloodied by the encounter. He had been so close to losing everything. Had it not been for Calipha, bless her tail-feathers, Engar would have wrested control of the Council from him, and all that he had worked so tirelessly to achieve would have been for nothing. Tomar's head sank wearily onto his chest at the thought, and he pecked listlessly at his feathers. Could he survive again? No, he couldn't bear even to think about it at the moment. There would be time enough to worry. One owl's vote had bought that precious time, and Tomar knew that he would have to use it well. But all he wanted to do right now was sleep.

'Give yourself time. You're not as young as you were, and that's the truth!' he told himself. Time was marching on, setting a pace that he found hard to match. Come to think of it, he couldn't remember being anything but old! But there had been a time...

Tomar's huge eyes closed as sleep took hold, and he dreamed about the distant days of his youth. Cerival appeared to him. But a Cerival of agile wings and firm, young talons. Other owls were there, too, and Tomar felt the warm glow of their attention.

Cerival was speaking, welcoming his friend. 'This is a time for which I have waited with some impatience, my friends. For I am sure everyone here will agree that Tomar is a valuable addition who will strengthen the Council of the Owls, not least with his prodigious mind. So, welcome, Tomar. Welcome, my friend. Take your rightful place among us, and may you serve Birddom faithfully and with distinction.'

And then all the members of the Council thronged around him, clapping him on the back with their wings. Tomar ruffled his primaries with pride. Then the scene changed, and he was surrounded, not by friends but by a band of savage, pecking magpies and crows. Caitlin was with him, and they were being herded inexorably towards the lair of his mortal enemy, Slyekin. Tomar was afraid, but was determined not to let his captors see such weakness. However they might abuse him he would not reveal his secret. Let them torture him. He would rather put his own talon into his eye and rip it from its socket than betray the one bird who could still redeem Birddom.

'Kirrick. Kirrick!' he called out in his sleep. 'Save me. Save us all.'

Then the horizon turned red as far as the eye could see, and a call so sweet and melodious shook the very skies with its precious notes. And Kirrick was among them, glowing sun-bright, and larger, more substantial and real than any other bird had ever been. And he scattered his enemies. Smote them down to left and right. None could stand before his righteous fury. The magpies were vanquished from the skies, and dark clouds rolled back to reveal a glorious dawn.

Then Tomar woke, and knew that there was always hope.

Merion was troubled at what he was being asked to do. Although, until now, he had offered unquestioning support to Engar, he felt guilty for betraying Tomar's trust in him. He had broken Tomar's law. Defied the edict against taking an insect for food. And the venal pleasure had been tempered by the knowledge of his wrong-doing. But he had consoled himself with the thought that what he did – his small act of defiance and subversion – was of little consequence in the overall scheme. No one would know. Especially now that the insect population was being devastated by Man. He could keep his little pleasures to himself, and no one would be any the wiser.

But now Engar was asking for open defiance. Public support for actions against the law of the Council. Merion knew that it was hypocritical of him to differentiate. Wrong was wrong. And he was guilty. But Engar wanted him to promote the wrong-doing, to enlist his friends and neighbours in a revolt against the will of the Great Owl. Tomar would never forgive him. And his mother and sister would surely never speak to him again.

Engar interrupted his troubled thoughts. 'Are you with me, Merion? Or has it all just been a lot of talk? Do you have the courage of your convictions? Birddom is starving! Birds sit dying while food parades before their eyes and beaks. It is time to decide. Whose side are you on? You can't perch on the fence any longer. Are you for me or against me?'

The imposing frame of the barn owl towered over Merion, and the young robin shrank back, cowering as he replied, 'I am for you, Engar. Whatever you ask of me.'

Merion worked tirelessly amongst the incomers. At first he met with considerable resistance to his ideas, but a few months of severe hunger had eroded their support for the laws imposed by the Council of the Owls. After all, as Merion reminded them remorselessly, they were acting against their own natures. Birds were meant to eat insects as part of their natural diet. Nobody could deny that. Gradually the consensus of opinion altered, until many birds agreed that the young robin was talking a good deal of sense.

A significant ground-swell spread the message, and soon it was the talk of Birddom. Argument raged back and forth. Support for the Council held firm, until Engar played his second card. For, once Merion had laid the groundwork, he sent forth his most vocal cohorts on the Council itself, to speak in affirmation of every bird's right to choose for him or herself what to eat. Engar weighed in, at the appropriate moment, touring Birddom, and speaking to crowds made up of every species of small bird. He voiced his opinion, loud and long, that birds had the right to eat insects. That birds had the right to a full belly. That moralising words of ageing fools wouldn't feed their hungry children.

It was powerful and popular stuff, and birds across the land swallowed it whole, especially when reminded of Merion's antecedents. This was the son of Kirrick – hero of all Birddom. Merion was speaking to them, advocating a change in the law. Surely they could see that this fine young robin would do nothing to bring dishonour to his father's memory. It was Tomar who was tarnishing everything that Kirrick had fought and died for. By perpetuating the myth that an agreement made in a time of peril still remained valid in the modern era. Birddom had moved on, and Tomar's strictures imperilled them all. If the Great Owl had his way, the next hero of Birddom might die of hunger, and never fulfil his destiny of saving this great and beautiful land.

Engar's speeches were compelling, and, throughout Birddom, there were sporadic instances of birds taking the law into their own wings, and breaking Tomar's pact with the insects. But still they were isolated cases, and far too few for Engar's liking. Much stronger, however, was the voice raised in favour of a reversal of the law by the Council itself, which would release every bird from his moral duty, and enable him or her to eat with a clear conscience. Birds everywhere clamoured for the Council of the Owls to reconvene at the earliest opportunity.

Tomar knew that the tide was turning against him, but still he delayed. He had not thought of a way to combat his adversary, and now had to admit to himself that he had been thoroughly outflanked by Engar. This surprised him, especially after the barn owl's clumsy handling of the previous Council meeting, where Tomar had escaped, by the skin of his beak, from being ousted altogether. Something fundamental had changed, and Tomar was a very worried owl.

Kopa's journey north had been long and arduous. On setting out, the young chaffinch had had no specific destination. His choice of direction in which to travel had been determined solely by topography. But, as he had journeyed, his subsequent choices had been made for him by what he had heard. Fear was widespread among the small bird population, and that fear was crystallised by the specific rather than the abstract. Birds didn't fear the corvidae in general. They were afraid of the local coven, and of what direct action they might take, if once again they grew strong enough. Each bird that he spoke to was terrified of the threat to their own nest, their own young. Not a single bird had looked beyond their personal situation to see that there might be a wider threat to the very existence of Birddom itself.

Kopa could see it. As clear as daylight on the fringes of a wood. This was not merely a case of local issues with larger species. This was co-ordinated and organised. Somebody had a plan. And Kopa knew that it was vital to the future of Birddom that he should find out who was behind the corvidae's resurgence. By the time he reached the northern-most coast he had learned much, and had risked more in gaining that knowledge. He had needed to be incredibly careful to gain access to the illicit meetings of the rooks and crows, and he had required a great deal of luck to avoid detection. More than once he thought that he had been spotted. And every time he had sat, hidden and watching, he had feared that the pounding of his tiny heart would surely have carried to the ears of every bird gathered there before him. But, to date, he had not been discovered. The corvidae may have had sharp eyes and sharp beaks, but their eyes gazed inward to dreams of power and glory, and their beaks crowed of mayhem and murder to come.

Kopa's arrival at Cra Wyd was almost inevitable. As he had followed the trail of rumour and fear, journeying ever northward, the name came to his ears more and more frequently. Cra Wyd: the stronghold of the corvidae in the north of Birddom. Cra Wyd: the biggest rookery in the whole of the land. And expanding rapidly, if the fearful, whispered rumours were true. Filling with black birds, whose ever-increasing numbers had driven out all other bird life from the vicinity. A dark and dreadful place it had become. Stories of horror and evil deeds abounded, and the more Kopa heard the more afraid he became. But he knew that he must conquer that fear. For, surely, here was the answer. If he could be brave enough once more to put his head into the eagle's beak, metaphorically speaking, Kopa knew, in his heart, that he would learn the truth. He would find out what, or who, was behind the terrifying rise of the corvidae.

Tomar was relieved that Calipha had agreed to come and see him in Tanglewood. He would have gone to her home, of course. But it would have been an arduous journey for one so old and frail. Tomar felt safe in his own nest-hole. Here alone could he have privacy. Every-where else in Birddom was too public, and there seemed to be so few birds that he could trust now.

'Thank you for coming, Calipha.'

Her words, in reply, were sharp and jarring. 'When you are summoned by the Great Owl, it is necessary to attend.'

Tomar looked at the short-eared owl with compassion. 'My dear friend,' he said. 'What you must have gone through!'

'It has been horrible, Tomar. No one else is speaking to me. I have been completely ostracised. All of my family and friends think that I was a fool to give you my support at the Council meeting. And I'm not so sure that they aren't right.' Tears welled up in her beautiful dark eyes, and she wiped them away with her wing-tip.

'Calipha. You know, in your heart, that you did the right thing. And I admire you so much. It is the hardest thing in the world to stand up against the mob. Your courage was an example to us all.'

'I simply couldn't bear to see you ousted so unceremoniously, after all that you have done for Birddom. You seemed so utterly alone and friendless. It was downright unfair.'

A note of defiance had crept into her voice as she spoke, and Tomar felt encouraged that she still had a spark of resolve. Her actions at the Council had bought him a little time, but he would need her support again if he were to survive.

'I still believe that I have friends on the Council. But Engar's will is strong, and he is very persuasive. I must admit that I was surprised at how much support he had gathered in so short a time. But even I see the attractiveness of his arguments. At times I can even believe that he is right and I am wrong. But there is something else. Something that I can't quite put my primaries on. I simply don't trust that owl!'

'He will not give up,' Calipha replied. 'I saw the look in his eyes when he realised that his victory had been snatched away from him. It frightened me.'

'Fear of one's own kind is indeed troubling. We have so many enemies in the world, we do not need any more within our own family.

But although I too am afraid, I need to be strong. Time is against me. I must speak to as many of the Council as will come and see an old fool at the end of his days. But I chose to speak with you first. It is vital that I have your continued support. I need you to be strong, and to stay by my side in the face of all opposition. I must shore up my position. Even if I can convince one or two more owls to join us, I will be safe. Not that I care anything for my own safety. I have lived too long anyway. But I will not let Birddom be ruled by tyranny. And that is how I see Engar. For all his talk of egalitarianism, he is a tyrant at heart, I am sure of it. And evil, too.'

Chapter Five

'I want you to come with me.' Traska's voice was imperious, and the tone of his command unequivocal. It would brook no denial. 'You have done well here. By listening to my advice, you have repaired much of the damage done at the Council meeting. Support is now firmly behind you. But it is vital that you do not overdo it. You cannot risk being seen as too hungry for power. You have spoken well, now leave it to others to consolidate your position. I need you to show your face to different, but equally crucial, supporters. Come with me to Cra Wyd.'

'Isn't that very risky? I can't afford to be seen consorting with rook and crow, raven and jay. And especially not with magpies. My support would melt away like snow in springtime.'

'Of course you can't. I am not a fool. We will have to be very careful. You must never be seen with me. In everyone's mind I am dead. And it is better that I remain so. You must come up with a valid reason for such a journey.' Traska paused, and the wicked glint in his eye told Engar that the magpie had something in mind. 'You are the Great Owl elect, is that not so?' Traska asked the barn owl.

'Certainly,' was Engar's conceited reply.

'Well, I think that it is high time that you consulted with the great birds of the land outside of the Council. Their support will greatly strengthen your position. You must go and see Storne.'

'The golden eagle? You must be joking! He is Tomar's firmest ally. Even if I can get him to listen to me, he will never betray his old friend.'

'He doesn't need to,' said Traska, impatiently. 'Don't you see? You can't lose. The act itself shows great statesmanship. You are striving to unite the whole of Birddom. To bring harmony to the land. And it will give you the perfect reason to be in that part of the country. You will easily be able to slip away, and come to Cra Wyd. And, when you do, I will have an audience waiting for you. An audience the like of which you've never even dreamed.'

Portia dreamed of magpies. She was with Kirrick, and they were being pursued once more. Only this time there were dozens of the evil black and white birds, and no obvious means of escape. Moreover, Kirrick was seriously injured. Not to his leg or his wing. It was an injury that Portia could not see, but it was killing her loved one before her very eyes: an injury to his heart, to his courage. Kirrick was afraid, and his fear was shrivelling his body, hour by hour, as she watched, unable to help him. His flight became more laboured and he needed to rest every few yards. And the magpies were closing in. Soon they would be trapped.

'Leave me,' whispered Kirrick. 'It's over for me. I'm finished. Save yourself.'

'I have no self, my love. Without you I am dead. You must try, Kirrick. We can still escape, if we stay together.'

Kirrick managed a weak smile, and hauled himself to his feet once more. 'All right, my love, I will try. For your sake, I will try.'

Portia almost wept with relief, and gathered herself, ready to take to the air once more. But a terrible, dark shadow loomed over her. Light flashed from a black beak that plunged towards her. Portia screamed.

'Mother. Mother! Wake up. What is it?'

Portia opened her eyes to see Olivia gazing down at her, full of concern. 'It was just a dream. And yet... it seemed so real. I could feel the pain, just as Kirrick must have done. But even worse was the feeling of helplessness, as if I could do nothing to prevent it. And it isn't just the dream. I feel helpless all of the time now. I need to be doing something, anything, to help Tomar. He needs support, and we perch and do nothing.'

'That's not true, Mother. You've spoken out, far and wide, giving your support to Tomar.'

'And been shouted down, too, everywhere that I went. There must be something else I can do to help. If only I wasn't so small a bird. Tomar needs bigger and stronger friends than a pair of little robins.'

'But he *has* bigger friends!' Olivia cheeped, excitedly. 'That's a marvellous idea, Mother. We will go and see Storne, and ask him to come back with us to help his old friend. He will not let us down.'

'Storne!' gasped Portia. 'Of course. His voice will carry the authority that mine lacks. Birds will listen to him. We must not delay. We will leave right away.'

'Shouldn't we tell Tomar where we are going?'

'No, my dear. I think that he would counsel against it. Anyway, I'd like to surprise him. Imagine his face when he sees an eagle coming to his aid once again.'

Tomar would have welcomed a friendly face. He was meeting a stone wall in his effort to persuade his Council colleagues to change their minds and support him against Engar. Tomar knew that the barn owl would soon find a way to engineer another vote of no confidence. And he could not afford to go into that particular battle with Calipha as his sole supporter. Engar would use any means, fair or foul, to make the short-eared owl choose what was, frankly, the far easier option, and abandon her support for the incumbent Great Owl.

But, no matter who he spoke to, he received no joy. Every other owl on the Council was against him. Or, rather, *for* Engar. For Engar's vision of the future: equality for all, in a utopian world, without rule or government, where self-determination and restraint would create an idyllic society. Hadn't the fools realised that there would no longer be a Council of the Owls, no independent body to resolve differences between species, or combat threats to Birddom. What would they do about Man? Almost every day he posed them a new puzzle, which they had to solve in order to survive. Who would *think* for Birddom?

The answer was obvious. Engar would. He would gradually manoeuvre himself into a position of absolute power, while still espousing his clap-trap about 'everybird'. And they would beg him to lead them, so that they wouldn't have to think about their problems, or even think for themselves. They would replace a benevolent Council with a monarch. An absolute ruler. A dictator.

But none could see it. Creer, Pellar, Steele and Cerca – to a bird, they rejected his words as a jealous diatribe against the coming 'bird'. Meldra, Wensus and Janvar listened with more politeness, and were kinder in their refusal of him. But, in the end, it was the same. He had lost them all. Faron had got wind of his consultations, and had disappeared without a trace. His had been the penultimate vote, the tenth against Tomar, and he hadn't wanted to face the hurt behind Tomar's stoicism, the defeat in those once proud eyes.

Tomar had left Lostri until last. He had deliberately given his friend time to think. The Great Owl knew that an immediate attack upon Lostri's newly-discovered idealism would certainly have met with failure. He had hoped, in this way, that Lostri would have pondered the constantly-raging debate that was going on all around him, and would have heard, as he had, the note of falsehood behind the rhetoric. If any other owl had the capacity to perceive the lie, it would have been Lostri.

But the coolness in his friend's greeting, when Lostri had landed on the crooked fir, made Tomar fear the worst. Even so, he tried to persuade the other owl that Engar was not worthy of his support. That the barn owl's vision for the future was a sham. Lostri listened in silence and, when Tomar was finally done, left without a word.

Kopa was becoming increasingly frustrated. He had stayed in the vicinity of Cra Wyd for several nights now, and had been disappointed at the lack of activity. Every instinct told him that the answer was here, that he had not made his long journey in vain. Local chit-chat seemed to confirm this. There was much talk of secret meetings in the dead of night, of debauchery and ritual sacrifice. Many a bird there testified that one of their own relatives had disappeared, never to be seen again, and that it was most likely that they had been taken by the rooks and hideously slaughtered at special ceremonies. The lack of grief in the telling made Kopa suspect that most of the stories were apocryphal. But if even a tenth of them were true, it was undoubtedly a grisly and frightening place.

Each successive night, the chaffinch had had to steel himself to make his perilous excursion to the rookery itself, but Cra Wyd revealed none of its terrors. Huge though the community was, it portrayed merely a magnification of normal life in any forest or woodland. Corvidae ate and slept, squabbled and fought. There was mating now and then, and the sounds of young demanding food. But no evil deeds to chill the marrow of Kopa's bones. The young chaffinch began to despair, believing that he had undertaken a fool's errand. He felt very lonely, so far away from his family and friends, and began to long for the warmth and comfort of his own nest. Only a stubborn will had kept him from abandoning his mission so far, but his resolve was weakening.

And then, on the seventh night, he felt a change in the place. The whole atmosphere in Cra Wyd had been transformed. The air seemed to crackle with tension and excitement. It vibrated, like electricity from a gathering storm. The rooks and crows were much more active. Squabbles were more frequent and more violent. And everywhere there were the whispers: 'He is coming. Our Master will soon be with us. The time of our victory approaches.'

Storne was both astonished and delighted when, as once before, a pair of robins alighted on his nest-step.

'Portia, my dear friend!' he exclaimed, with genuine pleasure. 'And Olivia, too. My, how you've grown up. And every bit as beautiful as your mother.'

Olivia blushed at the compliment, and then stared around her, open-beaked. She had not realised that an eyrie could be so huge. But, seeing Storne up close, she realised that his massive frame fitted perfectly into such imposing surroundings.

'Forgive the intrusion, Storne,' said Portia. 'I know too well that one's home is a precious and private place, and that the arrival of strangers...'

'You will never be strangers to me, my friends,' Storne interrupted. 'You are as dear to my heart as family. It is wonderful to see you again. But tell me, what brings you on such a journey? You have had ill adventures in this land.'

'This land is my home,' Portia replied. 'And both of us have many good memories, as well as dark ones.'

'It is a beautiful land,' Olivia added. 'And one that is fitting for the lord of the eagles.'

'Your words of praise do me great honour,' Storne responded, courteously. 'There have been times when I have felt altogether too small for these mountains. They demand so much.'

'And you have given, in full measure,' Portia said, smiling.

'Enough of this mutual admiration, ladies. You have not answered my question. What brings you here?'

'All is not well with the Council of the Owls. Tomar is beleaguered, and his position as Great Owl is threatened.'

'How can this be?' asked Storne, anger rising in his voice.

'A new owl has been voted onto the Council. An owl full of ideas, and just as full of his own importance. Engar is his name, and, in him, I fear that I have met, for the first time, an owl that I do not trust.'

'How can such a one have been accepted onto the Council?'

'Engar is very persuasive, and very modern in his thinking. I believe that somehow he sensed the mood of the times, and was able to take advantage. His ideas seemed fresh and exciting. But his words felt wrong somehow. Tomar certainly is against him, but then Engar is trying to usurp his position as Great Owl.'

'But Tomar has been the bed-rock on which Birddom has been rebuilt. But for him there would be darkness across the whole of the land.'

Portia nodded. 'I know. We all owe him a debt that we can never repay. That is why we are here. Tomar needs your help. At the last Council meeting he survived by a feather. Control is slipping from his talons.'

'I can scarcely believe what I am hearing. But I do not doubt your word. Of course I will do whatever I can to help my old friend. I cannot leave immediately, however. I must make certain arrangements here to ensure that things run smoothly in my absence. But, rest assured, I will come – and soon.'

'Thank you, Storne. That is good news indeed. And my heart feels lightened by your assurances. I feel better than I have done for a long time. Oh, why can't life always be peaceful and happy? We had both, for a time. The corvidae were vanquished. The Council ruled the land with wisdom and justice, and we had peace. Why could it not last for ever?'

'Nothing lasts for ever, my dear,' Storne answered. 'The best that any of us can hope for is a brief reprieve from the trials that are put before us to make us stronger.'

'Well, in that case, meet the Hercules of robins!'

The golden eagle and the two robins laughed, then a look of puzzlement spread across Storne's face. 'You both made a dangerous journey, coming so far to see me. I'm surprised that Merion didn't accompany you. Where is he? There's nothing wrong with him, is there?'

The laughter died on Portia's beak, and it was Olivia who replied. 'There is everything wrong with Merion. He is utterly lost to us. He has chosen his own path, and has cast his lot with Engar. My brother has become one of his staunchest advocates. He has turned his back on his own family, has rejected Tomar, and has been ensnared by Engar's promises and lies.'

'Do not distress yourself,' Storne said, soothingly. 'I am sure that it is but a temporary aberration. Merion is a sensible, sound young robin. He will come to his senses. I am sure that he would do nothing that would bring dishonour to the name of his father, Kirrick.'

'I am terribly afraid, Storne. Afraid that things may have already gone too far. He makes speeches in support of Engar, in which he favours breaking Tomar's edict against taking insects for food. And I very much fear that he now practises what he preaches.'

'Surely not. The pact brought us to the peace that we still enjoy to this day, or so I had thought until your visit. Without the help of the insects, we would not have beaten the corvidae, and Birddom would be a very different, much darker place. Surely Merion would not be such a fool?'

'My brother is not the bird you knew, Storne. Indeed, he has become a stranger even to his own mother and sister.'

Engar looked around the circle of trees, his gaze passing briefly over the two unoccupied oaks. 'Thank you for coming to this informal gathering. I did not see the need to request an official session of the Council. This is just a meeting of friends, nothing more. I simply wanted to tell you about my plans, and to ask a few favours of you while I am away.'

A murmur of consternation rose among the other owls, but Engar quashed it immediately. 'Oh, don't worry. I won't be gone for long. But it is vital for the future of Birddom that I undertake my journey. The Birddom that we strive for can only be won with total support across the length and breadth of the land. We can sit here, holding Councils and making grand pronouncements, but unless we win the hearts and minds of every species, any laws that we pass will be unworkable in the real world.'

Engar paused and gestured dramatically with a sweep of his wing. 'We must influence the strong. We must enlist the bold. We must ally with the mighty!'

A cheer broke out from the gathering, and Engar preened himself briefly before continuing, 'Tomar is a stubborn old fool, if even we, his friends, cannot persuade him. But perhaps he will listen to the counsel of others close to him. So I am going to pay a visit to Storne, the golden eagle, once a member himself of our noble Council. Maybe he will be able to show Tomar the error of his ways. Anyway, for the sake of Birddom, I am prepared to try.

'But, while I am gone, we must not lose momentum here. The ground-swell of opinion favours our ideas for the future. It will be up to you to make sure that this does not diminish. Talk to the world. Spread the message that ours is the only way. The right way!'

The gathering broke up, and owls flapped off in all directions. But five lingered behind, as arranged earlier by Engar. When he was sure that they were alone, he addressed them in less flowery tones.

'You lot have two tasks to perform. Firstly, I want you to keep an eye on those others. Make sure that no one weakens or breaks rank. I want a united front out there. One message. One voice. Do I make myself clear?'

Pellar, Janvar, Wensus, Creer and Cerca all hooted in affirmation, and Engar bestowed a benevolent gaze upon them as they fawned.

'There is one other thing. We need to deal with Calipha. I don't like losing, and I'm not going to lose again. She must be persuaded that she made a misjudgement at the last Council. She must be made to see that it is in everyone's interest that she correct that mistake at the earliest opportunity. I want all of you to put some effort into this. Use whatever methods you deem necessary, but get her to change her damned mind! Find the point of leverage and put some pressure on it. She must have family, doesn't she?'

'A younger sister, I believe,' replied Wensus, submissively.

'Perfect! A younger sister is a precious commodity. Not something that one would want to see broken. See to it, all of you. I want some good news when I get back. Some very good news!'

Chapter Six

Engar was somewhat taken aback by the frostiness of his reception when he arrived at Storne's mountain eyrie. Although he had never met the great golden eagle himself, Engar was fully aware of the cordiality of the relationship between the leader of the eagles and the Council of the Owls. It was a link that had been maintained since their initial alliance at the Great Battle. Engar had expected a friendlier welcome.

'You must be Engar,' Storne said, curtly. 'What is your business here?'

Engar hesitated before replying, to cover his surprise and annoyance at the eagle's harsh words. 'And you are undoubtedly Storne, lord of the eagles. I am flattered that you know of one so lowly in Birddom. But tell me, how is it that you come to have heard of me?'

'Your fame precedes you,' replied Storne, cryptically.

'It is a modest fame at best,' Engar responded, with insincere humility. ' I hope that word is spreading about what I am trying to do to help Birddom in its hour of need.'

'Is Birddom in such need?'

'Indeed it is. Look around you, Storne. Consider the life of every bird residing in your domain. Not your eagles themselves, for they are the least affected by the malaise which is destroying our homeland. Birds are hungry, cold and sick of a quality of life turning ever more sour. The odds seem stacked against them. And why? Because they are under the yoke of oppression. I see your disbelief when I say that. Indeed, it is hard to force myself to accept such a reality. For it is altogether a benevolent oppression, directed with love, honesty and honour. But it is a misdirection, which I believe is killing Birddom. And I am one of its perpetrators.'

The barn owl paused, fixing Storne with a limpid, beseeching gaze. 'I am a member of the Council of the Owls, the law-givers, whose wisdom, or otherwise, shapes and moulds the future of Birddom and the lives of all of its citizens. I have spent all of my life believing in the rightness of that way of ruling our land. It has been hard to admit that I was wrong. But now that I am privileged to be a part of that decision-making process, I have the opportunity, not to mention the duty to every bird, to influence those decisions and to change them for the betterment of Birddom. Indeed, it has been of considerable encouragement to me to see how receptive the majority of the Council members have been to my vision for the future of Birddom.'

'There are some who are of the opinion that your vision is not necessarily in the best interests of Birddom.'

Storne watched Engar's face, acutely, for a reaction. But the owl's countenance betrayed nothing.

'As I said, the majority share my views, and I respect the opinions of those who do not. Respect them, but hope to change them by the force of my argument. The will of the Council must prevail.'

'Forgive me,' Storne interjected, 'but the last I heard, Tomar was Great Owl and leader of the Council of the Owls.'

'And so he remains,' Engar replied, cautiously. 'Tomar is held in the highest esteem throughout Birddom, and I too have the greatest personal regard and love for the Great Owl. I am proud to call him my friend.'

Once again, Storne was no match for his visitor when it came to hiding his reactions. Open astonishment registered on his features, and his beak gaped, dumb-struck.

'Why would it be hard to believe that I admire and love the leader of Birddom? He is a saint and has led us all, in good times and bad, with a purity and selflessness that should be an example to us all. His only failing has been an unwillingness to change, and therein lies our peril. I called the Council benevolent oppressors, and angered you in so doing. But it is my sincerely-held belief that the title is justified. The law that forbids taking any insect as food, has left every bird starving and dying. It was a law formed of dire necessity, but it is outmoded and now works against Birddom like no other. That is why I say that Tomar is resistant to change, much as I love him. And why I will continue to argue against him on this matter in Council. Do you not see?'

Storne found it hard not to be impressed by the barn owl's vehement convictions, and felt himself persuaded by the power of Engar's argument. Surely, Portia and Olivia had misjudged this owl. He could detect no falsehood in him. The robins were seeing Engar's sincere beliefs as an attack on their old and dear friend. But it was obvious that Engar felt nothing but reverence for the Great Owl.

However, the eagle sought to clarify this with his next question. 'Do you intend to replace Tomar as leader of the Council?'

Engar's next meeting differed greatly in the reception that he received. Waves of adulation replaced the frosty courtesy, and he contented himself in basking in their warmth, while Traska spoke.

'Brothers and sisters, thank you for your welcome. You do us great honour by inviting us here tonight. For Cra Wyd is held in high renown. If the corvidae are to regain their glory, and we *will* regain it, then Cra Wyd will be seen as a mighty jewel in the crown of the new Birddom. A Birddom ruled by its rightful leaders. You should note that I do not say ruled by magpies and crows, rooks and ravens. We will be the lords of this land, but not alone. We will welcome strong allies. We will embrace those who see as we see. Think as we think. And it is in this spirit that I bring my friend Engar here today. For he is a visionary owl. He understands that Birddom is a lesser place without the corvidae sharing in its leadership. Partners in rule.

'Do not mistake me. Many still revile us. We are hated for past deeds, although I feel aggrieved that we have been so misunderstood, and are tainted by association with that megalomaniac, Slyekin. We are a great race, a nation in waiting, although we must be patient, for the time is not yet right. But it is coming. And Engar here is the bird who will ultimately steer us home. For his time *is* come. He will soon be the leader of the high-and-mighty Council of the Owls. He will direct their thinking and alter their opinions of us. In time, we will be accepted once more not only as full citizens of Birddom but as influential and respected partners in power. We will rule the land, this I promise you. We will be the dominant force in Birddom, and we will rule for all eternity!'

The roar that greeted Traska's words shook the leaves from the trees, and sent a stab of terror into the heart of the little chaffinch, who lay concealed barely five wing-spans away from the perch where Traska and Engar bathed in the corvidae's approval. Kopa squeezed his eyes tightly shut, and prayed with all his might: 'Creator. Keep me safe. I must live. I must not be discovered. Tomar has to be told of this treachery. He must be warned without delay – if I can ever get away from this dreadful place.'

Tomar had not believed it possible that things could get any worse. As he listened to the awful news, his heart ached for his beloved Birddom. Yet he knew that it must be true. His position, tenuous at present, was threatened still further. The news had come in from several sources, and each affirmation of the facts seemed to put another nail into the coffin of Tomar's tenure as Great Owl. Man had stopped feeding the birds. A vital resource had been withdrawn across the whole of Birddom.

It was easy to understand why. It was another piece of the jigsaw in Man's war with the insects, and the logic was irrefutable. If Man stopped feeding the birds, the birds would eat more insects. And, in doing so, would become unwitting allies to Man, solving some of his problems for him. But Man could not know of the pact that existed between the birds and the insects, a pact under threat from within Birddom, but now liable to collapse utterly with this outside intervention. Tomar shook his head in despair. This was playing into the wings of his opponents. Engar would surely get his way, once knowledge of Man's actions became widespread.

But what of the insects? How would they react? Their world, improved immeasurably by the agreement with Birddom's leaders, had turned sour when Man had responded violently to their increase in numbers. Under attack, and dying in their millions, what would be the consequence of a new threat? Would their awesome power be unleashed against the lesser of two enemies? And if so, would a single bird survive their vengeance?

That was a future too terrible to contemplate. And Tomar knew that Engar would not allow any prolonged discussion on that aspect of this latest news. But he would hoot from the rooftops about the need for Birddom to feed itself and avoid starvation. Man's actions had helped Engar's cause considerably, and Tomar had no doubts that the barn owl would take full advantage.

*

It took the sight of two robins to put the smile back on Tomar's beak. 'Welcome. Welcome, my dear friends. How good it is to see you both. It seems so long since you last visited. What have you been doing with yourselves?'

Portia chuckled, knowing the surprise that she would give her old friend. 'Oh, we've been a busy pair of birds,' she began. 'We've done a bit of travelling, truth to tell.'

'Travelling?' Tomar asked, rising to the bait.

'We took a little trip to see another friend of ours. And yours, Tomar.' Portia was deliberately prolonging the suspense, and grinned at the look of curiosity and frustration on the old owl's face.

'And who might that be?' queried Tomar, playing along.

Olivia took pity upon him. 'We went to see Storne.'

'That was a long and perilous journey to make,' replied Tomar, gravely. 'What prevailed upon you to put yourselves at such a risk?'

'We were careful, Tomar. And it was a risk well worth taking. Storne needed to be told about your troubles. To know that the Great Owl was besieged by those who would usurp his position.'

'What did you tell him?'

'Everything. We told him about Engar, and of his machinations to get the other owls to vote you off the Council. He was very concerned, and promised to help in any way that he could.'

Tomar gazed lovingly at the two robins before him. 'I am not sure exactly what Storne can do. But I am grateful, more than I can say. Thank you, my friends. Your loyalty and support is of great comfort to me. And your actions *do* give me hope, where I thought that there was none. Maybe, with Storne alongside me at the next Council meeting, I can make the others see that I am right, and that Engar's visions are against the interests of Birddom.'

*

Kopa had waited for several hours after the gathering had split up and crow and rook had returned to their nests. Every bone in his tiny body ached from the enforced confinement and inactivity. Finally, he deemed it safe to emerge from his hiding place. However, he had scarcely moved a muscle when he heard a sound that froze his blood. A cat was prowling around the base of the tree. Kopa could smell its rank odour, and hear its spitting, growling voice. Although he could not understand the words, Kopa felt that the cat was calling to him, taunting him: 'You cannot hide from me,' it was saying. 'I will find you, and I will eat you.'

Kopa's heart pounded in his breast, and he held himself deathly still, mortally afraid of the claw that would reach into the crevice where he lay, and drag him, screaming, to his death. He could hear the cat scrabbling at the trunk with its extended claws, ripping at the bark, as it sought to gain purchase and climb up to his hiding place. Kopa wished that he had chosen somewhere much higher and much less vulnerable. He wished he were high in the sky, flying free and away from this terrible danger.

A loud snarling announced the arrival of a second cat and, shortly after, a third. Still Kopa did not dare to look. For he knew that, once he set eyes on the dreadful creatures who were hunting him, he would swoon and fall right into their midst, to be torn to pieces and eaten at a gulp. The cats circled the tree relentlessly for more than an hour. Occasionally, one would leap, in futile frustration, seeking to defy gravity in order to reach him. It was only by the purest good fortune that Kopa had chosen to hide in a tree which bore no lower branches and had a trunk so smooth that climbing was well-nigh impossible, even for such agile and determined predators. But at that moment, Kopa didn't believe in good fortune. He was certain that he was going to die.

Then a loud, deep-throated sound rent the air, and the cats

shrieked in anger and fear, abandoning their attempts to reach their prey, and turning their attentions on their own attacker. A huge dog bounded towards them, barking and slathering as he ran, drool spraying from his savage jaws. The cats stood facing the charge, with hackles raised and spitting defiance. But, at the last moment, self-preservation prevailed, and they turned tail and fled. The dog chased them for a short distance, but soon gave up, and wandered aimlessly about the wood, growling softly.

Kopa's relief was short-lived, as the dog returned to the base of his tree and began snuffling, round and round. Had one hunter simply been replaced by another? No difference between the jaws of a dog and a cat; both would mean death for the little chaffinch. The dog raised its nose from the leaf-mould, and sniffed the air. Then it yawned, turned sideways and cocked its leg up the side of the tree, relieving itself and marking its territory. The rank, acid smell nearly made Kopa choke, and he fought desperately not to give himself away. But the dog had lost interest in what might or might not be up the tree, and trotted off the way it had come.

Kopa waited for five more minutes before he felt that it was safe enough to take a look. Edging carefully out of his place of concealment until he stood on an open branch, the chaffinch surveyed the surrounding woodland for other signs of danger. Then, fearing to delay any longer, and not wishing to linger in the lair of his enemies, he took to the air, and flew off in the direction of home. In spite of the cramps that assailed him, he flew as fast as a chaffinch can fly. He flew with the urgency of need. Tomar had to be told about Engar's betrayal of Birddom, of his unholy alliance with the corvidae and, in particular, with the magpie called the Master. Kopa shuddered at the thought of that evil bird, whose very words had felt like poison dripping onto his wings.

Unclean. Utterly wicked.

'Tomar must be told,' he repeated to himself, over and over again as he flew. Tomar would know what to do.

Tomar was at a complete loss as to what to do. He had set great store on Portia and Olivia's visit to the great golden eagle. But Storne had not come. Many days had now passed since the robins' return, and each day a little more of Tomar's hope and courage had dwindled. He had told himself that Storne may have been delayed by the need to put his own nest in order prior to heading south. He had stilled his doubts by believing that some minor troubles might have needed sorting out, or that localised adverse weather conditions might have temporarily postponed the eagle's journey. But there came a time when Tomar simply had to face the facts: his friends had made a wasted journey, and the bird he had thought his staunchest ally was not going to be flying to his aid. Or, if he did so, it would now be too late.

For Engar had returned, and had demanded a reconvening of the Council of the Owls at the earliest opportunity. Tomar had prevaricated, claiming that it would take a little time to gather all of the Council members together, and it seemed that Fate was on his side: Calipha was nowhere to be found. Tomar made extensive enquiries, but it seemed that neither she nor her sister had been seen for over a week. They must have had a good reason for setting off together on a journey, without a word to any of Calipha's fellow Council members. It was almost without precedent. Communication of whereabouts was a requirement of the role and, under normal circumstances, Tomar would have been angered by such a breach. But in truth, he was thankful. He was not ready, physically or mentally, for another battle with Engar. He needed time to muster his wits, and to shake off the disappointment that he felt over Storne's non-arrival.

However, if the old tawny owl wanted a respite, Engar was in no mood to oblige. He harried and badgered all of the other owls, claiming that a state of emergency now existed in Birddom. Man's withdrawal of a vital food source was the last straw for a starving population. Birddom needed the Council to rescind Tomar's suicidal law. Every bird had to be allowed to eat insects without delay. Lives depended upon it, and the duty of the Council was clear. So what if one member was absent? Surely eleven of the best minds in the land were enough to decide such a simple and clear-cut issue. The same strictures could still apply. Ten against one would be as unequivocal as the old rule. And as binding.

Engar would not be denied, not that there was much opposition from his fellow members. The Great Owl stood alone against him. Engar's face wore an expression of extreme satisfaction when he came face to face with Tomar, and commanded his presence at the sacred meeting place at sunset on the morrow.

'If it is the will of the Council,' Tomar replied, with quiet dignity, 'I will be there.'

Chapter Seven

Kopa's tiny heart felt as if it would burst. One minute he had been flying, fast as an arrow. The next, he was going nowhere. Trapped in a fine mesh that tightened its grip with every struggle, he flapped and fretted uselessly in a vain effort to free himself, and cursed at his own misfortune. The little chaffinch had taken such care on his outward journey, for he, like every bird, knew of the dangers. But his haste, driven by the urgency of his message for Tomar, had made him forget his caution, and now he would seem to have paid the ultimate price. His headlong flight into the netting had torn through the gossamer-like mesh, but the inner core of plastic cross-wires held him fast. And the torn fabric wound itself around him as he panicked.

Try as he might, Kopa could not free his head or his legs from the deadly netting. With such limited movement he could only peck futilely at the harsh plastic strands nearest to his beak. But the mesh was un-yielding and, after a while, the chaffinch made fewer and fewer attempts to escape from the trap. He was overwhelmed with a deep and abiding sadness. Not for his own fate. But for the fate of the land that he had embraced as his own. The knowledge that he alone held in his head was vital to the future of Birddom, but in his head it would remain, unless some miracle could free him from a slow and lingering death.

'It is clear that we are getting nowhere with this old fool. I call for an immediate vote.'

The contempt in Engar's voice made several of the fairer-minded owls wince, but none spoke up against him. Those not actively involved had realised the significance of Calipha's timely disappearance. But, even when Tomar had raised the issue, in a direct accusation against Engar for corrupting the legitimacy of the Council for his personal gain, not one of the nine other Council members had offered a word of support for their leader. Tomar struggled to retain his composure.

He had been a fool, just as Engar had described him. A fool not to see that the barn owl had engineered Calipha's disappearance in order to guarantee a victory at the Council meeting. And that victory was now certain. Tomar had no doubts about it. All that remained was the ritual humiliation of facing each member in turn, and hearing them vote against the law that had been the central plank of Birddom's very existence since the war with the corvidae. It was a bitter pill to swallow. But it seemed that worse was to come. Emboldened by the absence of any support for the Great Owl, Engar spoke up once more.

'I believe that there was some unfinished business from the last Council meeting,' he began. 'It is obvious that Tomar no longer holds the respect and trust of the overwhelming majority of all here today. The will of the Council is made stronger now, with the latest news. Birddom cannot survive, unless we break our pact with the insects and take them as food once more. We will vote that stupid law out of existence. And we will vote its originator off the Council. And Calipha, too, if she can't be bothered to abide by the rules of the Council and wanders off without a word. We are better off without such a feckless owl holding a position of responsibility. Let the Council forthwith be ten. Ten are enough to make the decisions that will govern our future. Ten is a good number for the law-makers of our land. I call for a vote of no confidence in Tomar. He is no longer fit to lead us. We cannot permit the Great Owl to be so at odds with the wishes of the Council, and of Birddom as a whole!'

*

Kopa knew that he was dying. Severe thirst had parched his throat and almost gummed his beak together. Breathing was extremely painful, as he had wrenched many of his muscles in the struggle to free himself from the netting. His reserves of energy were very low. Without sustenance, he would not survive the night. Tears bled from his eyes and whetted his damask chest-feathers. Indeed, his weeping blurred his vision to such an extent that it took a moment for him to realise what he was seeing. Then he forced his beak apart, and cheeped out a warning: 'Beware! Keep away. You will be trapped, too.'

The female chaffinch beat her wings strongly to maintain her hovering position, close to where Kopa hung limply in the grip of the net. 'I will be all right,' she answered. 'I must help you to get free.'

'No!' Kopa screamed at her. 'You cannot save me. But you can give some meaning to my death. I need you to take a message for me. A message to be delivered to the Great Owl, and only to him.'

'But I can't just let you die,' she continued plaintively.

'What is your name?'

The question took the young female by surprise. 'Cian,' she replied.

'Well, Cian, I am Kopa. And there is nothing that you can do to save my life. But if you do what I say, you will help to save the lives of many other innocent birds like ourselves. Will you help me?'

'Yes,' she said, with solemnity. 'Tell me what I must do.'

'You must listen to my story. And you must commit every word to memory. You must become my voice and, in that way, although my body may perish, I will live on in your words and actions. You will carry my hope with you. A hope that Birddom desperately needs in such evil times.'

So Cian listened while Kopa told his story. He spoke slowly and, at times, the pain in his throat made his voice harsh. But he spoke clearly, emphasising any point that was crucial to her overall understanding. He also made Cian repeat what he was saying, to be sure that she had the story fixed in her mind. It was a long and laborious process. Several times, Cian had to take a brief rest in a nearby tree. But always she returned, as soon as she possibly dared, and hovered near him once more while he spoke. At last, it was done. Everything that Kopa had seen and heard on his journeys and at Cra Wyd was passed on to this bright young female. Relief flooded through the trapped chaffinch's weary body.

'Thank you,' he said. 'Thank you from the bottom of my heart. Go now, Cian. There is no time to lose, and you can do nothing more for me. I will never be able to repay you for your help. Your reward will be in the knowledge that you have played a part in saving this beloved land of ours. Delay no longer, my dear. Go. Go, I beg you. Fly as fast as you can, but take care. You must get my message to the Great Owl. Remember that – tell no one but the Great Owl!'

Tomar sat on his perch in the ring of oaks, silent and withdrawn. In the centre of the clearing, Engar strutted and preened in triumph.

'This is a great day for Birddom!' he announced. 'What we have done here today will have far-reaching consequences for every bird. We have made a momentous decision. Hunger will now be eradicated throughout the land. Every bird's life will be immeasurably improved, and all will thank us for having the courage of our convictions. Our names will reverberate across Birddom. And do not fear that the insects will somehow rise up against us. Only cowards and the weak-minded would give credence to such nonsense. The insects' enemy is Man. They are at war with him. They will not even notice our depredations. And if they do, we will surely defeat them in any ensuing battle. For they are tiny. And we are mighty. No, we have nothing to fear from the insects. Except, maybe, indigestion.'

All of the owls, with the exception of Tomar, hooted with laughter. The old tawny owl was seething with anger. This was no joking matter. Couldn't the fools see that? His worst nightmare was going to come true, and not a single bird would live to tell the tale. It was sheer folly to believe otherwise.

Engar spoke again, enjoying the general approbation. 'We have voted to restore our absolute right to eat whatsoever we choose. And we have voted for the future of this Council. A Council on which you no longer have a place, Tomar. I think that it is time that you left us to govern this land, and take it into a far brighter future.'

At this direct provocation, Tomar finally broke his silence. 'Yes. It is time. I cannot stay where I am not wanted. I cannot speak where I am not heard. So I will go, and trust to the hearts of those that I have long called my friends. Do not let yourselves become the mouth-piece through which one bird rules. Always I have led this Council by following its will. Be careful that the Council does not become a mere follower. Choose well, my friends. For the sake of Birddom, choose carefully.'

'Thank you for your advice,' Engar cut him off abruptly. 'And now, we will detain you no longer. Go well into your retirement. We have business to attend to.'

Tomar soon felt the full extent of Engar's petty cruelty. Exiled from the Council, and unable to leave his home in Tanglewood because of his age and frailty, the old tawny owl was virtually a prisoner, at the mercy of his enemy. And Engar showed precious little mercy towards his erstwhile adversary. Within days, the Great Owl elect had deemed it necessary to despatch all of the other Council members, and several other owls who served under them, on a country-wide fact-finding mission. The stated aim was laudable – to find out the extent of the difficulties that every bird was facing, and to spread the word about the rescinding of Tomar's law. But this was merely a pretext. Behind it lay Engar's desire to inflict further hurt upon Tomar; in sending the owls to far-flung destinations, he was, in fact, withdrawing the vital support that the old owl needed to provide him with sufficient food and warmth.

Alone, Tomar struggled to forage close to his nest-hole. But the pickings were meagre indeed. Catching fresh meat was beyond him, and an inadequate diet of seeds and berries soon saw his remaining flesh slough away to feather and bone. From time to time, Tomar was aware that Engar was watching him, and evidently enjoying the spectacle. The barn owl would alight in the upper branches of Tomar's own crooked fir tree – an affront in itself – and would sit gloating while his adversary pecked and scratched in the undergrowth below. Tomar did his best to ignore his tormentor, but the humiliation stuck, like burrs in his primary feathers. His sole hope was that some of the other Council members would come to see the real wickedness behind the mask which Engar presented to them, and would reconsider their choice when the time came to vote for the new Great Owl. But it was a forlorn hope. More likely that the next meeting of the Council of the Owls would see Engar's position ratified by unanimous approval. Engar would become Great Owl, and Tomar's fate would be sealed.

Merion could barely contain his excitement. At last he had something important to do. The young robin deemed it a great honour to have been personally chosen by Engar, and he knew that he would do everything within his power not to let his hero down. Merion's task was, in reality, a fairly simple one. He was to fly east, replicating a journey made by both of his parents, and visit Kraken in his coastal home. Once there, he was to reassure and placate the great gull, lest any rumours might have reached him about Tomar's having been overthrown.

Engar had realised that he had been lucky in having visited Storne so close behind whomsoever Tomar must have sent. That stroke of good-fortune had enabled him to allay the eagle's fears, and prevent a dissenting presence at the Council meeting. That achieved, the last thing that Engar wanted was interference from another of Tomar's legendary triumvirate of supporters. So the robin was chosen to feed words of reassurance into Kraken's ear, and to persuade him, if needed, to stay at home and tend to his own flock. A similar messenger would be sent to consult with Darreal, the kite. Engar would brook no obstacle in his path to power.

Merion knew that he should leave without delay, but he felt unhappy about embarking upon such a long journey without saying goodbye to his mother, in spite of the rift between them. So he made a brief detour to her nest-site and, arriving and finding no one at home, called out, 'Mother. Where are you?'

Portia emerged from behind a nearby bramble, and smiled when she saw who her visitor was. 'Merion, my son. How good to see you.'

'I had to come, Mother. I wanted to see you and say goodbye before I set off.'

'But where are you going?'

A look of pride gleamed in the young robin's eyes. 'Engar has chosen me personally to journey to the east coast and visit Kraken. I am to tell him all about the exciting new era into which our Great Owl is leading us.'

'Merion!' Portia snapped, angrily. 'What has got into you? I cannot believe that you have so little respect for the owl who saved your life. Tomar is Great Owl, until a successor is formally chosen by the Council. And in my eyes, he will always be the Great Owl.'

'Oh, Mother, stop living in the past. Tomar's day is done. Engar is the future for Birddom. And it will be a *great* future. Things have been stagnant for so long. But Engar will change all that. Birddom will become a place where every bird is equal. And where no bird is ever hungry again.'

'I will be hungry, if I so choose. For I will never break Tomar's stricture, even if my very life depends upon it. Insects are forbidden. That is the law.'

'That law is history, Mother,' Merion replied, angrily. 'Why deny yourself any longer? Why abstain from something that isn't deemed a sin any more? Let me fetch you something now. A worm? A caterpillar?'

'Begone with you, if you have to make your journey. We have both chosen, you and I, for good or ill. But take care, my son. And thank you for coming to see me. I would have worried so to have heard no news from you.'

'Goodbye then, Mother. Don't fret about me. I know how to take care of myself. Look after yourself while I am gone. I love you.' Suddenly embarrassed at his own words, Merion took wing, and flew off without looking back.

Portia's gaze followed him, until she could see him no longer. Then she sighed softly. 'There is still hope,' she said to herself. 'Thank the Creator that there's still hope.'

Cian was exhausted when she arrived on the outskirts of Tanglewood. She had flown without rest, following Kopa's instructions as to the route that she must take. But, now that she had made it to her destination, she was confused. Kopa had been very weak at the end, and the female chaffinch had been distressed by his imminent passing. Cian had stayed with him until the end, and had only left, tearful and grieving, when Kopa's body had finally relaxed, and his head had slipped from its prison so that he had hung by his feet, upside down in the indignity of death.

Cian had flown hard, repeating all the time the message that she had to carry. But the effort of memory had driven out vital information concerning the whereabouts of the Great Owl's home. Cian realised that she would have to find someone who she could ask. Plunging into the woodland without further delay, she soon spied an owl perched high in a crooked fir tree. At first, her heart leapt. This might be him. She had found the Great Owl. But, upon closer inspection, Cian's spirits drooped. This owl was ancient. His feathers were bedraggled and unkempt. He was emaciated, and altogether as unimpressive an owl as Cian had ever seen. This could not be the leader of Birddom. Still, he might know where she could find the Great Owl. Approaching closer, Cian was about to speak when she realised that the old owl was fast asleep.

'Poor old thing,' she thought to herself. 'He looks so poorly that he might never wake again. I must not disturb him. I'll just have to find someone else to ask.'

Tomar thought that he had heard the beating of a pair of wings close by, and struggled to rouse himself from the depths of sleep. On opening his huge eyes, he found that there was no one there. But he had heard something, he was sure of it.

'Kirrick. Kirrick,' he called, into the silence. 'Is that you?' Then he shook his aged head sadly. 'You old dotard,' he chided himself. 'You were dreaming, that was all. Kirrick is dead, as well you know. And by the state of you, you'll not be far behind him. It was probably that blasted Engar. Sometimes I wish he'd just finish me off, and get it over with.'

Merion had flown for many hours, but darkness had descended swiftly and early due to the inclemency of the weather. The robin sought a place to shelter and rest. Visibility was poor in the heavy downpour, and Merion could barely make out the vague outline of a copse of trees below and to his right. He swooped down, and flew a short way into the copse, where the leaves were more dense and provided better protection from the rain. But no sooner had he alighted than a change in the direction of the wind was driving stinging droplets into his face.

'This is no good,' he decided quickly, and looked around for a more suitable place to shelter. The tree opposite had a knot-hole, which, although a tight squeeze for the young robin, provided enough cover to keep off the worst of the rain. Merion forced his body as far back as possible into the hole, and there, in spite of the discomfort and cramped conditions, fell into a heavy sleep.

Harsh voices woke him. The rain had long since ceased, and the air was clean and fresh. Sounds carried clearly to where he lay, hidden in his small hole. Sounds of caws and crowing. Not from one bird, but from many. Merion was terrified. Childhood memories crowded in on him, of his capture by Traska. Of the brutality, and the fear of being so close to one so evil. From his limited vantage point, Merion could make out the shapes of a few of the large black birds on adjacent branches. They were rooks, so far as he could make out, and they were much easier to hear than to see. They were chattering incessantly among themselves, and the more Merion heard the more a sense of dread filled his heart.

It was not possible. It couldn't be happening all over again. Surely the corvidae had been defeated, once and for all, in the Great Battle? But Merion could not discount the evidence of his own ears. The rooks were talking about insurgence and killing. Nothing had changed. They still wanted power for themselves alone. And then he heard the name, and his blood froze in his veins.

'That old Traska will sort them out. He's waited a long time for his vengeance, he has. But he won't have to wait very much longer.'

'Shut up, you. Enough of your disrespect. You call him by his proper title, if you speak of him at all, which you shouldn't. The Master is our leader, and commands the respect of us all. He's given us back our pride. And because of him, we have a great future.'

'Which is more than I can say for the rest of bloody Birddom!' the first bird answered, with harsh laughter.

'What shall I do?' Merion asked himself, fretfully. 'I daren't move or I might be discovered. And that would be the end of me. But I must get away. I have to warn them. This is far more important to Birddom than my mission to Kraken. I have to go back. Engar has to be told that Traska is still alive, and up to his old mischief.'

Chapter Eight

Engar felt in a decidedly mischievous mood. He knew that there were places to go and birds to see. He knew also that it would not be long before the first of his fellow Council members returned from the mission on which he had sent them. Engar was glad of this. He was impatient to receive the title of Great Owl. His vanity required it. He deserved it. But, for now, he felt that he also deserved a little treat. After all, it might be the final time that he would get the opportunity. And humiliating Tomar gave him such pleasure.

Engar had decided that he would pay one final visit to Tanglewood. The old owl must be lonely. He'd surely be glad of some company. Grinning wickedly to himself, Engar set off at once. He flew in haste, eager to pile more indignity upon his adversary. But, when he reached the centre of the forest, a thought struck him, and he alighted briefly while he pondered the joke.

'Maybe Tomar would like some food,' Engar mused, cruelly. 'I'm sure that I could find a suitable repast for an ex-Great Owl. Some rotting, putrid carcass that even the flies wouldn't touch. Mind, I'd have to wash my talons in the brook afterwards. But it would be worth it. Just to see his face.'

'Excuse me. Can you help me?' The small voice of a chaffinch called to him from a branch some feet up, and to the left of where he perched.

Engar's huge black eyes fixed upon the little bird. 'That is just what I can do. Indeed, it is my duty to help *any* bird who is in need of my aid. Now, what can I do for you?'

Cian's relief was all too obvious. She was afraid of this place, but at least this owl seemed kind, and willing to help. 'I am looking for the Great Owl. Do you know where I might find him?'

'Your search is at an end, my dear. You need look no further. For I am the Great Owl.'

Engar saw a look of uncertainty flit briefly across her face. 'Does something trouble you, my dear?' he probed, gently. 'You look confused.'

'I am sorry,' Cian replied. 'It is just that I understood the Great Owl to be a tawny owl, and yet...'

'I am a barn owl through and through, and proud of it. But the fact remains that you have found the one for whom you were searching. Now, how can I help you?'

As he spoke, Engar hopped up and across to a perch much closer to the young chaffinch. If something were awry, he would need to have her within his reach. She seemed, however, unconcerned by his move, and he could see that she had accepted what he had told her. He might not have to kill her, after all.

Had Cian been in possession of the full facts, doubtless she would have fled in terror from the owl that now sat so close. But Kopa's message had been for Tomar's ears, and he had not thought it necessary to give a description of the birds of whom he was speaking. Tomar would know well enough from their names alone. So, while Cian knew that she had to tell the Great Owl all about Traska and Engar, she could have no idea that she might be addressing the latter. Kopa hadn't even told her that Engar was an owl. He had called him wicked and evil. A traitor in their midst. It had been terribly distressing, watching, helpless, while Kopa struggled to finish his tale before it was too late. And when he was done, his voice was weak with the exertion, as he told her, over and over, to take his message to the Great Owl in Tanglewood.

And here he was. She had found him. Looking at the magnificent barn owl, she told herself that it was obvious. He had such a presence. She must have been mistaken, that was all. She certainly couldn't be *sure* that Kopa had told her that he was a tawny owl. She was concentrating so hard, at the time, on keeping the message in her mind. No. She had got it wrong. But it was of no importance. The Great Owl didn't seem to have taken offence, and Cian was glad of that.

She began to recount all that she had been told by Kopa, and Engar's face became a mask of solemn concern and gravity. But, behind it, his brain was racing. It was only an incredible stroke of good fortune that had averted an absolute disaster. It seemed that she knew it all. His complicity with Traska. Their plans for defeating Tomar, and the eventual rise to power of the corvidae. Damn her. They thought that they had been so careful. But here she was, this little chaffinch, blurting out all of their secrets, pouring her heart out, in the deluded belief that she was helping to save Birddom. Well, she'd find out soon enough. He would tell her, of course, before he killed her. Just to see her face. But, for now, he nodded with sagacity as Cian told her story, and gradually edged even closer.

'Hunger has its compensations,' Tomar muttered to himself. 'It gives you more time to think.'

Indeed the old owl was in such a weakened state that little other activity was possible. But thinking was what Tomar did best. Since his defeat at the Council, he had despaired for the future of his beloved Birddom. But despairing wouldn't solve anything. In his lowest moments, he had wished for his own death. But Birddom still needed him. It needed him alive. Even in his present emaciated state, he could still serve. By thinking.

Birddom was in a parlous position and under threat on several fronts: led by an owl whose intentions Tomar instinctively had not trusted from the beginning, beset by a powerful enemy – Man, and soon to provoke a conflict with another, even more deadly foe – the insects. Tomar could not remember a time when Birddom was in such peril. Not even when Slyekin had dreamed his crazy dreams, and had unleashed murder and mayhem across the land. But at least that was bird against bird. Tomar had been able to think like his opponents. He had understood their desires. Had been able to guess at their plans, and so formulate his own, in order to defeat them. But to out-think Man? To out-guess the insects? It was simply not possible. There would have to be another way.

Tomar tossed the options endlessly inside his ancient brain, searching for inspiration. The sun climbed across the sky above the canopy of the treetops while the old owl sat there, still as a statue. But his mind was never still. Nor, for that matter, was his stomach. It growled and complained, paining the tawny owl with its urgent demands for food. Tomar did his best to ignore the hunger pangs, and struggled once more to regain his train of thought.

'Avia.' The word came unbidden into his mind. Avia. Of course! Why hadn't he thought of it before?

'Now calm yourself down, you old fool!' he told himself. 'Don't get over-excited. You need to think this through.'

But try as he might, Tomar could not help feeling a sense of elation. It would need all of his skills to see any scheme to fruition. But he just might have found an answer – a way by which Birddom could be saved, if it be the Creator's will.

*

Cian felt drained but, at the same time, greatly relieved now that she had told her story. She had fulfilled her promise to Kopa. He had not died in vain. She had passed on the responsibility to one who was in a position to do what needed to be done. The Great Owl would stop those villains, Engar and Traska. The little chaffinch looked once more into the barn owl's great black eyes. And then she saw the change within their depths. The compassion and concern had gone from them, and they were suddenly like deep, black pools of icy water. She felt as if by merely staring into them she was drowning. Cian jerked her gaze away. She seemed an instant from flight, but Engar's huge wing settled across her back.

'You must be so tired,' he began, soothingly. 'You must rest. But first I would like to offer you my humble thanks. You have done Birddom a great service today, Cian. I know how hard it must have been for you. You have been so brave. But it is all over now. I will take it from here, you can rest assured. I will consult with my brothers on the Council at the earliest opportunity. Indeed, I would like you to meet them all, so that they can have the opportunity to thank you themselves. I am sure that you are wanting to get back to your own home, but I hope that you will not mind delaying that pleasure by just one day. You will be our guest of honour, and deservedly so.'

The gentleness of his words were at odds with the pressure upon Cian's back as he pinned her to the branch. She felt that she had little alternative but to accept.

'Good,' he responded, easing the weight a little. 'Then it is settled. But we can't rest here. It is far too exposed. You just come along with me, and we'll find you a place of comfort where you can get a good night's sleep. And then tomorrow, when you are well rested, we will be able to show our gratitude in a manner befitting a true heroine of Birddom.'

*

When she awoke, Cian felt disoriented by her unfamiliar surroundings. She stared wildly around her for a moment, until she caught sight of the barn owl. The look of malice on his beak chilled her blood, and her one desperate thought was of getting away. But, even as she took to the air, she was knocked to the ground by a huge black wing. Momentarily stunned, Cian lay on her back and looked up, in terror, into the face of a magpie. Its unmistakable aura of pure evil left her utterly incapable of movement, save for the pounding of her heart.

'Let me do the introductions,' the barn owl called out, mockingly. 'Traska, Cian. Cian, Traska. Ah, I see that you recognise the name, little lady. And, while we are being so polite, forgive me for not introducing *myself* before now. I wonder if you can guess my name. No? Well, I'll put you out of your misery, in that much at least. I am Great Owl as I said, or at least I soon will be, and, together, we are the real rulers of your beloved Birddom. I am Engar. Now, what I would like you to do is to repeat your story to Traska here. I am sure that he would find it most enlightening.'

Fear constricted the chaffinch's throat, as Traska prodded her impatiently on her chest with his sharp beak. 'Come on. Get on with it,' he ordered her, harshly. 'I don't want to waste my time. Tell me everything that you know, and tell me quickly.'

Merion had been forced to remain in the knot-hole for several hours, until dawn had finally arrived and stirred the corvidae from their roosts. The robin had waited until the last of the rooks had flown off in search of food, then he had quickly emerged from his cramped place of concealment and had flown back in the direction that he had come. Merion ignored the agony in his wing-tips, caused by his night in such a confined space. He had to get back as fast as he could, so that he could warn Engar of the danger. He could still scarcely believe it himself. The corvidae were on the rise again. It was too dreadful to contemplate.

The little robin's urgency carried him swiftly to Engar's nest-site and, on arrival, he was just about to call out a greeting when he heard a voice that silenced his cry. Merion knew that voice. It was one that had haunted his dreams since childhood, turning them into nightmares from which he would wake in a cold sweat of terror. Traska!

Merion couldn't understand. What was that vile bird doing here? And then, another voice began to speak. A tiny, fearful voice, telling a story, which, as it unfolded, gave Merion his answer. It was an answer that he did not want to hear. No. It wasn't possible. Engar was a great bird. He was his hero. What he was hearing simply couldn't be true. But, as Merion listened to the terrified little chaffinch, he knew, in his heart, that she was telling the truth. Engar was a traitor, in league with Traska and the corvidae. And he, Merion, had helped the owl to gain his position of power. A position from which he could now do just about anything that he wanted to betray Birddom. As he himself had betrayed Tomar.

Merion realised suddenly that he hadn't heard Engar speak. Perhaps he was not there at all. Perhaps he knew nothing about all this. No, that wouldn't do. Merion couldn't fool himself any longer. The chaffinch had mentioned him by name. Engar was guilty and, therefore, Engar was evil. As evil as Traska himself. But where was he?

Merion looked behind him fearfully, lest the barn owl had somehow crept up and was waiting to strike. But no talon hovered over him, ready to deliver the fatal blow. The robin inched forward until he could see Traska's blue-tinged wing-tips, and long black back. The magpie continued to tower over the inert body of the little chaffinch and, at that moment, Cian stopped talking. She had told her tale, all over again, and now stared up at Traska in petrified silence.

'I told you that it was an interesting story, didn't I?' Engar hooted, and flapped across to land beside the chaffinch. 'And I think that it would be wisest if it wasn't told to anyone ever again. Don't you agree?'

The barn owl addressed his question directly to Cian, who replied in stuttering tones. 'I won't tell anyone else, I promise you. No one else need know. Your secret will go with me to my grave.'

'How prophetic,' Engar chuckled, cruelly. 'You have never spoken a truer word, my dear.'

Traska's foot suddenly gripped the little chaffinch like a vice, and his beak fastened about her neck, twisting Cian's head sideways. It was a position in which she could only watch as Engar's great talon swung inexorably down, and tore out her throat.

Merion watched, too, in utter revulsion. He gagged, as bile rose in his craw, and fought desperately not to make any sound which might give him away. Not that the two huge birds would have heard him. They were laughing loudly, as they tore the chaffinch limb from limb, bathing in her warm blood. Cian would never hear anything ever again. Merion turned from the carnage and crept silently away, afraid that, at any second, they would be upon him, too. But no beak rent his flesh. No executioner's talon descended upon his neck. He made his way slowly, not sure of his direction, just wishing to put as much distance as possible between himself and the horror that he had witnessed.

Tomar couldn't remember when, if ever, he had been so excited. There was frustration mixed with the elation, of course. Frustration that he was too old and too infirm to make the journey. Once again, he would have to rely on others. He thought back to the adventures on which he had sent Kirrick and Portia.

'Let it be robins again, then,' the old owl said to himself. 'It would be most fitting.'

But the more he thought about it, the more troubled he became. The journey that he would ask them to make was an arduous one. For Portia, at least, her days of flying hither and thither at his command were probably behind her. Olivia was a strong girl, of course – a fine robin in every way. But it was a dangerous thing that he would be asking her to do. Far more dangerous than the task that he had set for Portia some years earlier. Tomar knew that he could not send Olivia on her own. She would need a companion. If only Merion hadn't thrown in his lot with Engar. How he missed that robin and their discussions, their lively arguments, more often than not. He would feel so much happier if he could send the pair of robins. But it was not to be. He must face the unpalatable truth. Merion was lost to him.

The old owl still cherished the hope that his robin friend would wake up to the reality of what Engar was about, but it was a forlorn hope. Engar had succeeded in deceiving far wiser heads than Merion's. No, he must think of someone else. Olivia needed someone like Mickey, the chirpy bullfinch who had been Portia's companion when she had travelled to Wingland on the Council's behalf. His good humour and common-sense had been vital on their mission together, especially when it appeared that it had ended in failure.

'Olivia might fail, too,' Tomar told himself. 'It is asking a lot of any bird. But I have little choice. I can't even fly as far as the borders of this forest, in my present state. Olivia will have to do my flying for me.'

As he spoke these words quietly to himself, an idea formed in his mind. 'That would work,' he mused. 'Kopa would be the perfect choice. He could accompany Olivia on her travels. That young chaffinch knows his way around, all right. And he's got a brain on him.' Tomar clapped his old wings, in his excitement. 'I'll send word for him without delay, though, now I come to think of it, I don't remember having seen him for quite a while. I wonder where Kopa could have got to?'

Chapter Nine

Portia and Olivia had been most concerned about their old friend in the aftermath of the Council meeting. Word had spread quickly about Tomar's ousting as Great Owl, and his further banishment from the Council itself. Feeling helpless and embarrassed, the two female robins had delayed in visiting the old owl. What could they say? What comfort could they give?

Finally, they had plucked up the courage to face up to the reality. Tomar was Great Owl no longer. Instead, he was an ageing, frail but still dear friend. And anything that they could do for him they would do with a glad heart. However, when the robins arrived at the crooked fir in Tanglewood, they found Tomar in high spirits. Excitement glittered in his eyes, the years seemed to have dropped from him. He looked, once again, like an owl to be reckoned with.

'Portia. Olivia. My dears, it is so good to see you. I have been thinking about you both. Indeed I have. And that has given me hope. More hope than I have felt in a very long time.'

The two robins stared at the tawny owl, with barely concealed curiosity. 'What has happened, Tomar?' they cheeped, in unison.

'I have come alive again, that is what has happened. For far too long now, I have been so wrapped up in my own problems that I have forgotten that I am only here to serve Birddom. Well, better late than never, eh?'

The two females could scarcely contain themselves. 'What is it?' they cried out. 'Tell us. Tell us, please!'

'I've been an old fool. It should have come to me much sooner. But no matter. We should still be in time, if we act quickly.'

'In time for what? Don't be so cryptic,' Portia chided.

'Forgive me,' Tomar replied, in suitably contrite tones. 'I will not tease you any longer. Not that I was teasing. It's just such a wonderful idea, that's all. Quite brilliant, if I say so myself.'

'Tomar!' Portia screeched, impatience boiling over into anger.

'Sorry,' the owl said, soothingly. 'I'll tell you all about it. Have either of you heard of Avia?'

A look of incomprehension spread across both robins' faces.

'No. Well, I don't suppose that there is any reason that you should have. It's only something that has been passed down through the generations on the Council of the Owls, although it has not been spoken of since Cerival was Great Owl. Maybe we should be thankful for that, because now it is a secret that few if any but myself know.'

'What is Avia?' Olivia asked, with a rising sense of excitement.

'*Where* is Avia? That is more to the point. Avia is a place. A land, in fact.'

'I've never heard of it,' Portia interjected. 'Is it very far away?'

'No one knows. Or, at least, no one in Birddom that I am aware of.'

'Don't you know?' Portia asked.

'I only know what I have been told. What has been talked of at the Council. Avia is a *wonderful* place, a paradise, where every bird is safe. A land where there is no hunger, and no enemies to fear. In Avia, the skies are always blue and the worms are fat and juicy. Above all, in Avia there is no Man.'

'Can such a place really exist? Mightn't it just be old wives' tales, made up to give comfort in times of trouble?'

Tomar looked quite piqued. 'Oh no, it exists, I am sure of that. The

Council is too solemn and austere a place for old wives tales.'

Portia spoke placatingly to her old friend. 'I am sorry, Tomar. It is not that I do not believe you, and I did not mean to give offence. It is just that Avia sounds like a dream.'

'It is a dream. It's a prayer. But nonetheless it is real. And you have to help me to find it.' The tawny owl's great eyes fixed upon the younger of the two female robins as he said this.

'Me?' Olivia replied, somewhat shakily.

'Yes, Olivia. Now, don't be afraid. I have a plan that I think will work. And Portia, like you I do not mean to give offence. I have thought long and hard about this. In the long road that is history, we all have a part to play. Great or small. And you have played yours, my dear, to Birddom's great benefit. Oh, I know that you would do anything, fly anywhere, out of love for me. But this task is not for you. Let the next generation take their turn. You have done enough.'

'But won't it be dangerous?' Portia asked, only somewhat mollified by Tomar's speech.

'Danger is all around us, you must know that. Birddom is no longer a safe place to live. And yet I won't try to deceive you. It is a desperate chance. But no more so than sending Kirrick flying across the length and breadth of the land. No more so than sending a plucky female across the seas to Wingland. No, my dear, I will not play down the dangers, but merely hope that Olivia here can find the courage inside herself to accept the quest.'

'What do I have to do?' the younger robin asked, quietly and calmly.

'I need you to go on a journey.'

'But you said that you didn't know where Avia is,' Portia interrupted.

'That is true, my dear. I don't. The door to that land is hidden from me. But I know of someone who is in possession of the key.'

'We have been lucky,' Traska said, hopping up and down in the clearing. Traces of blood still adorned his beak, from his earlier exploits with Cian. 'A lot of planning has gone into defeating Tomar, and it was nearly all for nothing. We are not yet ready, and all will be lost if that dratted owl gets wind of anything.'

'Stop worrying,' Engar replied. 'You said it yourself, we've been lucky. The only two birds in Birddom who bore this tale are no longer in any position to tell it. Our secrets are safe.'

'Can you be sure?' Traska's eyes flashed angrily. 'What if someone else knows? What if Tomar has sent out a whole network of little birds, flitting far and wide, and gathering gossip. If it was easy for one young chaffinch to find out so much...'

Traska left the sentence unfinished, but the barn owl met his stare with humorous defiance.

'If so, then we can have some more fun tearing them apart, can't we?'

The evil magpie laughed, in spite of himself, but then continued, more seriously.

'I still don't like it. We need to take precautions. What if I gathered all of our brethren together in our place? Cra Wyd could hold a vast host.'

'I think that would not be a wise move,' Engar replied, cautiously. He was nervous of igniting Traska's anger. The magpie scared him, in spite of his own size advantage. 'It would draw too much attention. If rooks and crows upped sticks and disappeared, questions would be asked, you can be sure of that.'

'Oh, all right,' Traska sulked. 'I suppose that what you say makes sense. We will just have to be more careful. And more secret, until we are ready. Then there will be no more need for secrets. All Birddom will know of us and will quake with fear!'

'You will have to find Septimus. He alone can tell you of the secret way. He, among all of the Creator's creatures, is the only one who can show you the gateway into Avia.'

'But who is Septimus, and where will I find him?'

Olivia's questions underlined her eagerness for such an adventure, and Tomar smiled at her before continuing.

'You are so like your father. Well, Septimus is revered in legend as being wise beyond any other. He must be very old indeed, if the stories are to be believed. For he has always been the guardian of the way, even from before the inception of Birddom. But here's a case of the rook calling the raven black! And yet, compared to him, I must still be a nestling.'

'How can any bird live to be so old?' Portia wondered.

Tomar shot her a swift glance of approval. 'Robins are nobody's fools,' he thought to himself. Aloud, he said, 'Septimus resides on the western fringe of the Isle of Storms. The stories are vague as to the exact location of his home, though I know it to be high on a mountainside. But I am sure that one so ancient and so revered will be well known among the local bird population. Once you get to the Isle of Storms, it should not prove too difficult to find him.'

Picking up on her mother's intuitive question, Olivia probed further. 'You didn't say what type of bird this Septimus is.'

'No. I didn't, did I? Actually, I didn't exactly say that he was a bird at all.'

'Not a bird?' cheeped Olivia, startled by such a revelation. 'What is he, then?'

'He is the oldest and the wisest...'

'Oldest and wisest what?' both robins asked at once.

'Well. Wolf, actually.'

'Wolf!' cried Portia, making Olivia jump with fright at the very word. 'You want my daughter to fly all the way to the Isle of Storms and pay a social visit to a wolf?'

The older robin was incredulous, while the younger one was near to fainting.

'I know that it is a lot to ask. I wouldn't let her go on her own. I have chosen a companion for her. His name is Kopa.'

'And who is Kopa? Is he a dog? Or a bear?'

'Kopa is a chaffinch,' Tomar answered, lamely.

'So now the wolf gets two little snacks, instead of one. Are you mad, Tomar? How can you even consider this?'

'We have no choice!' The anguish in Tomar's voice checked Portia's retort. 'I am sorry, but there is no other way. Don't you think that I've tried to find an alternative? I've thought of nothing else for days. But we have to make the attempt, or else we shall all die.'

Mother and daughter were silent for a while, giving the old owl time to compose himself once more.

'Forgive me. I am just so frustrated at my own weakness. If only I were able, I would take this burden upon myself.'

'On that long road, that you spoke about, you have played your part many times over, Tomar.' Portia went across to the old owl and stroked his heart with her wing-tips. 'You have done enough, my friend. This burden is one for others to carry.'

'I am so afraid,' Tomar responded, with tears in his eyes. 'Afraid for the future of Birddom. For Man is set against us, in his casually brutal way. And, when the insects rise up against us, as they surely will when they realise that we have broken the pact...' The old tawny owl's great back seemed to slump, as if his wings carried too great a weight to be borne. 'When that day comes,' he continued, 'it will be the end for all of us. Large or small. Brave or cowardly. It will not matter. Not a single bird will survive their onslaught.'

'Then I must make sure that I succeed in my quest,' Olivia said, simply.

At that moment, the three of them heard a cry. It came from a point some distance away, but they all recognised the voice.

'Merion,' they called together. 'Over here.'

An exhausted robin emerged from the undergrowth, and all but collapsed at Tomar's feet. 'Thank the Creator that I found you!'

'But what has happened?' Tomar questioned him gently. 'You look completely done in. Why are you in such distress?'

Merion broke down and wept at the old owl's words. 'Forgive me,' he gasped, through the tears. 'Please forgive me, Tomar.'

'There is nothing to forgive.'

'Nothing!' Merion exclaimed. 'I have been such a fool. I have betrayed you and have rejected everything that you taught me. I have brought dishonour upon my mother and sister, and have shamed the name of my father, Kirrick.'

At this, the two female robins closed to Merion's sides and tried to comfort him.

'It's not so bad,' Portia said. 'You chose the wrong path for a while, that is all. What is important is that you are back with us once more.'

'But I have seen such horrible things...'

At the sound of his own words, Merion seemed to be jerked back to his former urgency.

'Tomar!' he cried. 'I have terrible news. I have seen Traska!'

*

'What are we going to do with Calipha and her sister?' Engar deferred to Traska in asking this question, tacitly acknowledging the magpie's position of power in their relationship.

But Traska was in playful mood. 'What do you want to do with them? After all, you are Great Owl. Their fate is in your wings.'

'I have a mind to be merciful,' Engar announced, struggling to keep a straight face. 'Perhaps my first act on being proclaimed Great Owl will be one of clemency. No one who knows me could believe that I mean them any harm.'

'How noble and virtuous you are, Engar. Maybe you will sanction their release?'

'That might not be such a good idea at this stage. Questions might be asked. Awkward questions. Best if they remain where they are for the time being. I am sure that you have made them most comfortable!'

'They don't seem as grateful for my hospitality as I would have expected,' Traska smirked. 'Well, they will just have to get used to it. They won't be going anywhere for quite a while, until we decide the time and the place. Certainly, I don't want Calipha anywhere near the next Council meeting.'

'We must come up with something to prevent Tomar's presence, as well. I know that he has no real right to be there any longer, but you know how sanctimonious he is. He might still consider it his duty to interfere. It's only the remotest chance, I'm sure, but, if he does know something about us, I don't want him gate-crashing and spoiling my moment of glory.'

Traska merely smiled, but it was a cold, hard smile. Engar shuddered, just to look at it. The magpie had not uttered a word, but his message was unmistakable. Under no circumstances would Tomar be allowed to show his face at the Council meeting. Traska's smile said it: the old owl wasn't going anywhere.

Tomar's face was a mask of horror at the mention of that name. Portia and Olivia cried out, as if in pain.

'It is not possible, Merion. Traska is dead. We were told that he had been shot. You must be mistaken.'

'Do you think that I could ever make such a mistake? I will never forget that voice. His shape inhabits my nightmares. I would know that evil magpie anywhere!'

Tomar looked at the robin with pitying eyes. 'I am sorry. Forgive me, my friend. I do not doubt that you are correct. It is just that your words were such a shock to me. To us all. But I see that you speak truly. So, Traska is alive. That is ill news indeed. But now is the time for me to listen, not to make speeches. Please, Merion, tell us everything.'

So the robin recounted all that he had seen and heard in the rookery, and at Engar's nest-site. Tomar's sorrow at the news of the death of Kopa was matched by his anger at the barbaric execution of Cian. It was an evil act, and demonstrated the depths of Engar's depravity.

It was Portia who voiced that anger for them all. 'You were right, Tomar. You never trusted that owl. And here is the proof. He is a traitor and an enemy of Birddom, in cohorts with the corvidae. It is beyond belief.'

'Sadly, it is all too believable,' Tomar replied. 'Traska still lusts for power. His kind have tried for total domination, seeking to rule by overt acts of slaughter. Now it seems that he has found another way. Covert action and an alliance so diabolical that not a soul in Birddom would suspect it. A tryst between magpies and owls. Allowing the corvidae to rule from within. Oh, Creator, what will become of us all?'

'Do not despair, Tomar,' Olivia said, reassuringly. 'You still have your plan. Can it be carried out without the knowledge of the Council?'

'It can, and it must,' responded Tomar, positively. 'Engar and Traska must not be alerted, in any way. Secrecy is our only chance of success.'

Merion looked questioningly at the old owl. 'What plan, Tomar?'

'Before you arrived with your dreadful news, we were discussing an idea of mine. I feel that, in the not-too-distant future, we will have no option but to evacuate Birddom!'

Tomar then proceeded to tell Merion about Septimus, and the hope of a future in Avia. That same hope shone in the robin's eyes as he listened to Tomar's description of a paradise for birds.

'Can such a wonderful place exist? It sounds too good to be true.'

'Indeed it does, and yet I believe that there is such a place. Will you help us to find it?'

Merion looked at his sister, and his smile held all the warmth of a summer's day.

'I am not sure that I deserve the chance. But I will be proud to undertake such a journey with my sister. I will do everything in my power to protect her and to make sure that she succeeds in her quest.'

'*Our* quest, brother. Ours.' Olivia responded, throwing her wings around Merion, and hugging him to her.

Chapter Ten

The owls had all returned from their country-wide missions, and had reported back to Engar. Their message was unanimous and unequivocal. Throughout Birddom they had received an almost ecstatic response to their news of the rescinding of Tomar's edict. It seemed that birds across the land were in no mood for moral niceties. They were hungry, and here were the rulers of Birddom telling them that a feast awaited them. Few birds gave a single thought to the rights and wrongs involved in taking insects for food once more. Tomar's pact was shattered for ever.

Engar was exultant. The news of such a positive response swept away the last of his fears concerning Tomar's continued influence in Birddom. The old owl was finished, once and for all.

'Can't we kill him now?' Engar asked Traska. 'I would really enjoy that.'

'Don't be such an impetuous fool,' the magpie scolded. 'Tomar will die when I say, and not before. You always underestimate him, don't you? It is one of your biggest failings. Killing him now, before you are even voted for as Great Owl, would be a stupid mistake. You would make a martyr of him. No, we must stick to my plan. I will keep Tomar out of the way. He will become invisible. You will say nice things about him, in your acceptance speech, wishing him well and pledging to see to it personally that he is taken care of. Then, when the time is right, you will be able to announce, with all due solemnity, the sad demise of the former Great Owl.'

*

'You must go, without delay,' Tomar said. 'Time is pressing in upon us. Oh, has Birddom ever had three such enemies? Forage well, my young friends, though I fear that the fare hereabouts is scarce. Eat your fill. You will need every ounce of your strength to make the journey.'

'We will do as you say,' the pair of robins replied together. 'But do not fear for us, Tomar. We will succeed in our mission. We will find Septimus, and he will show us the way into Avia.'

With that, the two younger robins left their mother and Tomar, and flew to a more-densely foliated quarter of Tanglewood, where food might be more plentiful.

'I am so worried for them,' Portia said. 'They have no idea of the perils that they may face.'

'Neither did you, my dear, before you departed for Wingland. But you did not let it daunt you. Moreover, you left behind your children. At least they do not have to make that choice.'

'That is true, my friend, and I am grateful for it. I do not know whether, given the choice again, I would have the courage to risk all for Birddom's sake.'

'That is not even in doubt,' Tomar answered, firmly. 'You have proven your bravery beyond any reproach. Yours is the stoutest heart in Birddom, my dear.'

'Well, it doesn't feel very stout at the moment. But hush, here they come.'

Merion flew back onto one of the branches in Tomar's tree, his beak bulging with berries and nuts. These he deposited on the bough, and flew off again in search of more food. Olivia swiftly followed suit, and soon a large pile was gathered.

'Let us take our meal together,' Merion suggested. 'It is a long time since we have had the opportunity to do so, and we may be gone for quite a while.'

'A splendid idea,' replied Tomar. 'And a thoughtful one, too. I am humbled by your kindness. You are the ones going off into potential danger, and yet you think of a useless old fool like me.'

'There is no creature in the land who is less like a fool, Tomar, and well you know it,' Olivia countered. 'Without you, we would not even know where to start. But no more talk. Our feast awaits.'

Replete from their meal, the three robins and the owl slept for several hours. They awoke again at dusk, which seemed to Tomar to be a propitious time to be embarking upon a journey.

'These are dark times,' he said. 'It seems appropriate that you should leave under the cover of night. If you fly hard, my friends, you should be well beyond the boundaries of Tanglewood before the moon reaches its zenith. You must then plan your progress carefully, according to your needs. You must balance the urgency of your mission against the risk of exposure to the many dangers that you face. Take great care of yourselves, my dear, dear young robins. Birddom is depending upon you.'

'We will not fail,' Merion answered.

Olivia nodded in agreement. 'We will not be beaten, by Man nor bird. Nothing will prevent us reaching the Isle of Storms.'

'It is time to call the Council to order,' Engar announced, with due solemnity. 'This is the dawn of a new era for Birddom. We have serious business to attend to. Your journeys, in recent weeks, have been vital to the future of our land. Each one of you has reported back to me, and I know all of your news. But everything is not known to all here. Let us rectify that, if time permits. Be brief, be concise, but let every Council member know of the reality of the world that we serve.'

This lengthy, and somewhat pompous opening speech nevertheless drew admiring glances from all around the ring of oaks. Not a single owl there dared to question Engar's right to open the proceedings of the Council. His appointment to the position of Great Owl was yet to be ratified, but it was seen as a fait accompli. However, it was not until the fifth owl had made his report that the subject was broached.

Creer, the long-eared owl, had flown far to the south of Birddom, and his report highlighted the ever-increasing threat of Man in the conurbations that were his stronghold in this part of the country. Spraying or netting had killed or injured thousands of small birds in the south. Food was scarce, even in the arable-rich areas, due to Man's jealous possessiveness of his crops. Creer reported the delight of every bird in response to the news of the lifting of sanctions against eating insects for food. The softer southern climate, and the previous adherence to the ban, meant that there was now a vast proliferation ready for harvesting.

'And it is down to your foresight and wisdom, oh Great Owl,' Creer finished, 'that Birddom is now in a position to reap the rewards. You have saved our land from starvation.'

This comment drew a murmur of general approval, and one or two of the owls broke out into a ragged cheer. Engar held up his wing, and silence fell upon the other Council members.

'I would like to thank Creer for his kind words. But although they are undoubtedly sincere, they are also somewhat presumptuous. In this present Council we are all equals. My voice is but one amongst ten. I stand no higher than any of my brothers and sisters here. It might even be asked whether we need a Great Owl at all. This new Birddom was ever intended as a democracy, and, at best, the Great Owl should be merely a gatherer and garner of the wishes of the entire Council, a summariser, not an autocratic law-giver. A voice to the thoughts of the ten wielders of power in the land. But it is dangerous for power to be wielded without responsibility, and it has always been the wisdom of the Council of the Owls that has led Birddom along the right path.'

Stirred by the nobility of Engar's rhetoric, Creer could not help but call out, 'Will you lead us?' and this call was taken up by every owl there. Nine voices, raised in unison, demanding that the barn owl should acquiesce. Engar called for silence once more.

'Thank you, my friends. Your belief in my abilities humbles me, and I am deeply moved by your loyalty and passion. I will serve Birddom as its Great Owl. It is an honour which I did not seek, but one that I am proud to accept. Particularly proud, as it means that I will be able to lead such a fine bunch of owls as yourselves. Thank you again, my friends. But we must once more move to business. Steele, we will hear your report next.'

The old owl sat contentedly beside Portia, as they watched her children fly away, Portia's chest swelling with pride. 'So, the story carries on,' she said. 'Like a river flowing through time.'

'Yes,' agreed Tomar. 'First Kirrick, then you. And now your children. It is fitting.'

'And beyond them? What does the future hold?'

'Who knows?' the owl replied. 'But they will shape that future. They carry it with them, in their wings. And who knows? Their children and their children's children may play their part also, helping that river on its journey.'

'I hope so, Tomar. It comforts me to think so, especially in these dark times. But what part will I play? I may be getting old, but I am not yet nest-bound. Is there anything that I can do?'

'It may seem arrogant of me for saying so, but I believe that you can serve Birddom well by keeping me alive, my dear friend. I still believe that I have one final part to play in the drama to come. My enemies believe that they have diminished and side-lined me. As such, I am sure that they will not long feel any need to keep these old bones from the earth. I need your help, Portia. Sustain me against their cruelty. I have been given a glimpse of the future. Not for me an honourable death. Engar and Traska want to see me suffer. I am sure that their plans for me involve a slow starvation, and an ignominious end.'

'Well, I will not let that happen, not while there is a single breath left in my body, Tomar. I will protect you and keep you alive, as best I am able, so that you can, at the final end, save us all.'

'It is all going exactly as you planned!' Engar exclaimed.

'Did you doubt it?' Traska asked, with a sardonic tone. 'I have thought about this for a long time. Did you think that I would have left anything to chance?'

'Not for a moment,' said Engar, placatingly. 'You are a genius, Traska. Evil and twisted. But a genius, nonetheless.'

Traska's harsh laughter echoed around the clearing. 'Thank you, my friend. Your compliments will undo me, if I am not careful.'

Engar clapped his friend on the back with his great wing. 'One thing did surprise me, though. I had half-expected that meddlesome old fool Tomar to turn up at the Council meeting. I am amazed that he has given in so easily.'

'Let us just say that he was unavoidably detained,' replied the magpie.

Engar hooted with pleasure. 'Oh, do tell. Please, Traska. Don't keep me in suspense. What have you been up to?'

'Come with me, and let me show you.'

With that, magpie and owl took to the air, and flew off in the direction of Tanglewood. They encountered the first crow when they were still a mile distant from Tomar's home. The black sentry stiffened to attention at the sight of the pair.

'Anything to report?' Traska asked.

'Nothing, sir,' the crow replied. 'I've been around the perimeter twice this morning. No sign of any activity from the prisoner. Mind you, from the sight of him, I don't reckon he'd get past a ring of wrens. He'll not be causing us any trouble.'

'I'm glad to hear it,' Traska said. 'But keep on your guard. I won't look too kindly on any failure, especially now that you have reassured me that Tomar is a spent force.'

The crow nodded uneasily at the veiled threat, but blustered on. 'He is too old and too frail to attempt anything, but, even if he did, he'd be no match for my lads. They'd finish him in a minute.'

'I don't want him finished,' Traska cut in, sharply. 'Not until I am good and ready.' Then, turning to Engar, he continued, more calmly. 'Shall we go and take a look? After all, we must do all that we can for the welfare of our old friend.'

Engar looked doubtful. 'Is that altogether wise?'

'What?' snapped Traska.

'I can see that he is being well guarded. Tomar is certainly not going anywhere. What is to be gained by showing ourselves to him at this stage? Don't forget, he doesn't know that you are even alive. It's surely not worth the risk.'

'I'll decide what risks are or are not worth taking. And, anyway, we *have* shown ourselves to him. Where will he think that the guards have come from? He is no fool, Engar. Don't ever forget that. Anyway, I *want* him to know. That is why I have showed our hand. I want Tomar to worry. I want him to fret. Let him lose sleep. I want his mind torn apart by the thought that I am back, ready to defeat him in the end.'

'Let him think it, then. But don't let him know it for sure. Leave the doubt there, to fester alongside the worry. Don't show your face to Tomar.'

'Are you giving me orders?' Traska asked, in an unnervingly mild voice that made the feathers rise on the back of Engar's neck.

'No,' he answered, hurriedly. 'Of course not, Traska. I would never tell you what to do. We are partners, you and I. Equal partners in this enterprise.'

A smile spread across the evil magpie's beak. 'You think that, if it gives you comfort,' he muttered, under his breath. 'Until the time comes.'

When Tomar realised that he was being guarded, that he was a virtual prisoner in his own home, he was not surprised. The old owl was merely thankful that he had been able to set Merion and Olivia off on their journey before the net had closed. It made him fearful for Portia, but, at this stage, he had no way of knowing if the corvidae were in place to keep him in or others out. He hoped fervently that he would still be allowed to see his friend. But he knew, from bitter experience, that he could not rely on the generosity of his captors.

Tomar was well aware that Traska was behind all of this. He knew also that the act was designed to keep him isolated from those that he had formerly thought of as his friends on the Council of the Owls, to minimise any continuing influence that he might have. Traska and Engar could not know that he had any knowledge of their complicity. His life would be forfeit, in such circumstances. Of that he was certain. And that knowledge was power, after a fashion. It gave the old owl an advantage, and one which he was unlikely to squander. It was more important to the future of Birddom that he kept his powder dry for future use, if at all. The guards were not a great inconvenience. He was not going anywhere. He was old, infirm and had no need to travel. All he needed to do was think, and no amount of sentries could limit the compass of his mind. No, he would not provoke them. But he would focus every ounce of his remaining strength on defeating them.

Dawn was breaking over the gently-rolling hills, and promised fine and favourable weather as the pair of robins flew westward. They had made very good progress, although their journey had only just begun. Their hurried departure had left little time for the robins to begin to worry about any dangers that might lie ahead, and, now that they were on their way, their exuberance pushed any thoughts of foreboding to the back of their minds. They flew with ardent hearts and youthful vitality. And they flew with the joy of reunion. Olivia had missed her brother, and held no recriminations for his recent follies.

And for Merion, his errors of judgement were mistakes to be put behind him. He had been given the chance to start afresh, an opportunity for atonement. He would not fail. He would rather die than let down those who loved him.

Swooping closer, he called to Olivia. 'Keep up, sis. We have a long journey ahead of us. I know that you are weaker than I, and I will try to accommodate your slower pace. But I fear that I will fall out of the sky if I have to fly this slowly!'

Olivia laughed. 'Save your breath for your flying. You'll need it to match my speed. I can fly rings around you, and well you know it. And the only reason that you'll fall out of the sky is because you're too fat!'

It was Merion's turn to laugh now, as he chased his sister in a pretence of annoyance. 'Let's see your best then,' he cried. 'We've got two more hours of good flying before Man wakes to his mischief. Let's see how much distance we can put behind us before we rest.'

So challenged, Olivia excelled herself in her exertions, and her brother matched her. They flew as if the very devil were pulling at their tail-feathers and, after some time, they alighted on a twisted hedge of blackberry, collapsing in an exhausted heap amongst the brambles. There the robins allowed themselves a couple of hours sleep. They woke, refreshed and famished. The blackberry was in full bloom, but some months away from bearing fruit, so they were forced to forage farther afield for a meal. Merion and Olivia flitted here and there, gleaning a few seeds from the nearby vegetation. Then they alighted side by side on a substantial bough, along which crawled a bright-green caterpillar.

Merion looked at his sister. 'Do you remember, Olivia? When we were fledglings, and Tomar was teaching us about the world?'

'I remember the tool that he used to teach you with. It was a painful lesson, as I recall.'

'Yes. A clout from an owl's wing is a powerful way of getting a message across. It's a lesson that I've not forgotten.'

'Haven't you?' asked Olivia, looking at her brother with reproach in her eyes.

'No!' he replied, earnestly. 'It might have slipped my mind for a while, but I remember it well enough now.'

Merion turned away from his sister's gaze, and bent his head towards the wriggling creature in front of him. 'Off you go, my little friend. You'll come to no harm today. Excuse us for not stopping and chatting, but we've got food to find.'

*

It seemed that finding food was an issue that Tomar would no longer have to face. If he had thought that Engar and Traska had planned for him to starve, he was indeed mistaken. For he was provided daily with sufficient food to feed far more than just a solitary, ageing owl. But therein lay the cruelty. For the diet so solicitously provided for him was made entirely of insects. Bugs of every kind were brought to his nest-site by the crows who were guarding him. And those insects that were living soon made a hasty and thankful departure. Tomar would not eat them, living or dead.

It was only Portia's ingenuity that ensured Tomar's continued survival. Her initial attempts to see the old owl were thwarted by the guards, who had evidently been briefed about Tomar's friendship with robins. So Portia decided to overcome her fastidiousness and ingrained habits of personal cleanliness. She bathed in mud and dust, concentrating on her tell-tale chest feathers. After much effort, she managed to conceal her red breast and, in doing so, became simply another dun-coloured little bird. The subterfuge worked splendidly, and her passage about Tanglewood was unhindered. Even Tomar had not recognised her immediately when she had arrived at the crooked fir bearing a beakful of sedge grass. And Portia's reward at fooling her old friend was doubled by hearing his hearty laugh once the disguise was breached.

'Truly, my dear Portia. You are magnificent. Kirrick would have been proud of you.'

'Well, I would be a poor kind of robin if I failed in the one task that you set me. I will keep you alive, even if I am never able to wash again!'

Chapter Eleven

Olivia stared out over the vast expanse of water that barred their way. The sea was slate-grey in colour, with only the white caps of the rough, tumbling waves providing a relief from the uniform dullness. Crossing it was not an enticing prospect. But the pair of robins had two advantages over their mother, Portia, when she and Mickey, her bullfinch companion, had faced a similar journey some years earlier. For one, the distance of the crossing was considerably shorter, landfall on the Isle of Storms being less than twenty miles from where Merion and Olivia now sat. More importantly, the two robins knew the trick that Portia and Mickey had used to achieve their seemingly impossible task. It was merely a matter of plucking up the courage.

Their journey, thus far, had been uncomplicated and free from danger. It had taken them swiftly across the breadth of Birddom, without incident. They had not encountered any magpie bands, and had judiciously avoided any larger predators. The only delay during their travels had been the result of a squabble between brother and sister when they had reached the western mountain home of Darreal, the red kite.

Both robins remembered the awe that they had felt when they had first seen the magnificent leader of the falcons. He had been one of the honoured guests at the first Council of the Owls to be held after the Great Battle, which had seen the defeat of the corvidae. The pair, then young fledglings, had hidden behind their mother's tail, peeking out at the red kite who, along with Storne, the golden eagle, and Kraken, the great black-backed gull, discussed weighty matters of state with the leaders of Birddom.

Of course, the years had lessened the awe, and it was not fear that made Merion argue against visiting Darreal in his mountain stronghold. He reasoned that time was of the essence, and that their hard work, in coming so far in so short a time, would be undone if they delayed now. Olivia understood that her brother's argument was a sound one, but she longed to see the great falcon again, if only to reassure herself that, with such mighty birds on her side, nothing was impossible. Also, she felt a long way from home, and from the wisdom of their mentor, Tomar. But Merion's logic prevailed. They could not afford to waste any time. Their journey was too crucial to the very future of Birddom, and of every bird that lived there. So, reluctantly, the two robins had by-passed Darreal's home, and had continued on to the coast.

'Come on then. What are we waiting for?'

Without waiting for a reply, Merion flew across the small gap of swirling water, and on to the rail of the ship. Olivia had little option but to follow her brother.

Unloading long over, the ferry was deserted for the moment, although, further along the jetty, an eager crowd waited noisily for the barrier to be removed and embarkation to begin. Two children spotted the robins, and tugged excitedly at their father's sleeve but, by the time that they had attracted his attention and pointed, Merion and Olivia had disappeared. The robins had flown off swiftly in search of an isolated place to hide. They discounted the fore-deck, where seating promised a plethora of people. Aft, there were similar arrangements, for those who felt the need to wave farewell to their homeland. There was no convenient coil of rope, such as had served their mother so well during her sea crossings. There was rope everywhere, of course, but it was all too close to the areas of public access for the robins' purposes.

It was Olivia who spotted the small tear in the canvas covering of the lifeboat, which hung suspended high above the walkway on the starboard side of the ship. The wind had caused the coarse material to flap, and the movement had caught her attention.

'Look, Merion. What about in there?'

'It's worth a try,' he replied, flitting swiftly through the gap in the cloth.

Inside the lifeboat it was dark and cool under its covering. There was plenty of space, and, at one end, a pile of blankets, which would provide a soft bed for the journey. Merion poked his head out through the hole, and called to his sister.

'It's perfect, Olivia. Much better than mother's hiding place. And we won't even get wet from the sea-spray. Well done, sis.'

Olivia smiled at the compliment and quickly joined Merion in their safe-haven. She was not a moment too soon. Seconds later, a large, bearded man came along the walkway and paused beneath the lifeboat, leaning over the rail and checking that all the ropes that held it aloft were securely fastened. The pair of robins peered cautiously out through the hole in the canvass, but the seaman did not look up, and after a few minutes, contented, strolled off along the deck.

'He's gone,' Olivia cheeped, with relief.

'Good. We may as well make ourselves comfortable, then. It shouldn't be too long before we are on our way. We should make the Isle of Storms well before nightfall.'

Merion's prediction proved unerring. The crossing was a rough one in the heavy seas, and the lifeboat rocked alarmingly in spite of the restraints holding it in place. But the journey was not prolonged by more than half an hour, and it was late afternoon when the ferry docked and began disgorging its human and mechanical cargo. Once again the robins were thankful for their chosen hiding place, as it offered some protection from the overpowering stench of petrol fumes, as a steady stream of cars rolled off the ferry and drove away. Merion and Olivia waited patiently for all noise and activity to abate, then they emerged from the small boat and flew gratefully onto dry land.

'OK, sis. Where to now?' Merion asked cheerily. But it was a serious question. Where were they to go? They knew that they had to find Septimus, but Tomar's instructions had been very vague. A mountain 'somewhere in the west' was not a very precise location. Still, it was all that they had to go on. Simultaneously, they raised their eyes to the horizon. The sky was a clear blue and the late-afternoon sunshine bathed their faces.

'The west it is, then,' Olivia replied. 'And don't worry, brother. The Creator will help us to find the way.'

It was well into the next day before Merion and Olivia allowed themselves to stop and rest. Much of the coastal area was heavily populated by Man and, by choosing to follow the course of the river, whose mouth housed the ferry port, the robins had to fly inland for many miles before the houses petered out into scattered dwellings and then isolated farms.

Olivia was exhausted and fell swiftly into a deep sleep, almost before her feet touched the branch of the heavily-leafed beech in which they had chosen to rest. However, sleep came much less easily to her brother. His conscience over his months of folly pricked at him uncomfortably. What a fool he had been! How had he allowed himself to be so easily swayed, and won over, by such an evil bird? And yet

Engar's words seemed to make so much sense at the time. In a way, they still did. But it was not so much the words that were at fault, as it was the foul creature who spoke them. For they concealed a deeper truth: a lust for power, and a willingness to abandon all moral certitude for the sake of personal glory. Merion believed in a better Birddom for every bird. But Engar did not, and never had.

'I will not fail in this,' the robin promised himself. 'If it only makes amends for a tenth of the wrongs that I have done, I will learn the way to Avia. Even if I am not worthy to go there myself.'

Merion looked over at his sister, sleeping soundly, and he smiled, with a protective fondness.

'Sleep well, Olivia,' he whispered, adding, to himself, 'take her lead, you foolish bird, and get some sleep. You will need all of your strength in the days to come.'

Traska had a plan for his oldest adversary. One that even Engar was not privy to. Indeed, if the barn owl were to find out the nature of Traska's strategy, it would shock him to the core. But the strength of the magpie's plan was in its secrecy. No one else knew what he intended. He had made the mistake in the past of confiding in others. Never again. He had entrusted no part of it to any of his lieutenants. Even in his tours around the country he had spoken in generalities, raising the expectations of the corvidae by jingoistic rhetoric. None of them knew a single detail of how they would achieve what he consistently promised them.

But Traska knew every detail, every nuance, and, in his plan, it was essential to keep Tomar alive for the time-being. However, this had to be on his own terms. He wanted the ancient tawny owl to capitulate completely, robbing himself in the process of any moral high-ground.

But Tomar's guards reported back that he was refusing to eat the insects that they were providing. The obstinate old fool was unable to yield an iota of his principles, even if it meant starving to death. Traska's fury at the old owl's intransigence gnawed away at him, eroding the caution that Engar had counselled. He had to see for himself. So the magpie flew deeper into Tanglewood, fully prepared to confront his foe, to reveal himself to Tomar, as he had wished to so often, ever since this adventure had begun. But ill-fortune dictated otherwise. For his arrival at Tomar's home coincided with that of Portia, in disguise, bringing her old friend another life-saving meal. The robin did not see her evil enemy approach, busy as she was gathering food for Tomar. And, initially, Traska did not recognise her. To his eyes, it was just another small bird going about her business. But, as he watched her, something about the small bird's movements and manner jarred. The way that she carried herself. The distinctive bobbing of her head, as if nodding in acknowledgement of some universal truth, were unmistakably robin.

Traska laughed mirthlessly to himself. It was cleverly done, he had to concede that. A trick of her own ingenuity, or born of Tomar's intellect? It mattered not. He knew her now.

'Well, well, Portia, my dear,' he gloated, silently. 'This is an unexpected pleasure. We really must get together soon. To reminisce over old times. And absent friends!'

It was a sight to strike terror into the hearts of the pair of robins, a nightmare recalled from their childhood. And it had only been the merest stroke of luck that had prevented total disaster. The cool, green shade offered by the solitary ash tree had proved irresistible to the tired birds, and they had gladly taken advantage of shelter from the hot sun. But barely an instant after they had alighted, Merion had frozen, motionless, on the well-camouflaged branch. Instinctively, Olivia had mirrored her brother's actions.

'What is it?' she whispered. 'What do you see?'

Merion gestured minutely with his beak, and Olivia's gaze followed where he had indicated. The pretty robin's heart constricted with shock and fear as she saw what had caused Merion such distress. Hopping across the field in front of them were two huge corvids. Many years earlier, their father, Kirrick, had hidden in an ash tree when being hunted by a pair of cruel magpies. Now his children faced a similar danger. But these birds were not magpies. They were huge and menacing spectres from Merion and Olivia's past: a pair of giant hooded crows.

And worse was to follow. For the two corvids were soon joined by four more of their own kind. The immediate reaction of the robins was to fear that a trap had been set for them. That somehow, Traska had sent word and arranged this deadly reception committee. But it seemed that there was no urgency in the actions of the hooded crows. They were merely foraging in a leisurely manner, and calling raucously to each other while they fed.

'What are we going to do now?' Olivia asked quietly.

'What can we do?' replied her brother, equally softly. 'We'll just have to stay where we are, and hope that they don't spot us.'

'Do you really think that they would harm us?'

'That's a stupid question. They would kill us in a moment, if they found us. You've seen them before. You know what they are capable of. Now no more words, I beg of you. Our safety lies in our silence.'

Portia was in even greater danger than her two children, but unlike Merion and Olivia, she was unaware of the threat. It was not until she had almost bumped her beak into the huge black chest that she registered the presence of the massive crow towering over her. The robin's eyes darted right and left, quickly confirming her worst fears. Two more of the black sentinels hemmed her in.

And then a voice spoke from behind her, soft and coercive, but full of menace. 'Portia, my dear. It's been such a long time.'

The robin whirled round to confront her tormentor, and looked into a face of pure evil.

'I must say, you do seem to have let yourself go since I saw you last. You look as if you need a *really* good bath. I barely recognised you. Still, there must be red under there somewhere.'

Portia's reactions jerked her off her feet as she fell backwards to avoid the savage thrust from Traska's sharp beak. The magpie laughed contemptuously, looking down at her on the ground.

'Don't you want to die like your mate? Such a noble death, I always thought. And one that gave me a great deal of satisfaction. But not for you, it seems. So, my dear. Just how do you want to die?'

Portia's desperation seemed to give the evil magpie an almost sensual satisfaction.

'Take your time. I'm in no great hurry. We can take as long as you like. In fact, I think that I'd like that best of all. A nice, slow, painful death. Wouldn't that be the perfect end to such a lovely day?'

Tomar was getting worried. Portia had promised the old owl that she would come this evening, and she had never yet let him down. It wasn't the hunger that troubled him. That was a fact of life. Even the rations that Portia so diligently provided for him made barely a dent on his constant hunger. But he was used to the gnawing pains in his stomach, and had conditioned himself to ignore them. The robin gave him enough food to keep him alive, and it was sufficient for his needs. But Portia gave Tomar something else also: company. Another thing that Engar and Traska strove to starve him of. To have someone to talk to was as important as a partly-filled stomach. Portia kept him in touch with reality and provided reassurance when Tomar began to doubt the wisdom of his plans.

The old owl glanced up at the skies, noting, with despondency, the fast-approaching onset of evening. Where could she have got to? He shuffled painfully along the bough of the crooked fir, peering out into the gloom for a sight of his friend. But the robin was nowhere to be seen. Tomar's head lowered miserably onto his chest, as loneliness overwhelmed him. It was an act of great cruelty on Traska's part to keep the old owl in such solitary confinement. And it added greatly to his sadness that none of his old friends on the Council had, to his knowledge, made any concerted effort to visit him. Although they had rejected him and ousted him from his position as Great Owl, Tomar held on to the belief that one or two of the Council members still felt fondness and respect for him personally. But it seemed that none had demonstrated the courage to defy the new regime. Portia, alone, had kept the old owl in contact with the outside world, and Tomar felt a renewed surge of fear for his friend's safety, as the hour got late and still no one came.

The pair of robins felt a huge sense of relief when the six hooded crows finally finished feeding in the field, and flapped off in unison to the south. Merion and Olivia relaxed the tense muscles that had held them inert for over an hour, and flapped their wings to circulate the blood once more.

'Let's move,' Olivia cheeped to her brother. 'I don't want to be here if they come back.'

'No. One close encounter with that lot is more than enough. Aren't they terrifying?'

Olivia let out a nervous laugh. 'Not to their mothers, perhaps. But seeing them brought it all back so clearly. Being held prisoner. Thinking all the time that we were certain to be killed, when we had barely begun to have a life at all.'

'I remember, sis. Indeed, it is something that I will never forget. But can you imagine how I felt, when I went back looking for Engar, and heard Traska's evil voice?'

'I think that I would have dropped dead on the spot,' Olivia replied. 'But we're still very much alive, Merion. And if we want to remain so, I suggest that we get on our way without further delay.'

So saying, Olivia took wing and, followed by her brother, sped westwards once more, towards the distant mountains where, if their luck held, they would finally meet the ancient wolf, Septimus, and would learn the secret of the gateway into Avia.

The magpie flew in slow, processional circles around the crooked fir, giving Tomar every opportunity to see the trophy that he carried between his talons. Then he flew down, landing awkwardly because of his burden, and hopped imperiously over towards the old owl.

'Greetings Tomar, my oldest friend. I expect that I'm the very last bird that you thought you'd ever see again. But here I am, alive and well. And I've brought you a present.' Receiving no reply, Traska continued, in taunting tones. 'I thought that you might be hungry. I had heard that you had been a bit fussy over what you would and would not eat. I cannot blame you. Insects aren't very appetising, are they? Although beggars really shouldn't be choosers. But I'm sure, like me, that you much prefer to feast on fresh meat, don't you? There's nothing quite like the taste of still-warm flesh, is there? So, as I said, I've brought you a little present. Not more than a mouthful for a hungry owl, I'd guess. But enjoy it anyway.'

Tears welled up in Tomar's old eyes as he looked down upon the limp little body of his friend.

'I would like to comfort you by telling you that she didn't suffer. But that really wouldn't be true, as you can imagine. In fact, she suffered a great deal. But she was a brave little bird, I'll give her that. Right up until I broke her back. She screamed then, and it was the sweetest sound that I have ever heard. But it didn't last, of course. No stamina, these small birds. No threshold for pain.'

A murderous anger filled Tomar's throat, and he roared with violent outrage as he lunged towards the magpie. But his aged body denied him just revenge, and he overbalanced, toppling from his perch and landing, winded, on the leaf-strewn ground below.

Traska looked down at the prostrate owl, and sneered venomously. 'Now that wasn't very sensible, was it? And you are the one who is supposed to be so wise. You're a bit long-in-the-beak for such melo-dramatic heroics. You ought to be careful, you know, you might hurt yourself. And hurting you is my prerogative, I'm afraid. Actually, I'm not at all afraid. But you, dear Tomar, you should be very afraid indeed!'

Chapter Twelve

Up close, the great black bulk of the mountain was a daunting sight for the pair of tiny birds. It towered above them, seeming to block out what little light remained in the evening sky. They had exercised extreme caution during their travels across the Isle of Storms, after their chance encounter with the hooded crows. Both Merion and Olivia realised that they had been extremely fortunate to have avoided contact with that particular troop of corvidae. They had witnessed first-hand, in their infancy, the casual brutality of which those huge birds were capable.

However, in the days of their subsequent travels, neither robin had dared to risk even the briefest contact with any of the local small bird population, though their journey did not pass unnoticed. Several birds called out to them in their passing, either in greeting or as a challenge in response to territory invaded. But the robins maintained their silence and flew on, even though avoidance of such contact hampered them greatly in their search for the home of Septimus. For surely they would have been able to receive word of the great wolf from the indigenous populace. His legend would have loomed large indeed in these parts. But caution reigned supreme, so the robins trusted to luck. And fortune did not desert them.

Merion and Olivia had chosen a gorse bush, smothered in glowing yellow petals, as a suitable place to rest, while they considered what they should do next. They were not even sure if the mountain that stood so imposingly before them was the one that Tomar had told them about. Several other smaller mountains were dotted about the region, but instinct told them that this was the most likely home for so great a creature as Septimus.

So engrossed were the two robins in discussing their immediate plans that they were completely unaware of the pair of eyes that watched their every movement and the pair of ears that heard their every word. The eyes twinkled with barely-contained merriment; the ears twitched with ill-concealed curiosity.

'So old Septimus is going to get a run-out after all this time, is he? And not before time. He has been dormant for far too long. But now it seems that Birddom needs the old wolf's help.'

Ears twitched once more with excitement, and muscles bunched in eager anticipation. Then, with effortless grace and athleticism, the watcher launched himself into the air. His bound carried him easily over the bush where the startled birds squatted. Landing with equal ease, he turned quickly to face Merion and Olivia.

'Welcome!' the rabbit said, mirth crinkling his nose and shining from his huge eyes, ringed in black fur in an otherwise white face. His body fur was white, too, save for a ridge of black along his spine, and a dark tip to one of his ears.

'My name is Hobo,' he continued. 'And this is my mountain.'

'Your mountain?' Merion queried, in an incredulous voice.

'Indeed,' Hobo replied, with frosty dignity. 'And why would it not be so?'

The robin was immediately contrite. 'Forgive me, Hobo. I did not mean to give any offence. We are strangers here, my sister and I, and we do not know the locality. We had been told to seek out a venerable wolf called Septimus, and had thought this to be *his* mountain.'

'Old Septimus lives here, all right. He lives with me, in fact. But it is my mountain, all the same.'

Sensing that her brother might make another clumsy remark, Olivia interceded. 'It is a beautiful place, and we thank you for your welcome. I am Olivia, and this is Merion, my brother, as he has already said. We have come a long way, having journeyed from Birddom in the hope of seeing Septimus and asking for his help.'

Without warning, the rabbit leapt clean over their heads, turning in mid-air and continuing the conversation, without pause, upon landing. 'And what help could a wolf be giving to a pair of robins?'

Merion's head swivelled round, body following until he once again faced the right way. Olivia followed suit, and answered Hobo's question. 'We have been sent on a mission by Tomar, the tawny owl who until recently was leader of Birddom.'

A glint of recognition showed in Hobo's eyes at the mention of that name, and Olivia continued with renewed hope. 'I see that you have heard of him. He is a great and wise owl who has nurtured the land that we live in, and ourselves personally, for all of our lives. We owe him everything, and now seek to help him triumph over evil by succeeding in our mission. Can you help us?'

The female robin's eyes looked beseechingly into those of the rabbit, and Hobo smiled reassuringly. 'I can, and I will. But all in good time. It is not often that strangers visit my mountain. I am eager for news of the wider world. You spoke of evil in Birddom. We had heard tales about the rise of a dark wing over the land some years ago, when the corvidae strove for power. But surely they were defeated, and their threat broken in two?'

'They were defeated, yes. Thanks to the genius of Tomar, and the bravery of many, including our father, Kirrick, and our mother, Portia.'

It seemed, from Hobo's reaction, that he had heard of these names also, and the rabbit confirmed this immediately. 'Honoured guests indeed, of such parentage. But accept my apologies. I interrupted you. Go on with your story, please.'

'The corvidae rebellion was crushed, and their covens scattered. Slyekin was killed, but his lieutenant, Traska, disappeared. He returned, however, to make mischief in Birddom once more, and it is only thanks to Tomar that the evil magpie did not murder us, as he has so many before. He fled Birddom again, and we thought that the threat was ended once and for all. But Traska has returned, as wily as ever and more powerful than before. For now he has made an alliance with Engar, the new Great Owl and leader of Birddom. The corvidae are on the rise once more, and our land is in great peril.'

The rabbit looked distressed, but not surprised. 'That is sore news indeed. That an owl should so betray the trust of Birddom! Grave tidings, my little friends. But set aside your worries for a while. I am sure that a way can be found to help you in your hour of need. For now, come with me. There is someone whom I think you may be eager to meet.'

Engar was facing something of a revolt from a faction of the Council of the Owls. This was the first challenge to his authority, and the barn owl was determined to deal with it swiftly and decisively. There were three owls opposing him, but only one provided Engar with any misgivings. Wensus and Janvar were vacillators, easily swayed by whichever owl was speaking to them at the time. He could bring them back into line. No, it was Lostri who was the obvious ring-leader in this conspiracy. What was it with these damned tawny owls? It was almost as if they had been sent to plague him. Somehow, Lostri had gotten wind of disturbances in the wider world of Birddom that were being attributed to corvids. The events in themselves were relatively minor, isolated breakdowns in the iron band of discipline forged by the will of Traska. Indeed, that magpie had ensured that swift retribution had been carried out against the perpetrators, angry that their actions might jeopardise his plans. But, limited though they may have been, small birds had been killed, and the spectre of Slyekin loomed large still in Birddom. Every bird's fear was for the rise of the corvidae, and a return to darkness and despair.

Engar knew that he had to be careful. He could not simply dismiss Lostri's information out-of-wing. But he had no intention of acceding even an iota of his authority. In the last Council meeting he had broached, without opposition, the notion that, for the sake of Birddom's harmonious future, the ostracised brotherhood of the corvidae be brought back into the fold as full and equal members. They had committed their crime and served their time. It was appropriate that the new Council should begin to heal the rift, he had argued persuasively. And the Council had fallen in line behind him.

It had been decided that a delegation would soon be sent to several of the known strongholds, where the corvidae had regained a small measure of their former power. Engar had chosen three owls for the job – to a bird his staunchest supporters, and owls least likely to question his decision. But it now seemed that Lostri had taken it upon himself to do some investigating of his own. Well, Engar would have to keep an eye on that owl in the future. But, for now, he had to act.

'Lostri, I would like to thank you for your diligence in this matter. Indeed, you have taken a great deal upon yourself, not having been investigating in any official capacity. But this does not diminish the importance of your findings. I am gravely troubled to hear of any acts of violence done to Birddom's own family, however minor these infractions are in the overall scheme of things. It is sad that this should cast a cloud over our future relations with an almost-wholly contrite corvidae. But evil is evil, and must be eradicated from our land. I believe that it is even more important now that we hold talks with the leaders of the magpies and crows. I am sure that we will find that they, every bit as much as ourselves, do not wish for any ill-will between us.

'I propose that you, Lostri, should join our delegation, and that the four of you should delay no longer. I think that time is of the essence, and, as there is no real danger, you should each make a journey – north, south, east and west – seeking out the corvid leaders and offering them our olive branch of reconciliation. What say you, Lostri? Will you accept our request, and serve the Council and Birddom, by travelling north as our emissary of peace?'

'It is not much further,' Hobo called out happily over his shoulder, as he dashed on ahead. Merion and Olivia found it hard to keep up with the bounding rabbit, flying as they were in strange terrain, where the chosen path twisted and turned, then disappeared into sudden fissures in the mountain-side. The pair of robins kept their eyes fixed upon Hobo's bobbing white tail, and managed as best they could.

When they suddenly emerged into a cool, silent vale, seemingly carved out of the gut of the mountain itself, Hobo hopped onto the summit of a pile of rocks and turned to address the breathless birds. 'Here we are then. Isn't my home a beautiful place?'

The robins looked about them admiringly. It was very beautiful and tranquil, the last place that they would have associated with so active and vibrant a personality as Hobo. Even now, as they watched him, his feet tapped restlessly on the rock, as if eager to be off again on an adventure.

'Your home is magnificent, Hobo,' replied Olivia. 'I feel a great sense of peace here.'

'Yes. Well, even rabbits have to rest sometimes, and where better?

Let me show you around.'

Olivia's sharp look stifled any protest from her brother, and the robins followed Hobo as he pointed out every one of his favourite places, regaling them, as he did so, with tales of deeds great and small that had happened at each spot.

Finally, Merion could bear it no longer. 'Does Septimus live here also?' he enquired, impatiently. 'We are both so eager to meet him.'

Hobo's countenance took on a sullen cast. 'Well, I'm sorry if I've been boring you...'

'Not at all, I assure you,' Olivia answered hurriedly. 'You have been so kind to show us around, and it has been fascinating, really it has. It is just that we have travelled such a long way to see him, that is all. But do forgive us for our discourtesy. We would both be devastated to lose your friendship, so newly won.'

The severity on the rabbit's face softened a little at Olivia's unctuous words.

'Yes. Well I suppose I do get a bit carried away. But I love this place so much, you see. It's the best place in the entire world!'

The rabbit's returning grin was like the sun coming out from behind a cloud, and he danced around and around as the irrepressible joy bubbled up through him once more. The pair of robins chuckled merrily and Hobo joined in, until the sides of the vale echoed with peals of laughter.

'What is the meaning of all this noise?'

The voice that spoke was soft, like a breath of wind, and old, as if the hills themselves had asked the question. Olivia and Merion looked all around them, but could see no one but the now rather chastened rabbit. It was he who answered.

'I have brought some friends to see you, Septimus. They have travelled a long way.'

'Then they will be in need of some rest. And I hope that they are more successful in it than I. All this racket and disturbance. Can't an animal even get a good day's sleep?'

The mutterings receded as the owner of the voice seemed to move away from them, though neither robin had even caught a glimpse of the wolf throughout the exchange.

'My, my. Someone got out of the wrong side of the den, that's for certain,' Hobo whispered, with unconvincing bravado. 'It comes to something when a rabbit can't enjoy himself with his friends.'

'Was that him?' Olivia asked eagerly. 'Where was he? Why couldn't we see him?'

'Oh yes. That was Septimus, all right. Sour old so-and-so. He's getting old, you see, and his bones ache so much more than they used to. He's not usually rude to guests – not that we have many nowadays. But don't worry. You'll see him tomorrow, if he wants you to.'

'But will he help us?' Merion queried anxiously.

'He will, sure enough. Septimus always does as I tell him.'

The guards had sent an urgent message to Traska the moment that they had found Tomar stretched out on the ground at the base of the crooked fir tree. Without Portia's help, he had not been able to find anything to eat since Traska's visit. On that occasion it had taken all of his remaining strength to fly from his ignominious position on the ground back to his nest, where he had lain exhausted for almost two days and nights, unable to move a feather. Even when he had recovered sufficiently to venture out onto the branch adjacent to his nest-hole, he had found that his hunger had weakened him severely. Caught in a vicious circle, the old owl hadn't had the strength to take off from his perch in order to forage for food. Finally, even the act of perching required too much effort from his emaciated body, and he had once again tumbled to earth in a pathetic heap, unable to move.

Traska looked down from his vantage point in a nearby tree, and tutted. 'This won't do. This won't do at all,' he said, gleefully. 'We can't have the leader of Birddom – or should I say ex-leader – in such a sorry state. We must look after him, until he is strong enough and well enough to look after himself.'

Traska called across to one of the guards, and gestured for the crow to join him at Tomar's side on the ground. Both birds flew down, and hopped across to the stricken owl.

'He's as good as dead,' remarked the guard, callously.

Traska rounded upon him, seething with anger. 'Well, I don't want him dead. Do you understand? I am not ready for this old owl to die. When he does, I will choose the time and the place. And I will take it very badly if he is allowed to leave this life before I am good-and-ready!'

The guard snapped to attention at the snarl in his boss's voice, but showed little understanding of what was required of him.

With an effort, Traska took hold of his impatience and, breathing with exaggerated slowness to calm himself, said, 'I want you to feed this old owl. He cannot do it for himself, so you must help him. Listen carefully. He is only on the very edge of consciousness. Don't go stuffing seeds and berries into his gullet. He'll choke for sure, and that will be both of you dead. Do I make myself clear?'

The guard nodded nervously, and Traska continued, 'Feed him small pieces of freshly-caught insects. Their juices will give him the sustenance that he needs to survive. Chew them up for him, so that the food slips down easily. And, if he refuses to swallow, persuade him.'

*

Septimus' fur was as grey as evening shadows, and his muzzle was white with age. Merion and Olivia had never seen so huge a creature. As they sat near his head and looked along the length of him, it seemed to the robins that they would have to fly to reach the tip of his tail. The old wolf's eyes regarded them with deep serenity. It was as if all of Time was held within their deep black pools. Merion and Olivia were struck dumb with awe in the great creature's presence, and it was Hobo who finally broke the silence.

'Come on, my young friends. I am a busy rabbit. Get on with it. Isn't this what you came here for?'

'Yes. Thank you, Hobo. We are sorry. It is just that your friend exceeds our imagination.'

The old wolf's lips curled in a smile at the compliment, as Olivia continued.

'Septimus, we are grateful that you have agreed to talk to us. We have been sent here on a mission by Tomar, erstwhile Great Owl in Birddom. He says that you alone know the way into Avia. He seeks to save all of bird-kind from the perils that beset our land. Birddom is no longer safe, and our friend foresees a time when we will have to leave. Avia is our only hope, and you are our only possible guide.'

The wolf closed his eyes, and it seemed for a long time that he was asleep. But, gradually, a deep thrumming resonated in his chest and his eyes opened once more as he began, very slowly, to sing:

'Avia's neither far nor near,
Not over there, but not quite here.
The path where you would choose to go
Is one that only a wolf might know.'

The singing stopped, and the pair of robins looked at one another quizzically. But, before they could speak, it resumed again:

'Avia is a state of mind
Which few if any bird can find.
Avia lies within your heart,
You'll find the end is but the start.
But peril lies at Avia's doors
If you're not true to Birddom's cause.
Choose any but the common good
And ever you'll be bathed in blood.'

The pulsing beat of the wolf's song mesmerised the two young robins, and they stood transfixed, staring deep into the great black eyes. Then Hobo coughed, and they turned to face him, startled by the interruption to their trance. When they turned back again, Septimus was nowhere in sight. But this did not seem to surprise the rabbit, who bustled on in business-like fashion.

'Well. There you are then. You got what you came for. I am surprised that it was all so easy. Septimus must really have taken a shine to you.'

'But what did it all mean?' gasped the robins.

'It couldn't have been much simpler,' Hobo replied, exasperated. 'You wanted to know the way to Avia and the old fella told you, plain enough.'

'But we didn't understand. It sounded as though Avia was every-where and nowhere.'

'That's it. Now you are getting the idea.'

'What idea? Is Avia a real place, or isn't it?'

'Oh, Avia's a real place, right enough. Just like you and I are real. But then, maybe we're just a dream in the mind of a great black cat sleeping in front of a roaring fire.'

Hobo seemed particularly pleased by his own imagery, and bounded around for a while, calling out, 'Wake up, you silly old cat!' over and over again. But gradually he calmed down and rejoined the pair of robins once more.

'Septimus can only help you to find the way to Avia. He can show you the gate, but he doesn't hold the key.'

Distress was plain on the robins' faces as Olivia spoke out. 'Who is it then that holds the key? Have we wasted our time here? Is there yet another journey to make?'

'Ungrateful though you may be, I will answer your questions, though back to front, as I choose. You have two more journeys to make. The first will be back to Birddom. The second, if you have learned by then a little grace and humility, to Avia. As for whether or not you have wasted your time in coming here, well, that's clear enough. You came seeking the way to Avia, and you got precisely what you came for. It is no one's fault but your own if you cannot understand something that is as obvious as the whiskers on my nose. And, finally, as to who holds the key – well, that's another simple answer: every bird does.'

The pair of blackbirds watched in increasing fascination as the men busied themselves around the huge metal objects. There were four in all, strategically placed at the corners of the field. All four were identical, each resembling a massive metal paper-clip. These had been installed in their present positions over the last seven days. Initially the arrival of the men, and their noisy activity, had disturbed the local populace of birds and wild animals. Many had fled from what they perceived to be an attack, only to return gradually when no violence came.

It seemed that the men were not intent on acts of aggression against the fauna, and so, emboldened by this news, the creatures watched as the men attached wires and ran cables back and forth between the four great machines. There was an air of purpose about their activities, and the wind was rank with the smell of human sweat as the men strove to complete the task before nightfall.

It was dusk when they gathered together in the centre of the field before performing what seemed to be an extraordinary dance of celebration. The men all began to rotate slowly and in ragged unison, heads and bodies turning to face each of the four metal monstrosities in turn, staring at them intently as if checking for some minute but crucial detail. Some of the men stood sideways on, swinging their heads back and forth, first looking at one machine on the diagonal and then the other. After a minute or two of this bizarre behaviour there was a general nodding of heads, and much back-slapping and shaking of hands. Then, en masse, the men left the field, climbed into numerous vehicles and drove away.

Animals and birds crept slowly into the now-empty field and, in the gathering gloom, stared in their turn at the giant machines. The male blackbird, bolder than the rest, flew up and landed on top of one of the metal structures. It felt cold and lifeless beneath his toes – its threat dormant. The blackbird began to sing defiantly, sparking a chorus of 'goodnights' from every bird on the ground and in the surrounding trees.

'Look at me!' he called to his mate. 'I am the lord of all that I survey. Man has built this perch especially for me.'

And the female looked on admiringly at her glossy black partner, yellow beak parted as he trilled into the darkness. Then, as if according the object acceptance as a part of his territory, the blackbird daubed its surface with a small faecal sack.

'There is nothing to fear here,' this gesture said. 'This thing will not harm us.'

Engar and Traska were huddled together in urgent consultation.

'We must not delay. This is too good an opportunity to miss. Have you spoken to Lostri since the Council meeting?'

Engar nodded, hooting with soft laughter. 'It was so easy. There was no way that he could refuse – not for so honourable an owl! He is to set off at dusk tomorrow, and his journey north will take him inexorably to Cra Wyd.'

'You did not mention that name to him?' Traska enquired, suddenly anxious.

'No. I am not a fool, and neither is Lostri. But it is inevitable. Any questions that he asks once in the north will lead him there for certain. Cra Wyd is already building a disquieting reputation. Lostri cannot fail to hear of it.'

'He will be cautious though. I can't see him going blundering into such an obvious place of danger.'

'You are right, Traska,' Engar demurred. 'We will need to bait the trap. What do we have that will lure Lostri there?'

'Not *what*, my friend. Who!' The evil magpie's eyes gleamed with vicious pleasure. 'You are forgetting Calipha and her sister. It is time that we put them to good use. They have been our guests for far too long. Now they must earn their suppers!'

The barn owl clapped his wings in delight. 'I had forgotten all about them. What a delicious idea. But how will Lostri get to hear about them?'

'They will be escorted north this afternoon by my band of hench-crows. They will ensure that the pair arrive safely and in time. I am sure that the local lads can find a secure place in which to hold them. I will give specific instructions to that effect. But you know these local birds. They can sometimes lack the necessary discipline. Mistakes can be made, and guards can become lax. And, let us not forget, two owls are not easy prisoners. It is just possible that one of them, the younger sister perhaps, might escape from her captors, and carry word to any friendly owl who might be in the vicinity.'

'You are unbelievable!' exclaimed Engar. 'You've thought this all out already, haven't you?'

'I never leave anything to chance,' the magpie snapped back. 'You don't get to live as long as I have unless you plan for every eventuality. Don't worry. Lostri will pay a visit to Cra Wyd. And we will make sure that he receives a warm welcome there!'

Merion and Olivia had expected so much more from their journey. They had thought that Septimus would lead them to Avia, that they would see for themselves the wondrous place of which Tomar had spoken. But it seemed that a solitary meeting and a few cryptic rhymes would have to be sufficient. But how could the two young robins go back to Birddom, and to Tomar, with so meagre a message?

However, this was the only option open to them. For, although the pair hung around for a couple of days, Septimus never reappeared to them. And Hobo, seemingly satisfied that he had done all that was required of him, ignored them altogether as he went about his daily business, full of bustle and bound and with little time, it seemed, for their continued company.

'What are we going to do now?' Olivia said. 'We can't simply stay here hoping for something to happen.'

'No. You are right, sis. We will have to go back, and tell Tomar that we have failed, though it grieves me to admit it. And it will grieve Tomar also. He had pinned all of his hopes on us, and we have let him down.'

'But what else could we have done? We managed to find Septimus, and we asked him to help Birddom. And all we got in return was a lot of nonsense for our troubles.'

'Did you understand any of what the old wolf said?' Merion asked.

'What was there to understand? It all seemed very vague to me. It was as if Septimus himself had no idea where Avia is. But that cannot be. Tomar was so certain that he would be able to provide us with the answer.'

'Well, if he has, it is beyond my comprehension. His rhyme is a riddle that I can't unlock. And, unlike the gateway to Avia, every bird doesn't have the key to this mystery.'

Merion paused, and his feathers drooped as the hopelessness of their situation overwhelmed him. Olivia realised that she would have to remain positive, even in the face of their failure.

'Well, I suggest that we head home without delay. I am missing Mother very much, and old Tomar, too. And who knows? Maybe the wisest brain in Birddom will be able to solve the riddle that Septimus has set.'

Chapter Thirteen

There was no warning. Only a shockingly brief moment in time. The pulse lasted but a few seconds. There was no noise. No light. Just terrible and instantaneous death. Carnage in a quiet field, in a quiet corner of Birddom. Nothing escaped. Every creature who, seconds before, had buzzed, chirped and snuffled within the perimeter formed by the four strange metal objects now lay dead on the ground where they had fallen. There was no blood. No wounds or injuries. But there were no survivors. Not a single creature crawled away from the scene to warn the unsuspecting natural world of what was to come.

The men entered the field from the gate at the far end, once the machines had been switched off. They each carried large black plastic sacks, and with gloved hands scooped the still-warm bodies from the ground and deposited them within. The men were meticulous in their work. No animal or bird was missed in their sweep across the field. Creatures such as badger and fox, too large to be placed in the sacks, were picked up by two of the men and carried away to the road, where they were unceremoniously thrown into the back of a van.

As the men cleared the field of the corpses they kept a tally of all the animals and birds that they collected: mice and vole, starling and toad, weasel and rat. Hunters and hunted, instantly extinguished. One man bent down, and closed his huge gloved hand around the inert body of the male blackbird – no longer lord of all that he surveyed. A carcass only, to be added to those within the sack. Dismissed. Irrelevant, save for being one of a hundred such unfortunate creatures, collected and counted.

The insects were too innumerable to be counted. And far too small to be collected. One man had fetched a spade from the back of a van, and had begun shovelling dead insects into his black bag. But it was a thankless task, and soon abandoned as a bad idea. 'Let them rot' was the general agreement. The animals and birds were to be examined and dissected back at the laboratory. Man needed to determine the extent of internal damage caused by the magnetic pulse. This would be crucial in determining the strength needed and the power required when the time came. But, for now, the men were ecstatic. Their contraptions had worked like a charm.

Tomar felt an overwhelming sense of betrayal and self-loathing. He had been force-fed for more than a week, and still remained too weak to resist his captors when they held his beak apart and slid another fat slug down his throat. There was no doubt that the nourishment was doing him good physically, but it was torturing him mentally. He had broken his pact with the insects. The very pact that he held sacred, even in the face of personal defeat on the Council of the Owls.

The old owl no longer felt able to wield any measure of moral authority. He was now like every other bird in Birddom. Eating insects, in breech of a solemn promise made in a time of direst need. And Tomar was fearful of the consequences that must surely result. If no bird kept the faith, what was to stop the insects rising up and cleansing the land of their false allies? Every bird would be devoured, defenceless against such an onslaught. Birddom was utterly doomed.

With an enormous effort, Tomar dragged himself out of the shallow scoop in the earth, which had served as a makeshift nest since his fall from his perch in the crooked fir tree. His eyes looked up wistfully at his nest-hole, now high and unattainable above him. It had been his home and his haven for most of his adult life, and he longed for its cool shade and protection from the elements. Tomar straightened up, and took his full weight onto his haunches, as he tentatively flapped his great wings. But, within a few seconds, he sank to the ground once more, utterly exhausted. Laying his head upon the baking earth, he let his mind drift away from his present sorry predicament and concentrated instead upon his solitary glimmer of hope: Avia.

It was the only possibility of any future for every bird, the only way to avoid the gathering storm. Tomar wondered how Merion and Olivia were faring in their quest. Had they managed to find Septimus? And would the old wolf help them? So much depended upon the two young robins. But history had taught the old tawny owl that no other bird was better-equipped, in heart and mind, to succeed at any task that they were set, however impossible it seemed.

The robins were preoccupied during their travels back to Birddom. As they flew, they pondered individually on the mysterious rhyme that Septimus had sung to them. And at each rest stop they fell into eager discussion, but any meaning to his words evaded them, and they remained frustrated by the puzzle that the old wolf had set.

'"Avia's neither far nor near, not over there but not quite here."' What does it mean? Neither far nor near. It sounds as if the place doesn't exist at all!'

Merion looked at his sister with a rueful grin, but Olivia met his doubts with a confidence that she did not truly feel, but wore for Tomar's sake. The old owl was no fool, she was certain of that. Avia *must* exist. And somewhere within the maze of the poem was the answer as to how to find it.

'He tells us that Avia isn't far. That must mean that it is at least attainable. That we can reach it if we persevere. If it was quite near it would be too easy, and wouldn't have to be earned. That's logical, isn't it?'

'Yes, sis. But Septimus also said that "Avia is a state of mind, which few if any bird can find." That seems to contradict the notion that Avia is real, doesn't it?'

'On the face of it, yes. But the words must mean something that we don't yet grasp. Anyway, you missed a couple of lines.'

'That's because I thought that they at least were obvious. "The path where you would choose to go is one that only a wolf might know." Septimus is telling us that he holds the key to the way into Avia, in spite of what Hobo said. But we knew that when we set out upon our journey. It seems pointless to taunt us in this way. And cruel, too.'

Olivia looked quite shocked at such an accusation from her brother's beak.

'No, Merion. I did not detect any cruelty in Septimus. Only an immense wisdom that outmatches our efforts. We must just strive harder to unlock his mysteries. But for now, a good sleep will refresh our bodies and our brains. Both have a long journey ahead of them.'

Lostri was weary after his travels into the far north of Birddom. His route had been dictated, as Engar had predicted, by constant news about the massive coven at Cra Wyd. Small birds from miles around spoke of it with fear and loathing. It was a dark and menacing place, from which a dark wing reached out on occasion to strike terror and mete out death.

Lostri had heard a different tale when he had consulted magpies and crows from other lesser covens in the vicinity. These corvids spoke with reverential awe, ascribing Cra Wyd with attributes of power and honour. From their beaks, it became a place to be aspired to, if one proved oneself worthy. And, constant to the mission given to him, Lostri knew that he would have to visit that stronghold, and learn what he could of its secrets. The owl quailed at the thought of such an adventure. It would be like sticking his head into a cat's mouth. But Engar had left him no choice. He *had* to carry the message of the Council into that dark place. It was a matter of honour, no matter how afraid he might be.

For now, though, he would rest and feed, and take comfort from friendly faces. There were still plenty of stories to be heard, and many a beak willing to impart them. Maybe he would wait for a couple of days before he visited Cra Wyd. It would still be there, and no less nor more of a threat than now.

Traska was bored with waiting. Once the initial excitement of setting the trap has dissipated, he fretted away the days necessary for Lostri to journey to the north and fly into it. Initially the evil magpie contented himself with mocking Tomar at every opportunity. Now that the ancient owl had recovered consciousness, Traska would visit him daily, taunting him from the vantage point vacated and now unattainable to the unfortunate bird.

'I hope that your new home is comfortable, Tomar,' he called out, smiling wickedly. 'It seems so much more fitting to your newly acquired status. Although I am sorry to see that you have fallen on hard times, as well as hard ground.'

'Spare me your concern, Traska. I do not deserve it.'

'Indeed you do. You and I are virtually alone in Birddom as sages who can see beyond the end of their beaks. I hate to admit it, but we are old, you and I. You more so, of course. But there is undoubtedly still life in us, or at least in one of us. Your life may soon be forfeit. But not until I have had my moment of glory. And you, your moment of ignominy.'

With such sallies, Traska had toyed with his prisoner, hurting Tomar every bit as much as if his hench-crows had beaten the old owl. But inflicting wounds with his tongue soon lacked sufficient thrill for the evil magpie. His lust for physical violence could not be sated by these small mental pleasures. It was a pity that he had despatched Portia from this life so swiftly. How he would have enjoyed more time with her in his clutches. Alas, it was not to be. However, Portia and her accursed mate Kirrick were not the only robins with whom he was personally acquainted, were they? Traska thought back to a time when his plans were built around a younger pair altogether. Had he not been betrayed by Katya, the one magpie, other than his mother, that he had ever loved, and then distracted by his deadly duel with his own son, Venga, Traska would have torn those little brats wing from wing, and laughed doing it!

These thoughts only fuelled his desire for brutality, and the magpie flew off in search of some small and defenceless prey. Initially he thought of Olivia. Merion, he knew, was away on an errand for Engar. Moreover, he was taking a devil of a long time about it. Kraken's clifftop home was a fair journey, but not far enough for an energetic young robin to have flown there and back less than three times in the time that Merion had so far taken. What could have delayed the young robin? Traska realised that he would be sorry if any harm had come to the little messenger. He treasured his right to be the instigator of any ill to befall each bird belonging to that family. And, for now, that meant the female offspring. But she could wait for just a little while. His desire for violence needed an immediate outlet at present, and he wanted to take his time when it came to dealing with Olivia. He would get his jailers to search her out, and invite her to join him later. There was little need to guard the old owl. He was in no state to be going anywhere.

'Let's consider the next lines,' Olivia suggested.

The pair of robins had decided to land on the blossom-laden bough of an apple tree, the fragrant blooms providing both shade and concealment on a cloudless afternoon.

'"Avia lives within your heart, you'll find the end is but the start." It's like us, sis. It is going round in circles. And, in doing so, it keeps coming back to my greatest fear: that there is no such place as Avia, that it is only an old fool's dream.'

'How dare you!' Olivia screamed, cuffing her brother roughly with her wing. 'Never talk that way about Tomar. We are the fools for not being able to unravel Septimus' web of clues. Now, let's start again. "Avia lives within your heart." Well, what do we hold in our hearts? Love for one another. So it is love that keeps Avia alive. Or it is a place where only love exists. That would fit with Tomar's description of it as a paradise.'

'There are other feelings that can be held in the heart, besides love,' Merion interrupted. 'A heart can feel jealousy and even hate.'

'They do not naturally reside there. No, there can be no negative answer to this particular riddle. Only love will do, in this instance. Not romantic love, though. But love of an ideal, belief in Avia as a final home for every bird.'

'Faith. That's what needs to live in our hearts. Faith in the very existence of Avia. I think that we may be approaching the answer, to that one line, at least. But what of the next? "You'll find the end is but the start." What end? The end of a journey? Well, I for one will be glad when this journey ends, and I certainly want a good rest and some home comforts before I start another. But a journey to where?'

'It could be speaking about the greatest journey that any of us have to undertake,' Olivia intoned solemnly. 'The words make sense then. If death is the journey, then that is the "end" that Septimus speaks of. But what starts after death? It is all that there is. Can Avia really only be a place in which to have a second life?'

'No. I cannot believe that Tomar would have envisaged the death of the whole of Birddom. Life itself is too precious to him. He has always done everything in his power to preserve it. And anyway, following your thoughts, if death is the end then the start must surely be birth. Do you expect each one of us to climb back into our eggs?'

Olivia rubbed her head to relieve some of the pain that these mental contortions were causing, and Merion laughed, unsympathetically.

'It should be me with the headache after that great cuff you gave me!'

Lostri's best-laid plans of delaying his necessary visit to Cra Wyd were thrown into utter confusion by the abrupt appearance, at his temporary nest-site, of Calipha's younger sister, Claudia. She came to him in a state of great distress, gabbling incoherently, so that the tawny owl had to place his wings firmly on her back to calm her down. Looking deeply into the eyes of the young short-eared owl, he hooted softly.

'What is the matter, Claudia? How can I help you?'

'They've got her!' she cried, in anguish. 'I managed to escape. It's been so horrible. They've done such terrible things to us. You can't imagine what we've been through!'

'Slow down, my dear, and tell me all about it from the beginning. Who has got who?'

'Calipha, of course. They've got her, and they will kill her for sure if we don't get her out of there.'

'Try to compose yourself, Claudia. I know that you are upset, but I need to know who has your sister in their clutches.'

'I am sorry, Lostri. I know that I am not making much sense, but it is just that I am terrified for Calipha's sake. They will punish her for helping me to escape. But I will try to tell you everything.

'Calipha and I have been prisoners for a number of weeks now. They took us shortly after the vote on the Council that tried to oust Tomar from his position as Great Owl. I think that their original intention was to capture only me, and to use my imprisonment as a means to coerce my sister into changing her vote at the next Council meeting. But, as ill-fortune would have it, Calipha chanced to arrive at my home at the very moment of my abduction. Of course, she fought to save me, but was soon overwhelmed and forced to come along. Since that horrible day, it has only been her great strength and dignity that have enabled me to survive. I lack her courage.' The short-eared owl's head drooped in shame.

Lostri lifted her beak tenderly with his primaries, looking at her compassionately. 'Claudia, my dear. Who were your abductors?'

The female owl could not help but notice the exaggerated patience smothering the frustration in Lostri's tone, and tried to pull herself together. 'Forgive me, Lostri. We were taken by a large band of magpies and crows, but the abduction was organised by a vile creature called Traska.'

Lostri gasped involuntarily at the mention of that heinous name, but Claudia shook her head, silencing him. 'That is not the worst of it. For Traska has an ally, and this act was undertaken for his benefit. Engar is the traitor who has undoubtedly gained from my sister's absence, as he would have done from her enforced silence or change of heart. We never saw him, so we cannot be absolutely certain. But Calipha is convinced. Engar and Traska have formed an unholy alliance that threatens the very future of Birddom!'

The announcement caused a huge public outcry, but it was largely noise without substance. The proposals were put across in such a stark way that even the most ardent nature-lover realised that the bottom line was a choice, between a drastic but short-lived upheaval or an agonisingly slow but inexorable deterioration of the quality of life for everyone in the country. After the initial trials, experiments had been carried out in laboratory conditions to see if the required dosage could be lessened so that only certain species would be killed by the pulses. After all, the war *was* against the insects. Birds and animals were innocent by-standers, caught in the magnetic cross-fire, so to speak. But it simply could not be done. To achieve the government's stated aim of total eradication of the insect population, it was inevitable and unavoidable that the pulse would have to be of such a magnitude that no living creature would survive.

Fortunately, Man would still be able to consume the bodies of any livestock. The dissections had shown that no mutation or spoilage to the quality of meat would result from the power surge. The volume of carcasses would be overwhelming, and plans were already afoot to convert hundreds of stables and farm out-houses into refrigerated warehouses for the safe storage of the dead animals, or at least those considered edible. It was this aspect that triggered an initial emotional reaction from certain more-liberal sections of the media, who touted their ecological headlines for a few days, adorning their front pages and their television screens with cute pictures of robins and rabbits.

But Man is largely a pragmatic and self-serving creature, and the announcement of the date for evacuation focused everyone's mind on the forthcoming disruption to their own lives, and relegated the plight of the rest of the natural world to an unimportant necessity in ensuring the future for the whole country. The cost was immense, but not prohibitive. Several vast conglomerates had realised that sponsorship of this venture would be hugely advantageous in terms of visibility and public good-will, and more than two-thirds of the overall funding required had been generated in this way. The rest was to come from the pockets of every man, woman and child in the country, and the spin-men went into overdrive, painting pictures of clear blue skies, free from the omnipresent insect netting that blighted everyday life.

Only a few more observant men and women noticed the irony in the images being used to persuade the population that this was a right and proper course of action. In the promotional videos, birds flew in the clear blue skies, sheep grazed languidly in green fields, and even the lazy drone of a bumble-bee was used to enhance the idyllic picture of a future life that awaited one and all – if sufficient contributions were forthcoming.

Politicians spoke in jingoistic and patriotic terms about the national sacrifice for the good of all and recalled public-spirited acts from the past, claiming that this would top them all for a place in history. Long before the public pronouncement, behind-the-scenes haggling with foreign neighbours had taken place to agree the three-month residency of the entire country's population on their soil.

Building was already well underway, erecting temporary shanty towns on every available patch of land, and a rudimentary infra-structure of transportation networks to allow the exodus to take place. Existing under-sea tunnels would be used to the full, supplemented by a vast flotilla of home-owned and foreign ships and boats. The preparation and evacuation would take about a week, and would test to the limits the renowned stoicism of the nation. The repatriation of the country would only be possible after the massive clear-up that would be required when the machines of death had done their work.

Fire-sites had been chosen across the length and breadth of the land, and a voluntary workforce would complete the grisly task of disposing of all the bird and animal bodies as swiftly as could be arranged. And an army of bulldozers would be used to plough the billions of insect corpses into the ground.

To minimise discomfort to the populace as a whole, the insect netting would only be dismantled in the final two weeks before evacuation. Then normal life would cease, and all commerce would be suspended, while men and women everywhere joined together in working for the nation's good. This would revive a community spirit that would be sorely needed during and after the evacuation. Until then, the most important task would be the erection, at regular intervals around the coastline, of the thousands of monstrous magnets required. There was no turning back. The die had been cast, and the clock was ticking towards the deadline for the extinction of every living creature in the country.

'What could the "peril" be "at Avia's doors"?' Olivia asked.

The two robins had reached the coast of the Isle of Storms, and were nestled amid the leaves of an oak, waiting patiently for the unnatural sound of a ship's klaxon to announce the arrival of their transportation home.

'"But peril lies at Avia's doors if you're not true to Birddom's cause."' Merion quoted the passage back at his sister, adding. 'How can there be peril? Avia is supposed to be paradise for all of bird-kind. What danger can there be in reaching paradise?'

'The peril is only threatened for those who are "not true to Birddom's cause." That's what the rhyme says.'

'But how can that be judged? Who will make that decision? Is there some sort of test to be passed before a bird can enter Avia?'

'I don't know, Merion. At the outset I envisaged Avia as a secret land. I was never sure where it was supposed to be, but I believed that it was as real as Wingland. Now it seems as if Avia is a kind of dreamscape – not real at all. And, moreover, guarded by a gate-keeper wielding death for the faithless.'

Merion nuzzled closer to his sister as they rested on the bough of the oak, and held her tightly in his wings.

'Don't fret so, sis. There must be a sensible explanation. Tomar is too old and too wise to have sent us on a fool's errand. Yes, I know that I voiced something similar a while back. But we are both just feeling the frustration of being a not-very-clever pair of robins.'

At that very moment, the sound that they had waited for echoed across from the stretch of water where the car-ferry chugged its slow passage towards port.

'Let's leave it at that, sis,' Merion continued. 'We both need to catch up on some sleep during the sea voyage. Once we land back in Birddom, we must waste no time in more useless speculation as to the meaning of Septimus' riddles. We must fly as fast as we can back to Tomar and to Mother. So long as we can remember the rhyme we will have done the job that was asked of us.'

'You're right, Merion. It will be so good to be back in Birddom again. How I am longing to see Mother. I have missed her so.'

Chapter Fourteen

'I simply can't believe what you are telling me,' Lostri said, incredulously. 'Engar a traitor? No, it is too much. You must be mistaken.'

'Am I mistaken that my sister and I have been held in captivity? That we have been starved? Beaten and abused? Am I mistaken that we have been brought here under heavy guard? Forced to fly with little or no rest? That for the last weeks we have had none but corvidae for company?'

'But why?' asked the tawny owl. 'Why would they go to all the trouble of bringing you here, to Cra Wyd?'

'Who knows what foul plans that evil magpie has hatching inside his warped brain? But it doesn't matter. All that is important is that we rescue Calipha without delay!'

It was not for nothing that Lostri had been a respected and long-standing member of the Council of the Owls. And now he stilled any further words from Claudia with a soft rebuke.

'No, that is not all that is important. I do not underestimate the danger to your sister, but I must think this through. Much of what you have told me is shocking in the extreme. But the implications could be more far-reaching than we currently envisage. I need only one more thing from you my dear, and then you must rest. You cannot help your sister in your present state. You look completely exhausted.'

'What do you want from me?' Claudia asked, abjectly.

'Tell me about how you managed to escape.'

'It was the merest chance. As I have said, we have been heavily guarded ever since our capture, and, although we talked of little else, there had been no chance of escape then or on our journey to Cra Wyd. But since our arrival, we had been largely ignored, as if our distance from our own home rendered us incapable of positive action. I am sure that they believed us to be thoroughly broken in spirit. And, without Traska around, the guards were soon bored with their continued duties, and much preferred carousing with the local thugs.

'Well, last night there was some sort of celebration going on, and by dusk only two rather weedy-looking crows were left with the task of guarding us. Bruised and battered though we were, Calipha and I realised that there would never be a better chance of escape. Launching at them without warning, we managed to overpower the crows and began our flight for freedom. Calipha was slightly behind me, as she had insisted on despatching the injured crows herself, knowing that a far worse fate would befall them if they lived to tell the tale of their failure.

'I quickly gained height, but as I looked back from treetop level, I was aghast to see six huge hench-crows surround my sister and force her, once more, to the ground. I thought about turning back and trying to fight, but she screamed at me to get away, to find help. There was nothing that I could do, but it almost broke my heart to leave her there in such peril. I flew as fast as I could, not knowing what to do next. But it wasn't long, in speaking to other birds, before I heard your name mentioned and realised, with joy, that you were in the vicinity. I came to find you with renewed hope, that Calipha might yet be saved.'

Lulled by the gentle rocking motion of the ship, Merion soon fell into a profound sleep. And, in sleeping, dreamt. It was as if he were walking down a long, dark tunnel. Merion had never been underground himself, but had heard tales from his mother about the time that she and Kirrick had escaped into a rabbit warren when fleeing from Traska's band of magpies. He did not feel afraid, not even when the walls and roof of the passage closed in on all sides, leaving barely enough room for a bird to hop through with head held low. The darkness did not trouble him either. There was a rightness about the place, and about his being there. His journey was a good one, he was sure about that. And, if it seemed that he wandered for hours, he didn't for a moment doubt that this was what he was meant to be doing.

Then, in the extreme distance, a pin-prick appeared ahead of him. A tiny, brilliant point of white light, which strengthened as he walked towards it, and grew larger, banishing the shadows all around him, vanquishing the dark, until he emerged, suddenly, into a world of purest white. Initially, there was nothing but the light. His claws made no sound on the ground, if there was any ground beneath his feet. But gradually, as he continued forward, the whiteness became a thing of texture. Soft as the down on a chick's breast. Warm, like milk straight from the cow's teat. And there was sound. A deep rumbling sound, as rhythmic and reassuring as a heartbeat. Merion knew, instinctively, that it was breathing he could hear all around him, but he did not feel frightened. Not even when the softness around him started to move, the pure whiteness altering, dappled by grey.

The creature stirred, and Merion felt as if he were at once inside and outside as it slowly turned. The white diminished as grey predominated, and soon became only a frame for the redness of the giant's open mouth and huge lolling tongue. The eyes that fixed upon Merion were black in the centre, like pools of unfathomable depth, but the iris in each was grey in colour and flecked with amber, like shafts of sunlight at dawn. The brave robin met their stare with a calm heart, even calling out a bold greeting.

'Septimus. It is good to see you. I did not think that we would meet again.'

'Oh, you can be sure that we will, my young friend,' came the reply, although Merion had seen no movement from the old wolf's lips.

'Did we forget something?' the robin asked. 'I thought that you had told us all that we needed to know at our last meeting.'

'You are no one's fool, my little robin. You seek more knowledge from me by your disingenuous questions. But you are right. I have been troubled since you left me. Troubled that I had been too vague, and that my very purpose would in the end be thwarted by my predilection for obscurity. I have one further message for you to carry to Tomar.'

Excitement mounted like a dammed stream inside Merion's chest, but he struggled to maintain his silence in spite of his desperate curiosity. This Septimus noted with some approval, nodding and smiling as he continued, 'Tell my friend, and wisest of owls, that the entrance into Avia is a gateway in time as much as in space, and that to miss the opportunity would be irretrievable.'

Merion was unable to contain himself. 'What opportunity? How can we know when the gateway will be open if you don't tell us?'

In reply, the ancient wolf's eyes closed as if in meditation, and the ensuing silence stretched the young robin's nerves to breaking point. Finally, speaking once again with a voice that seemed to arrive directly inside Merion's mind, Septimus began to breathe another stanza of the rhyme:

'When all is lost and hope is gone,
Think back to former battles won.
Make ready all who chance the gate,
For courage will decide their fate.

151

Don't fear the tunnel, black as night,
For darkness comes before the light.'

Engar looked around the ancient circle of trees with barely-disguised contempt for the owls gathered there to fawn upon him. 'They will do everything that I say,' he thought. 'No one here will challenge me. They haven't the guts. With Lostri otherwise engaged, there is nothing to stop me.'

The barn owl's face wore a look of extreme self-satisfaction, which the other eight Council members, feeling relief to a bird, mistook for a warm welcome. They smiled in return and waited, in respectful silence, for their leader to speak.

'My friends and fellow Council members,' Engar said. 'I have called today's meeting, as I believe we need to hear what three of our brethren have to report. Pellar, Cerca and Creer have all shown great diligence and loyalty to the Council. They have carried out their missions with the utmost celerity, as befitting the task that was set them. Would that the same could be said of Lostri. I find it hard to hide my disappointment that he has not returned. I, for one, was eager to hear about the situation with the corvidae in the north, where, as you all know, their strength in number is the greatest. But let that not lessen the worth of our successful delegates. We must hear their reports without delay. And maybe there is a very good reason for Lostri's tardiness, which I am sure he will explain if and when he ever decides to return.'

Creer, the long-eared owl, was the first to give his account of his travels and his discussions with the corvidae in the west of Birddom. He intimated that things had gone very well, with a mutual respect being noticeable at the meetings with the corvid leaders. They had been most anxious to co-operate and, at the same time, to reassure Creer that their aim was not to drag up the past, so distasteful to all, but to live in harmonious co-existence with the rest of Birddom, subject to its laws like any other birds and grateful for the leadership of Engar and the Council.

'I think we can safely say that, whatever may have happened in times long gone,' Creer expounded pompously, 'we are now able to look to a future where corvids will be our allies and not our enemies; our partners not our foes.'

Engar smiled once more, as he heard his own words coming from the mouth of his fellow Council member. Creer was word-perfect, having been so carefully coached, and had set just the right tone for what Engar had in mind. The barn owl thanked Creer effusively for his excellent work, then called upon Cerca to give his report.

Cerca had travelled east, and his story was much the same. The corvidae were eager to look to the future, to a world where black and white could live happily alongside birds of every colour. Pellar's visit to the south of Birddom yielded a remarkably similar picture, the only point of interest coming when he reported on a disturbing incident that he had learnt of from a distressed female blackbird. She had travelled for days without rest, and her exhaustion made her barely comprehensible. But, from what Pellar could gather, it seemed that she had set out from her remote home near the south coast with the aim of finding the Council of the Owls, but on hearing that one of their number was in her part of the country, had sought him out to regale him with her sorry tale. Apparently, Man had been making his mischief in a field near her nest, and her mate had been one of many birds killed, almost instantaneously, though what caused these deaths she could not explain.

Not wishing this distressing but irrelevant news to dampen the mood of the Council, Engar dismissed it as an isolated incident and brought the attention of the Council members back to the happier news about the corvidae.

'My friends, I am greatly encouraged by the reports from our three esteemed colleagues. I think that the corvids across Birddom need to be congratulated for their willingness to become a useful and integrated part of the great family of birds, which is the strength of Birddom itself. But I propose that we do something more than merely offer our congratulations. The magpies and crows, once reviled, have taken a monumental step towards rehabilitation, and we should give them a reward commensurate with their efforts. Firstly, I ask all of you not to dismiss what I am about to say, without due consideration. For I believe that now is the first true test of our mettle as a Council that is fit to lead Birddom into the modern era. And that era can only prosper, I am sure you will agree, with peace for every bird.

'I wish to bind the corvidae to us as brothers, and leaders of this our beloved land. And so, it is my respectful suggestion to the Council that we offer an olive-branch of friendship to their leadership to come and join with us in marching together towards a glorious future. I say that we should offer the corvidae three places upon this very Council. Circumstances have reduced our numbers to ten, from the traditional twelve who have always made up the leadership of Birddom. And Lostri, having failed in his duty to this body, should relinquish his place on the Council. I am confident that the substance of his findings will bear out all that has been said here today and, when he deigns to return to us, we will hear him. But his actions have forfeited his right to be a part of the highest, most noble body in the land.

'What say you to my proposals? For we are a Council of equals, you and I. Do we admit three worthy members of the corvids to our number, and, in doing so, sew up an alliance that will ensure peace for all time in Birddom?'

Eight heads nodded, though some less vigorously than others, and eight voices called out a unanimous 'Aye'.

Lostri was no fool. It had occurred to him immediately that a trap was being set. But he could not understand why. The news that Engar was a traitor, and, moreover, in cahoots with Traska, was shocking to the noble owl. And it was the newly-elected Great Owl who had specifically chosen him for this mission. But would Engar have sent him into danger deliberately?

No, he could not believe it. And yet the evidence that Claudia had set before him could not be denied. The birds with whom he had been sent to parlay were the very same birds holding Calipha captive, and brutalising her, to boot. Lostri knew that he had no choice. He had to help his old friend. But it obviously could not be done by force. The sheer numbers of the corvids at Cra Wyd precluded any attack. And, if Claudia was wrong, unprovoked aggression could have severe repercussions for the whole of Birddom. The tawny owl realised that he needed to think things through very carefully. Well, he had all night. Claudia was long-since asleep, and Lostri envied her the rest. But that was a luxury which he could not afford tonight. He must come up with a plan to save Calipha. It occurred to him that he had been sent empty-winged on this mission. He had been tasked with talking to the corvidae leadership, in Cra Wyd and elsewhere, but he had been given nothing positive to offer them as an incentive to co-operation.

What could he offer them? What would these birds want? What did they desire? Power, for one thing, if they were still true to their past. The magpies and crows, rooks and jays had not for nothing been Birddom's deadliest enemy in times gone by. Their lust for power had allowed the rise of Slyekin and his terrible, destructive regime. And it had fostered the emergence of Traska, the very essence of evil in bird form, who was still alive and, if Claudia was to be believed, now part of a calamitous alliance with the Great Owl himself.

Lostri shook his head violently, forcing himself to concentrate on the task which he had been sent here to perform. If the corvidae wanted power, what could he dangle in front of them that would ensure the release of Calipha? He could pretend that he had come with more to offer than was actually the case, that there had been a real purpose to his being an emissary of the Council. What if he said that a place on that Council could be obtained by a gesture of good will to all birds? That, in releasing Calipha, there would, in return, be the reward of establishing a power-base within the legitimate leadership of Birddom? The corvidae would be recognised as valued participants in partnership, with a voice on the Council.

'No, that is absurd!' Lostri chided himself. 'What are you thinking of? No honourable owl would agree to such a thing. And I will not be false with them. I will not betray the integrity of the Council, not even for Calipha's life!'

Merion woke his sister with a violent shake. 'Olivia! Olivia! You'll never guess. I've had such a dream!'

'You mean that you woke me in the middle of my own dreams to tell me about yours?' she replied, angrily.

'But my dream was important. Septimus came to me in my dream. And he spoke to me, giving me a message to take to Tomar.'

'We already have his message.'

'I know. I know. But Septimus told me more, not that it makes much more sense than his original rhyme.' Quickly, before he could forget, Merion repeated the rhyme that he had heard in his dreams.

'What can it mean, sis?'

Olivia blinked the remaining sleep out of her eyes, and pondered the mystery. 'It seems to be telling Tomar that he needs to trust in himself. That he has triumphed over adversity in the past, and is equal to the needs of Birddom in helping every bird escape to Avia. Septimus might be telling him to have courage, and to give that courage to all in the land who wish to attempt "the gate". What I simply don't understand is the meaning of the last line – "the tunnel, black as night." It seems to have no relevance to what has gone before. Septimus has never mentioned a tunnel before, has he?'

Merion almost leapt from his perch, clapping his forehead with his wing as he did so. 'I was in a tunnel! In my dream, sis. I was walking down a long, black tunnel, and it led me to the light. It must have been the gateway into Avia. I have seen it, sis!'

'What was it like?' Olivia asked, awed.

'It felt as if the very earth had swallowed me up. But it did not feel bad. Not frightening, I mean. It felt wonderful, actually. If that was Avia, then it is a beautiful place. But...' Merion stopped in mid-sentence, and a frown furrowed above his beak. 'I'm not sure that I know how to explain it, Olivia,' he said, urgently. 'It sounds crazy, even when I think it inside of my head. But when I came out of the tunnel and into the light, the light became Septimus. Avia was Septimus. Or he was Avia!'

'Don't be silly, Merion. Avia is a place. A paradise. Tomar told us so. It was a dream, that is all. And dreams can be confusing.'

'I suppose so. But I didn't get confused about Septimus' message, did I?'

'No, and Birddom may yet be thankful that you did not. This new rhyme seems to fit well with the rest. But we must not waste a single moment more, Merion. Let us fly like the wind, back to Tomar and Mother.'

*

The pair of young robins were distressed to find that Portia's nest was cold and empty. There was an air of abandonment about the place, as if their mother had not been there for some time.

'Where could she be?' cried Olivia.

'Perhaps she has gone to stay with Tomar. You know that she was looking after him. Maybe she found it more convenient to make a temporary nest in his tree, rather than travel back and forth all the time.'

Olivia's countenance brightened considerably at this thought, and she clapped her brother lightly on the back. 'Well, what are we waiting for? Let's go!'

Merion followed his sister as she flew off towards the heart of Tanglewood. But what they found there left them open-beaked.

'Tomar has gone, too!' Olivia exclaimed, looking into the bole of the crooked fir. 'His nest looks as abandoned as Mother's.'

The robins looked around in bewilderment, and it took a few seconds before either registered the low, feeble call from the ground below. Seeing Tomar prostrate on the forest floor, they stared in disbelief before stirring themselves and flying down to the old owl's side.

'Oh, thank the Creator! I thought that my eyes were deceiving me. But it is you two. You are safe.' The relief in Tomar's frail voice was unmistakable.

'Where is Mother?' Olivia asked, then cried an anguished, 'No!' as Tomar's eyes filled instantly with huge tears.

'What has happened to her?' Merion's voice was icy, as he envisaged the worst. But even he could not help gasping aloud at Tomar's grief-stricken reply.

'Traska murdered her! Oh Portia, my poor, dear friend. I would have gladly given my own life in your stead.'

Merion instinctively hugged his sister while she wept, his own glacial anger keeping all other emotions at bay. 'How, Tomar? How did she die?'

'Your mother was the bravest robin who ever lived, and I include your father, Kirrick, in that assessment. For he relied on her utterly, and would not have achieved a fraction of his heroics without her courage. Portia was looking after me, risking all to keep these miserable old bones alive. She brought me food, and I suppose that Traska must have got wind of what she was doing. He trapped her, tortured her and then...'

The owl's voice trailed away, unable to finish the words as a fresh stream of tears bled onto his chest-feathers.

Merion let go of his sister, and tried to comfort Tomar as best he could. 'Let us make sure then that my mother's death was not in vain. For you alone can give her sacrifice meaning, Tomar. You must become strong again, and lead us all. We have done as you asked and have brought back the words of the wolf, though much of their meaning eludes us. But you are the Great Owl. No, I do not recognise the right of the usurper. You are Great Owl still, and charged with the duty of saving Birddom from its doom.'

Olivia looked quite shocked at the severity of Merion's tone in speaking to the frail old owl. But she realised that her brother was right, and fought back her own grief to give him support.

'Yes, Tomar. Only you can unravel the mysteries of Septimus' puzzles. And, in doing so, ensure the future of Birddom.'

Tomar responded bleakly. 'Birddom's days are numbered.'

'Then our journey was folly, as was my mother's death!' Merion shot back, angrily.

Tomar's eyes shone suddenly with compassion, as he pulled

himself together. 'Forgive me, my young friends. And thank you both for fighting so hard to make me realise once again who I am. I am no longer Great Owl, but I am charged nonetheless with a sacred duty. I will not fail you, not while a single breath remains in my body. But I need your help, my friends. Note that I call you young no longer. For you are fully grown in my eyes and equal to any task, as you have already proved. I need food. I have barely eaten in the last two days. My guards seem to have deserted me. But it is fortunate in one way. You yourselves would have been captured if they had kept up to their duty. Be careful, my dear robins. For I can achieve nothing without you. Find us all a meal, then we will sit and grieve for Portia. But tomorrow you will tell me all about your journey to the Isle of Storms, and together we will decipher Septimus' coded words.'

Word had got back to Traska that everything was going according to plan. The younger of the two owls had been allowed to escape, as he had requested, and the corvid spies had followed her to her rendezvous with Lostri.

'I must make my move while he dithers,' Traska told himself. 'I must set off without delay for Cra Wyd. It is a pity, for I was looking forward to another joust with that old fool, Tomar. I so enjoy seeing him grovel. And those stupid guards haven't brought me that juicy young robin to play with, either. Still, no matter. I can't spare the time. There will be ample entertainment awaiting me in the north. And more of a challenge too. Killing a robin is *so* easy. But to kill three owls, now that is something that will tax even my ingenuity!'

Smiling wickedly, the evil magpie hurled himself into the air and flew off, with relish, over the treetops, northwards. And, as he flew, he chuckled maliciously to himself, thinking, with satisfaction, of his achievements so far. Slyekin had been such an arrogant fool. Power wasn't only to be won by battle, or by brutality. Oh, they were sometimes necessary, and often enjoyable. But, ultimately, power was won by stealth. By guile and cunning. By superior intellect. 'I could almost be describing myself!' Traska crowed, laughing once again with malevolent glee.

Chapter Fifteen

Lostri found that sleep did not come easily. His brain was too active, racing in desperate haste to solve the tortuous problem of how to rescue Calipha. He dismissed dozens of ideas as too fanciful or impractical. He had nothing to bargain with. He could not appeal to the honour of the corvidae, for they had none. And he could not try to take his friend from them by force. Two owls made for a paltry army, and it was an army that Lostri needed if he was to succeed in such a mission. So it went on, round and round inside his head, until the tawny owl was too exhausted to think any more and sank, at last, into a fitful slumber. He was woken almost immediately by Claudia, but his irritation was washed away by the look of anguish on her young face.

'What are we waiting for?' she cried, plaintively.

It was a good question. The delay had not improved the situation for Calipha one iota. They still had no plan for her rescue. And every hour that passed increased the likelihood that the magpies and crows would tire of their captive, and kill her rather than expending the effort of guarding her.

'It is probably a hopeless thing that we do,' Lostri replied, quite calmly now that his mind was made up. 'But let's get to it. Come along, my dear. Let's go and save your sister.'

The pair of owls flew off on an easterly heading that would, at their present rate of flight, bring them to the boundary of Cra Wyd within the hour. They informed no bird of their destination. For what aid could they seek from the small bird population against such a foe? It was true that many a brave heart beat inside a tiny breast, but individually they would be no match against even the smallest of the corvids. Besides, most would be reluctant to risk any confrontation that might break the albeit uneasy truce that existed in the locality. No, it was better that they go alone, regardless of the danger.

Once they reached the first tree at the edge of the daunting woodland, Lostri let Claudia lead the way. There was no point in being heroic. His female companion knew the way, and speed and sure-footedness might give them an element of surprise which they could use to their advantage.

Certainly there were no indications that they were expected. Neither owl spotted so much as a jackdaw in their silent flight through the wood. It was almost too good to be true. Perhaps the corvidae had been called away. Many a local bird had spoken, in great fear, of their massive gatherings – many hundreds of corvidae collecting together for their own nefarious purposes. But these were usually held in the dead of night, and the sun had set less than two hours ago.

Lostri's head turned fearfully this way and that as he flew. His huge eyes scanned the dense foliage of the deciduous trees, alert for the flash of a beak or the flutter of a wing. Suddenly, Claudia called to him with a soft hoot of warning.

'Lostri. We are near the place where they held us. What should we do?'

'We must go on,' he replied, urgently. 'We have no choice in any case, having come so far. But maybe the luck that has travelled with us thus far will hold awhile. Show me where your sister is being held.'

Dipping her wing, Claudia banked to the right and disappeared through a narrow gap between two great oak trees. Lostri followed, reckless now, as fear sent adrenaline coursing through his veins.

'I can't believe it!' Claudia exclaimed. 'The whole place is deserted.'

'Calipha,' Lostri called out into the gloom. 'Where are you? Can you hear us?'

But, as he called the words, he knew the answer with a sinking heart. The stench of death was unmistakable, and a strangled sob from Claudia confirmed the identity of the corpse that the night had hidden from them initially. It was a kindness in a way. For full daylight would have borne harsh testimony to her torture and brutal slaying, whereas twilight shadows covered her like a cloak, or a shroud. Claudia wept openly, her anguished sobs echoing through the sleepy woodland. Then the moon peeped out from behind a bank of cloud, and its clear, silver light was reflected in a hundred pairs of eyes which formed an impenetrable ring around the unfortunate owls.

Lostri was the first to react, surging off the ground in a desperate flight for freedom. Claudia followed suit, but not before the trees erupted with noise as a huge phalanx of corvidae took to the air. It only took a matter of seconds before the owls were forced groundward once more, but it was time enough for sharp beaks and claws to do their potent work and inflict grievous injuries upon the pair. Lostri and Claudia landed in pools of their own blood, adding to the crimson with each second that passed.

The magpies, rooks and crows could easily have finished them off then and there, their numbers were overwhelming. But they refrained, their blood-lust held in abeyance by something far stronger, which was revealed when a frustrated young rook called out to the gathered assembly, 'What are we waiting for? Why don't we kill the pair of them? Look at them! They're no match for the lot of us!'

His exhortations were cut off abruptly by another voice in the darkness. 'Don't be a bloody fool! You know our orders. We've done what we were supposed to do. Now we wait!'

Tomar looked considerably better after being well fed and rested. Something of his former sparkle returned to his old eyes, and his movements were less restricted and painful. 'Thank you, my friends. What would I do without you?'

'So far as I am concerned, that question need never arise again,' answered Merion, a shade of defiance in his voice. 'For we will never leave your side again, Tomar. I, for one, have had enough of journeys and errands, however important.'

'We all serve Birddom, and it is our duty to do everything that is asked of us in its service.'

'Then I hope that what we have found out is sufficient for Birddom's needs. Surely we have done enough? Given enough?'

Tomar wrapped a wing around his agitated friend. 'You have indeed, and if every bird knew of your trials and sacrifices they would not ask for more. But I may yet call upon you one more time. There may still be another task for a reluctant robin. But for now, all that is required from you is your story, from beginning to end.'

Tomar and the two robins talked long into the night, and the old owl soon realised that Olivia was deeply wounded by her mother's death. She was sombre and withdrawn, and it took all of his considerable skill to begin to draw her out of her depression. Tomar questioned and probed her about the details of the journey, trying to distract her from her thoughts of her loss, but, at the same time, seeking out the implication in everything that was told to him. He chuckled with amusement at her description of Hobo, the black and white rabbit, with his bright eyes, twitching nose and inexhaustible nervous energy.

'I am sure that he would have worn me out, just watching him,' Tomar said. 'He certainly seems a strange companion for a wolf such as Septimus.'

'Is a rabbit ever a likely friend to any wolf?' Olivia asked, with some irony. 'Unless it is as a friend to their stomachs!'

'True. It is most unusual. Hobo's colouring is odd, too, for a wild rabbit, though not unheard of. There may be more to that fellow than meets the eye. I wonder...'

Even as he spoke the words, the old tawny owl sank into reverie, and was silent until Merion broke into his thoughts.

'Are you all right, Tomar? What is the matter?'

'Oh, nothing, my friend. I was just thinking. But those thoughts are of no consequence for the present. Now, tell me once more about old Septimus, and his infernally clever rhyme.'

Traska had pushed himself hard to reach Cra Wyd so quickly, and was proud of his efforts. 'Not bad for an old magpie,' he said to himself. 'No, indeed. I'd like to see many of the fools around here do better. They're a lazy bunch of scoundrels. Not one of them would have made it into my coven in the old days. But at least there are a lot of them. Now let's see if they have managed to capture me a brace of owls!'

Traska sought out Scrant, the magpie he had personally chosen to be the nominal leader of the Cra Wyd coven, in spite of the pre-eminence of rooks in the colony. He could tell immediately, by the unbearably-smug look on the other magpie's beak, that the plan had been successful. Traska rubbed his wing-tips together in anticipation. What pleasure he would take in watching his three enemies die.

'Senseless murder! There's nothing like it!' he thought, smiling wickedly. Then, addressing the other magpie, he snapped out a command. 'Take me to the prisoners at once.'

Scrant was not used to being spoken to so dismissively. After all, he was the leader here. He made a vain attempt to re-establish his authority and dignity. 'The prisoners are perfectly safe. We will go and see them shortly. But, in the mean-time, rest and share some food with me. You must be exhausted and famished after your long journey. Come, let us feast. And do not worry your head, my lads are more than a match for a pair of owls.'

'What do you mean ... a pair?' Traska roared.

Scrant shrank back fearing that the other bird would strike him. 'What's the difference? Two owls or three? We had to kill the older female. She was trouble, and the boys were getting restless. Anyway, the trap worked just the same, didn't it? And I made sure that no one disobeyed my orders a second time.'

'No corvid under my command would have dared to disobey me even once,' Traska sneered. 'Until now, it seems. I gave explicit instructions that all three owls were to be kept alive until I got here.'

'I am sorry, Traska,' Scrant blustered. 'I will bring the bird responsible to you for punishment.'

Traska nodded, in business-like fashion, all the while thinking, 'There is only one bird whom I hold responsible. And I will decide if and when you are to be punished!'

*

'Avia's neither far nor near,
Not over there, but not quite here,
The path where you would choose to go,
Is one that only a wolf might know...'

Hearing Septimus' words from Tomar's throat, both robins found that they had tears in their eyes. For the resonance and power of Tomar's delivery as he recited the poem, seemed to roll back the years for the old owl himself. He held his body straighter, and his eyes shone with a passion ignited by the hope contained within the rhyme that he spoke. Olivia and Merion waited eagerly for their friend to decipher the puzzle, and so unlock the gateway to Avia itself. But it seemed that there would be no easy answers. Indeed, once he had recited Septimus' words, Tomar looked to the pair of robins for their thoughts and opinions.

'Well, Merion, what do you make of it all? It's quite mysterious, isn't it?'

'Olivia and I have done little else but ponder the rhyme since we left the Isle of Storms, but I don't think that we really understand more than a fraction of Septimus' meaning.'

'Well, that's a start at least, my friend. But you said that the rhyme was delivered in two parts?'

'Yes. I do not know how the old wolf managed it, but he invaded my dreams in order to deliver a message to you. He stressed that most particularly. "Tell my friend, and wisest of owls, that the entrance to Avia is a gateway in time as much as space, and that to miss the opportunity would be irretrievable." That was what he wanted me to tell you, but it just gives us yet another riddle to unravel. We don't know where Avia is, or how to get there. And, moreover, we don't know when Avia is – that is, when we can get there!'

Tomar's reply was soothing, calming the robin's agitation.

'Oh yes, Merion, we do know. We just do not know that we know!'

Lostri had never come face to face with Traska before. But he knew immediately that the magpie who strutted and preened in front of him was the very villain who had blighted Birddom for so many years. He had a presence that the others lacked. It was an aura, Lostri realised with shock, of pure evil. Even if it hadn't been evident to him, Claudia's reaction would have told him. She gave a small, choking scream and blanched, her pupils contracting wildly with fear. She had had dealings with Traska before, of course, and her memories were dire indeed. Lostri decided to go straight onto the attack.

'What right have you to hold us like this, against our will? I am Lostri, a member of the Council of the Owls, and I was sent here as an emissary to parlay with the corvidae of the northern territories. I came in peace, and this is how I am treated?'

'Stop your blustering, you pompous fool. You are giving me a headache, and I can get quite nasty when I have a headache. You say that you came here as an emissary for Birddom. I say that you came here to spy upon us. Your two friends, one of whom is now sadly demised, have both admitted as much, and their lives are rightly forfeit.'

Lostri bridled at such arrogance, and responded curtly. 'No bird has the power of life and death over another!'

'Open your eyes, Lostri,' Traska whispered with menace. 'Look around you and then tell me again that I do not have the power to break you in two if I so choose.'

Of course, the vile magpie was right. Lostri saw that immediately. Indeed, in his present position, all that he could hope for was a quick despatch from this life. But he feared that Traska had other, more elaborate plans for him and his friend.

Engar waved his wings expansively to the assembled gathering. The remaining Council members were all there. Cerca, Pellar and Steele formed a tight knot close to their leader. Creer, Wensus and Janvar chatted amiably with two of the new-comers. Only Faron and Meldra had the grace to look shame-faced, and each stood alone and miserable, not speaking to anyone. The third new-comer had hopped over to Engar's side, eager to speak to the Great Owl. But the barn owl delivered a hushed 'later' before calling the Council to order.

'Thank you all for coming on such short notice. I believe that today is as momentous an occasion as has been seen in Birddom since ancient times. An historic day, which will pass into the folklore of our land, along with the names of all present. For today is the day when the democracy that was always my dream for Birddom becomes a reality. I was chosen as Great Owl – you yourselves chose me – for that vision of Birddom as a place where every bird lived as equal to any other. Today that vision becomes flesh. For we embrace those who in the past have been our enemies, but who we now call our friends. I welcome Drag, Smew and Chak into our fellowship. They are the chosen representatives of the corvidae, and they honour us with their presence.'

Engar paused, and looked around for vociferous approval, which was duly provided by six of the owls there. The barn owl noted the reticence of Meldra and Faron to join in the clamour of welcome. 'Well,' he mused. 'So not everyone on the Council shares my vision for Birddom, eh? So be it. This is a democracy, after all!'

Meldra caught his eye at precisely this moment and looked away quickly, appalled by the evil in the Great Owl's smile.

'Oh Tomar, my old friend,' she moaned softly. 'You were right all along. What have we done?'

The two naked bodies huddled together, desperate for warmth in the cold night. They were a truly pathetic sight, and thankful that darkness hid them for now from the ridicule of the world. Lostri and Claudia had been plucked while still alive. Traska had taken a great delight in removing those feathers where the pain was greatest, ripping them away from around the eyes, ears and breast. He would have liked to have torn away their tail-feathers too, but others were equally eager for such pleasure, and Traska had watched the owls' agony with immense enjoyment. Each primary and pinion had been fought over as a prized trophy, and Traska had personally overseen the removal of even the smallest feather from their prison-site. He wanted to be sure to leave nothing. A pile of feathers might be used to provide a warmth of sorts for Lostri and Claudia, and Traska did not wish to be known for such generosity.

When day broke, the owls were torpid and near to death. They had been given nothing to eat or drink. Their body temperatures had dropped dangerously low, and only sleep had provided a respite from the horrors that had been done to them. But now a different, equally deadly threat emerged with the rising of the sun. For the sky was cloudless, and the day promised to be hot. And, even at his most optimistic, Lostri had not the slightest hope that his corvid captors would show any mercy. No. Having barely survived freezing to death, it seemed that the two owls' fate was to be baked alive.

Merion could not help but feel alarmed. Both he and his sister had pinned their faith on Tomar's intellect. Neither had doubted for a single moment that the old owl would be able to solve Septimus' riddle. But Merion now realised, with dismay, that Tomar was having no more success than they had had. He had listened attentively to all of their theories as to the meaning of each stanza of the rhyme, but had not been able to come up with a single explanation of his own to help unlock the puzzle. Merion felt like crying. His dear old friend was obviously going senile. His faculties simply no longer had the capacity for such a task. 'All is lost!' he thought, with resignation.

Even Olivia was worried, although she had greater belief in Tomar's mental powers. But why was the old tawny owl so quiet and unresponsive? He seemed content merely to nod at each one of their ideas, often smiling in encouragement. Occasionally he would mutter, 'Yes, that might be it,' or 'That's certainly one way of looking at it,' but adding nothing constructive of his own.

Finally, the robins' enthusiasm petered out, and they gave each other eloquent looks, which Tomar noticed immediately. 'I apologise if I have been a little quiet. It is not easy to talk and listen at the same time.' The robins looked suitably abashed as Tomar went on. 'You have both done well, whether you know it or not. We have moved much closer to the solution than you realise, and it is thanks to your efforts that we have done so. Now, don't worry about me. My body may be old and frail, but my mind isn't quite ready for retirement just yet. You must leave me alone for a while, that's all. I need to think. Septimus is a clever old devil, but, hopefully, so am I!'

Traska had never eaten owl before, and he had to admit that it was delicious. Underneath the blistered skin the flesh was still warm – almost hot – and the magpie gulped it down with relish. Blood dripped down onto his chest, and more spilled from his open beak as he saluted his companions.

'Enjoying the feast?' he asked, laughing. The crows and rooks nodded enthusiastically, too intent on their own food to utter a reply. Traska realised that he was being rather greedy, keeping all the best bits of the two owls for himself. But they looked happy enough, didn't they? They had the scraps and, besides, there was more than sufficient meat on the body of Scrant to make up the meal, and satisfy a dozen hungry bellies for the moment.

The cruel magpie looked back with satisfaction upon a job well done. He had relished engineering the owls' death, knowing that he had sent them to their final rest tormented with the knowledge of his plans for Birddom. Traska would never forget the look of absolute disbelief on Lostri's face, as he had described, in detail, the future and the fate that awaited every owl on the Council.

'Yes,' he had repeated, spitting the words into Lostri's shocked face. 'Every owl!'

Chapter Sixteen

The date of the evacuation had been set for the first week in September. That was now only four weeks away, and it was a tribute to Man's efficiency, once properly motivated, that so much had been achieved to the set time-scales. The coastline of the country was ringed with huge magnets, and, on careful consideration, many more had been placed at the highest points inland to avoid topographical interference with the pulse. Nothing was being left to chance. Weather was the only variable, but long-range forecasters were reassured by the prospect of a warm, dry and sunny start to autumn. Flat, calm seas would make the naval operation a great deal easier, and government sources were optimistic.

A massive push on the refrigeration conversion programme for farm buildings meant that planned slaughtering of livestock could be scaled up. This would reduce the workload involved after the great machines had done their deadly work. Cattle, sheep and pigs had been force-fed over the last few weeks to increase their body-weight well ahead of natural progress, and the carcasses of those animals already slaughtered weren't far from their prime. This was a success story that was being trumpeted in the press, and the populace welcomed the idea of a plentiful supply of meat being available when they returned to their homeland.

However, only a government stranglehold on the media stifled a story that would have seen them greeted with derision and anger by that same public. An appalling lack of forethought meant that no proactive action had been taken by the government to procure a source of livestock, from the continent or elsewhere, to restock the countryside and maintain the nation's farming industry. Now the country was being held to ransom by several of its nearest neighbours who simply added purchase of the necessary animal breeding stock as a codicil to their agreement to temporarily house the evacuees. The additional cost of this lack of planning would undoubtedly run into billions, and senior politicians were frantically seeking creative ways to hide their blunder.

But, to the public at large, the news being spun to them was all positive, and the clarion-call of public-spirited effort towards the common goal sounded loud and clear across the country. In two weeks the nets would come down, and the countdown towards the destruction of their enemy would begin.

Meldra realised that she was taking a great risk in coming, but the look of joy on Tomar's face made the danger worthwhile. The old tawny owl was alone while his robin companions foraged for a meal, and his head was sunk low as he focused his great brain on Septimus' strange message. Meldra had to hoot twice to attract his attention, and Tomar started at the sound. It was so long since he had heard any call from one of his own kind. Tears sprang up at the corners of his eyes, but he wiped them quickly away and cried out happily, 'Meldra, my dear friend. How good it is to see you. How are you, and how are all my friends on the Council?'

'I marvel at your tolerance in calling me your friend still,' she replied, with genuine remorse. 'And I am sad to say that you have precious few friends on the Council nowadays. Come to that, neither do I.'

'Have things changed *so* quickly?' Tomar asked.

'They have changed beyond all recognition, and to the detriment of the Council and of Birddom,' Meldra answered gravely.

Tomar gave an impatient nod. What was so bad that she had taken the risk of visiting him? And then he realised, with a great rush of love, that Meldra was reluctant only because she wished to protect him from ill-tidings. 'It is all right, my dear,' he said, with a rueful smile. 'I am not as frail as I obviously seem to you. Whatever news you have brought, I am ready for it. Remember, it is not that long since I was Great Owl.'

'Yes, Tomar, my friend. And Birddom would be a much better place if you were still our leader. I realise that now. You were right all along. Engar is a villain, and nothing that he does is for the good of our land. He talks of every bird, but thinks only of himself. He has ousted Lostri from the Council, declaring him to be a wastrel and unfit for such high duty. Engar sent him on a mission to communicate with the leaders of the corvidae in the north, but Lostri is long overdue. I am very fearful that something dreadful has happened to him; something, moreover, engineered by Engar himself.'

Tomar shook his head, his eyes showing genuine concern for the fate of his friend. 'These are ill-tidings indeed. What do the other members of the Council think about it?'

'That is part of the problem. I cannot be sure that any of them care at all. They seem to have become mere mouthpieces for Engar. Oh, Faron seems to be less sheep-like than the rest. He appears to be having second thoughts about our great leader. But I am not sure that I can trust my instincts any longer, having failed to see Engar for what he truly is. However, that is not all. There is more bad news to tell, if you can bear it?'

Tomar nodded for his friend to continue.

'The Council is back to its full complement of twelve members.' Meldra quickly stilled Tomar's question. 'You want to ask me who has been chosen, and why. The names of our newest Council members are Smew, Drag and Chak. I see from your face that you do not recognise their names, but why should you? The reason that you do not know them is very simple: they are all magpies, my friend! Can you believe it? Magpies on the Council of the Owls!'

At that very moment, Merion and Olivia flew back to the fir tree, their beaks crammed with the bounty of the woodland. They were astonished to see two owls sat where they had left only one, but this reaction was superseded by distress when they saw the shock on their old friend's face. They quickly alighted and, depositing their food store, ran to Tomar's side.

'What is the matter, Tomar?' the robins cried in unison.

But no reply was forthcoming. The old owl was momentarily unable to speak. Merion and Olivia comforted him as best they could while he summoned his inner reserves. Finally, he gasped out a single word: 'Magpies!'

The robins looked around in alarm, but seeing no corvids in the vicinity looked to Meldra for an explanation. She swiftly repeated her story, and the robins' shock matched that of their old friend.

'Traska's behind this, he must be!' Merion cried.

Tomar stirred from his mute reflections. 'Yes, my dear friends. This is all undoubtedly Traska's doing. Engar is merely his dupe. As vain as a peacock, and as stupid as a pigeon. But this is certainly only the beginning. Traska is trying to outdo his mentor, Slyekin. He will not be satisfied until he perches as supreme ruler on the throne of Birddom!'

'We cannot let that happen!' Olivia blurted out in anguish.

'I am not sure that there is a great deal that we can do to prevent it,' Tomar replied.

Meldra and the robins were aghast at his words, but Tomar held up a wing to silence their protests.

'Let us be realistic. We have absolutely no power base from which to launch a challenge against Traska, who, remember, has the support of the Great Owl. Meldra's days on the Council are numbered, you can be sure of that. Indeed, my dear, I believe most strongly that your life is in grave danger already. And probably that of Faron, too. Engar may be stupid in some ways, but he is cunning as well. I am sure that he is well aware of your doubts. No, you have served Birddom as a member of the Council for the last time, my friend. But I foresee another road for you to take, in service of our land.'

'But what good would that be if Traska is going to be the ruler of Birddom, as you say? I can scarcely believe it. If anyone other than you had voiced such an opinion, I would have called them a fool.'

'I have been labelled such many, many times, by those who do not know any better,' Tomar responded proudly. 'But I stand by what I said. Things have gone too far to be redressed. It is inevitable that Traska's power will increase. I am sure that it will not be long before more corvids are chosen for the Council. The magpies' grip will tighten. And Engar will let it happen, not realising where it will lead.'

Tomar shuddered, then composed himself and surprised the other three with a smile.

'It is all of no consequence, anyway. Birddom as we know it is finished. I have long said as much. That is why I sent the pair of you to Septimus. We are beset by enemies. Indeed, crazy as it sounds, Traska is the least of our worries. Avia is the only hope for any bird, and only then if we are able to find the way in!'

Engar's hoot of greeting was answered by Traska's salutary caw, as the magpie swooped down into the barn owl's lair. 'Welcome back, my friend,' Engar called. 'What news from the north?'

Traska landed, and strutted over to the Great Owl's side. 'Am I your missive, that I must make my report to you?' He sketched an ironic bow, before continuing, 'My name is not Lostri, you know.'

Engar stammered an apology. 'Forgive me, Traska. I did not mean to imply anything. I was merely glad to see you, and eager to hear your news.'

'My news is mainly about Lostri, as it happens. He has failed on his mission, and won't be coming to you with his report. He was unavoidably and permanently detained in Cra Wyd!'

Engar giggled delightedly. 'Tell me more,' he begged.

So, Traska regaled him with stories of cruelty and brutality, gloating over the gory details of the deaths of the three owls. Engar couldn't help but admire his friend's imaginativeness – put, as it was, to such depraved use. But he also felt a twinge of unease when hearing of how the magpie had dealt with Scrant, making a promise to himself never to get on the wrong side of his partner.

'But what about our progress on the Council?' Traska asked, and this time it was Engar's turn to report to his superior.

'Everything has gone according to plan. I anticipated Lostri's shameful neglect of his duty, and banished him from the Council. In his place now sits Smew, just as you requested. Drag and Chak have replaced Calipha and Tomar. The Council is twelve strong once more. But I am worried about the loyalty of at least one, maybe two, of the remaining Council members. Faron was not in the least enthusiastic about our introducing corvids onto the Council. And I caught Meldra watching me with a very strange look on her face.'

Traska was decisive. 'They must both be replaced, and the sooner the better. I will find two suitable candidates from within our brotherhood.'

Engar's manner was at its most ingratiating. 'What about you,' he simpered. 'Won't you honour us by taking a place on the Council?'

Tomar, Meldra and the two robins were deep in conversation. The food, for which Merion and Olivia had so patiently foraged, lay discarded and ignored. There was an air of excitement around the crooked fir, generated by the urgency of Tomar's words.

'My friends, do not despair. When I spoke of the end for Birddom, I meant only the loss of our physical home. We carry Birddom in our hearts, and its truths and philosophies will endure while any bird still lives who is faithful to its cause. Remember the rhyme, Merion? "But peril lies at Avia's doors, if you're not true to Birddom's cause." Doesn't that also mean that no harm will come to any who are true?'

His three companions nodded eagerly, as Tomar went on. 'Each one of us has work to do. Work that is vital for our future survival. I know that I place a heavy burden upon your backs and wings, but I am too old and too weak for such a task myself. I need each of you to undertake a journey, and I do not underestimate the peril that each of you may face. Birddom is a dark and ominous place once more, with the corvids wielding ever greater power. Indeed, it seems that my sole role, as Great Owl and now, has been sending others into danger. But there it is. I will not shirk it. Nor, I know, will any of you. But you will all need to take the greatest care. For Birddom's sake, you cannot fail.

'Meldra, I need you to fly far to the west, to the mountain home of Darreal, leader of the falcons. You recognise the name, no doubt. He has long been our ally, and a great force for good in Birddom. Olivia, you will return to Storne. Having visited him so recently, you will know the way.'

A shadow of misery passed over the female robin's face, and Tomar said, sympathetically, 'You grieve still for your mother. I am sorry to cause you pain by bringing out memories. But your journey then was not an ill one, even though nothing came of your efforts. And do not be angry with Storne. There must have been reasons for his choice not to help us. Indeed, looking back now, I cannot say what he could have done, if he had flown to our aid. But, this time I need him. And, this time, I am sure he will come.'

'What about me?' Merion blurted out, impatiently.

'You have already been given your mission, though your task was set with other, darker purposes in mind. You must carry out the very journey that Engar asked of you. I want you to visit Kraken.'

Merion's eyes lit up with understanding. But then, as he gave it a little more thought, doubt clouded his mind. 'I am not sure that I understand, Tomar. Are we preparing for another Great Battle against the corvidae? Like the one that you orchestrated with the help of my father? It seems that way, when you send us all to ask for aid from your allies in that triumphal time. But why should we do battle if Birddom is finished, as you say? And how will a war with the corvidae help us to find Avia?'

The old owl's eyes brightened with sudden revelatory under-standing, and he clapped his wing to his forehead, as if admonishing himself for his erstwhile stupidity. Then he smiled at his bemused friend. 'I will always seek to do battle against evil, Merion,' he replied. 'But this will be a battle of the mind – the only one that I am likely to win at my age. I need the help of Darreal, Storne and Kraken for two reasons. Firstly, they must help me to solve the riddle that Septimus has set us. They are each, in their own right, great leaders with years of wisdom and experience between them. But that will only be a part of their efforts. With them, and each of you, I want to create a Council fit to lead Birddom, and one which can organise our journey into Avia. We will have to persuade every bird of the justice of our cause, and the voices of those mighty birds will carry great weight when the time comes.'

'But we do not know when that time will be!' Olivia cheeped, in her frustration.

'Oh yes, my dear. Thanks to your brother here, we know exactly when that time will be! Reconsider the second part of Septimus' rhyme: "Think back to former battles won." Yes, Olivia. We may still not know how to get into Avia. But we do know when!'

Engar hooted for silence, and then called the Council meeting to order. 'We seem to be very busy just at the moment,' he began. 'But is it not right and proper? Birddom is in a state of change. Things move at a pace unheard of to the more sedate of our predecessors. I am not sure that they would have been able to cope. But we are a strong Council, reinvigorated by new members and new ideas. If it is not too strong a word to use, I will say that there is a revolution in this land of ours. But it is a revolution that we are leading, not fighting against. And that is because it is a revolution for good.

'Change for the better should never be feared but, rather, embraced by all right-minded and progressive birds. Our Council has changed, and changes even more today. For Meldra has deserted the cause. She has disappeared, and so failed to answer the summons to duty. Such an owl has no place on the Council, and I have asked Traska here to take her place.'

The sound of his name, spoken of as an ally at Council, and his very presence among them, caused a sense of shock to resonate through the six owls who stared, open-beaked, at their leader. But only one owl dared to raise his voice in protest.

'Engar!' Faron cried out, in dismay. 'Have you taken leave of your senses?' Ignoring the murderous look from the Great Owl, he continued, without pause, 'All of Birddom knows Traska to be the most evil magpie ever to hop his way out of hell. Now I've kept silent while good friends of mine were ousted from our Council. I've supported your vision for the future of Birddom, and still do. But your original plans for leading us into that future never included alliance with our enemies. You have gone too far.'

Faron cast his eyes around the Council ring, appealing to every owl there. 'Ask yourselves a question, my friends. Before it is too late. Ask yourselves what has become of Calipha. Of Lostri. And now Meldra. Each of them was an honourable owl. I say was because I fear that none of them are still alive. Tomar, our Great Owl, was banished, and I am ashamed of my part in that act of treachery. Now, three more of our Council have vanished without trace. And in their places perch four magpies! Think for a moment about the gravity of those words. Four magpies sit on the Council of the Owls!'

While Faron had been talking, Engar had sat speechless and impotent. But Traska had not. On his signal, Smew, Drag and Chak had begun to edge closer, inch by inch, towards the brave owl. Faron realised his predicament too late. His attempt to launch himself from his perch was thwarted when the group of magpies fell upon him in a savage attack. It was an unequal contest, and would have been over in only a few moments. But, even as the first blows were struck, Traska rebuked his cohorts in authoritative tones.

'Magpies! I am ashamed of you! Stop this at once!'

The three attackers were bemused by their leader's sudden apparent change of heart. Hadn't he given them the signal in the first place? Each magpie had known exactly what he had wanted them to do. Or had thought that they had. Unsure of what to do next, they backed off shame-faced, as Traska continued to reproach them.

'That type of act is the very reason why we have been Birddom's enemies for so long. I have worked so hard to make the peace, and to build a future for our own kind – a future of integration and harmony with the rest of the birds in this beloved land.

'Now, apologise to Faron. He has every right to express his views at Council, even if they are contrary to our own. We may not like what we hear, but we must resist against such a violent response. For that is not the way of the Council, and it will not be our way either. Please accept my own apologies, Faron. Are you hurt, my friend?'

Faron was as bemused as his attackers. He had been certain for a moment that he was going to die, and he had gloried in the knowledge that the magpies had gone too far. His own death would not be in vain. For surely Engar and the rest would indeed come to their senses, and abandon this absurd and dangerous alliance, now that the corvids had shown their true colours. But, astonishingly, Traska had defended him. Had saved his life! The owl was amazed and confused. He had been so sure that Traska was up to no good. But now, that belief was undermined by the generous actions of one he had called evil.

'It is I who should apologise to you, and to my fellow Council members. I am no longer worthy of that name. I ask your permission to relinquish my place on the Council. For I am out of touch with its needs, and, because of this, saw malice where there was none. I was so sure, and yet I was wrong, and so can no longer serve Birddom in honour.'

The remaining owls sat stunned by what they had witnessed. Not a single owl had moved as much as a wing-tip to help their friend, and, but for Traska, Faron's body would now be laying, discarded and bloody, at the foot of the great oak which had been his Council perch for so long. That thought alone was sobering to one and all. But they were dumb-struck by the whole scene that had played out before them, and had no response to their colleague's announcement. Looking around the circle with regret, Faron knew that there was no more to be said, and simply turned, and flapped painfully away over the trees.

It was Traska himself who broke the silence. 'That was regrettable, and the actions of my friends were inexcusable. But Faron did speak treason. Treason against your chosen leader, Engar, and treason against Birddom. For Birddom is all of us, including the corvidae. Things that we have done in the past are just that – in the past. I was deeply moved when the Great Owl did me the honour of inviting me to join the Council. For I felt that I had at last been forgiven for ancient crimes, carried out, remember, under a tyrannical leadership. Faron called me evil, but is it evil to obey your leader? Perhaps I should have stood up against Slyekin, but it would surely have cost me my life. Maybe the bird who stands before you today would have done so. For I believe that I am a changed bird. I am stronger and wiser, and I propose to use that strength and wisdom for the good of Birddom.

'Yes, I was proud when Engar chose me to join the Council. Note that I do not call it the Council of the Owls. For the current leaders of Birddom are much more representative than the Council of old, and I believe that, because of this, we can serve Birddom better than in the past. I know that I am new to the Council, but I would like to make two proposals. Following the unpleasantness in our midst today, these may be difficult words to hear. But our Council needs to be strong. Engar spoke wisely when he said that things move at a rapid pace, and that change for the better should never be feared.

'We need to choose a replacement for Faron, for I fear that he will not return. His is a great loss, but the fact is that he was lost to us before he left here today. You all heard him speak. Who can deny that his words were treasonous? He even realised it himself, in the end. I propose that another corvid be chosen to take his place and, before you over-react, I will give you my reasons. It seems to me that Birddom is like a single huge bird, and any bird has its left and its right wings. If they are of equal size and strength they give the bird balance, and allow it to fly true. I believe that five corvids and six owls will provide a greater balance for the body of the Council who rule Birddom. The Great Owl, of course, is the head, and his huge eyes see clearly the way ahead for our land.

'But I spoke earlier of a representative Council, and I believe as passionately as Engar does in equality for all. So I do not want to foist another magpie upon you. Cronyism has no place in democracy. I will consult with my own community, and place five names before the Great Owl. The new Council member will be a jay or a rook. A jackdaw or a crow. But he will not be a magpie. This is the best proof that I can offer that we do not wish to control the Council but to serve it.'

It was a long speech, and even Engar was surprised to see how spell-bound Traska's audience were. The magpie had managed to dissipate their shock at seeing what had happened to Faron. He had even managed to slip his second proposal, unnoticed, into his rhetoric. And now it was time for the barn owl to provide his support.

'Thank you, Traska. You have shown great courage in speaking so openly to us here today. Courage befitting one chosen for our Council. I feel also that 'Council of the Owls' is too insular a title, and, now that you have joined us, its continued use is a slight on your worth, and that of your – nay, our – colleagues. So, my friends, I propose that, henceforth, we call ourselves merely 'The Council'. It is a simple title, but sufficient for our needs. We need no aggrandisement, no trappings of power. We are servants of Birddom. We are its Council, and as such we shall be known!'

The three magpies could scarcely wait until the Council had disbanded before they fell upon Traska with questions. But he silenced them with a vicious hiss.

'Don't make me regret that I chose you, and don't be such bloody fools. Everything went perfectly, and according to plan. You couldn't have done better if you had tried. I've got them eating out of my primaries now, thanks to the three of you. You did just enough to scare Faron into shutting up, and I promise you that we will make that very permanent in the next couple of days. You scared the rest of the Council, too, and allowed me to play the hero. They think that I can control you, which I can, of course, but not in the way that they mean. You do my bidding, and, by reigning in your desire for blood this time, you have opened the door to something that will be much more fun, when I deem that the time is right!'

Chapter Seventeen

Merion was the first to reach his destination, his being the shortest journey of the three. He had exercised extreme caution, following Tomar's warning, and had needed to hide on several occasions while roving bands of crow and rook took to the skies, as if parading their new status to the rest of Birddom. However, he avoided any altercation with the corvids, and flew on. He eventually crossed over the same estuary that had caught the eye of his mother, Portia, with nearly disastrous consequences, when she and Kirrick had travelled this same path several years earlier. But Merion knew the story of Portia's folly only too well, and he had learnt, almost from hatching, to distinguish between fresh and salt water.

He sought out Kraken, the great black-backed gull, on the rocky promontory overlooking the shimmering sea. The day was fine and gloriously hot, and the seagull flock basked lazily in the afternoon sunshine. Every ledge on the sheer cliff was occupied by black, white and grey bodies, and the clamour of their conversations and arguments were deafening to the little robin.

Merion flew to the highest spot on the cliff, a place of honour which held the best vantage point for watching over the colony. Kraken should have been there, but instead a young but still very impressive seagull lounged in his place.

'Excuse me,' Merion ventured, timidly. 'I am looking for Kraken, the leader of your flock.'

The gull stared at him with an imperious eye. 'You are not from around here, are you?' he asked.

'No,' Merion replied. 'I have travelled a long way on urgent business with Kraken.'

The gull ignored Merion's insistent tone. 'If you were from around here, you would know full-well who is the leader of the flock.'

'You mean that Kraken has been deposed? Is he dead?'

'No, little one. Kraken is not dead. And neither was he deposed as our leader. Illness overtook him late last year; an ague that he shook off fairly quickly, for Kraken is a strong bird. But his eyesight was affected by the disease, and Kraken is now blind. Even with only one eye there was never a gull to match him, but the total loss of his sight has left him almost helpless and utterly dependant upon his family. We care for him, of course. How could we ever do otherwise? He was our leader for generations, and he is a great bird still. I am his son. My name is Pagen.'

'I am Merion, son of Kirrick, and I have been sent here by Tomar, formerly Great Owl of Birddom.'

'You call forth impressive names,' Pagen replied, nodding. 'Your father is a legend to the flock, and Tomar is still revered for his great wisdom. Is he well?'

'The years have taken their toll upon his body, and he is undoubtedly frail and old. But his mind is as lucid as ever, and works tirelessly for the good of Birddom. He asked me to come and seek your father's aid.'

'Alas, you came too late for that, unless the aid is something that can be given from the confines of his own nest.'

Merion looked pityingly at the massive gull, who obviously still dearly loved his father. 'At least yours is still alive,' he thought, sorrowfully, 'and you have known him every day while you have grown. I only know my father through the tales of others. How I envy you!'

*

Darreal was still very much in charge of the falcons of the west. Meldra did not have the robins' disadvantage in terms of size, when coming face-to-face with the object of her visit, but the owl felt a sense of awe, nevertheless. The red kite was a magnificent specimen, and the years since the Great Battle sat well on him. He bridled at her news about her journey, for Meldra had not been as successful as Merion in avoiding a confrontation with the corvids. Part-way through her journey, she had chanced upon a dozen powerful magpies, who, bolstered by their numbers, had surrounded her in a most menacing fashion. The owl had shown the quickness of mind to inform them in a frosty tone that she was a member of the Council, and was travelling on important business with the full permission of all of its members. This bluff was sufficient to make the magpies back off and allow her to go on her way. But the encounter had shaken her badly, and the red kite tried to take her mind off of the unpleasant experience by asking about Tomar, Portia and the others. Darreal was eager for news of his friends, and listened attentively while Meldra told him as much as she knew about the events in recent years. He never once tried to mask his feelings, which were all too plain upon his face. Sorrow at the death of Portia, sympathy for the current plight of Tomar and burning anger at the unholy resurrection of Traska. Here was a bird who clearly wore his heart upon his wing-tip. Meldra had no doubt that she would be able to persuade him to come to their aid.

'Tell me once again about Septimus' rhyme and Tomar's ideas about Avia,' the falcon requested, eagerly.

'Well, the rhyme remains something of a puzzle, even to that wisest of owls. I am sure that Tomar understands parts of it, but he cannot grasp the whole. It seems that we will only be able to gain entry into Avia on the anniversary of the very hour that your falcons, and the eagles under Storne's command, began to do battle with Slyekin's corvids. And Septimus' warning is clear. There will not be a second chance. So, every bird must be made ready, but ready for what? I fear that we are little further forward in answering that question. And, until we know how to get into Avia, there seems little point in knowing when!'

'Trust in Tomar,' Darreal replied, soothingly. 'I have never known of a problem that he could not surmount, with that astonishing mind of his. Yet I fear that I will be of no help at all, when it comes to solving Septimus' riddle. I cannot compete with my old friend in brain-power, that is for sure.'

'You underestimate yourself,' Meldra said. 'Tomar certainly believes that you can help him. Trust in Tomar.'

'*Touché*,' replied Darreal, smiling. 'Yes, Meldra. I will come with you, and will do the best I can.'

It took every ounce of patience that Olivia possessed not to turn around and fly home. He might be the leader of the eagles, and the most impressive bird still alive in Birddom, but the robin could not help feeling frustrated by Storne's seeming childishness. In the short time that she had taken to tell her tale, the golden eagle had gone from guilty sheepishness to seething anger. And now he was busy in a show of pompous self-righteousness as he sought, somehow, for a way to undo what could not be undone.

'If only he was my brother's size,' Olivia thought. 'I'd give him such a slapping!' But, to Storne, she said, guardedly, 'Tomar is looking to you to use your brain, and to help him find a way to save us all. You cannot right all the wrongs of the world, and no one is asking you to. You are not responsible for the death of my mother, any more than I am. Nor for those of the Council members whom Engar has betrayed into the clutches of Traska.'

Storne's eyes glittered dangerously at the mention of those two names, but Olivia persisted.

'You are not the first and will not be the last to have been fooled by our traitorous Great Owl, though I can hardly bring myself to call him that. He managed to turn the whole Council against Tomar, didn't he? He is very persuasive, but his vanity is his great weakness. He believes that he is infallible and, as such, can't see the danger that he is in.'

'Well, I wish it visited upon him in the fullest measure,' snapped Storne, through gritted beak. 'But if Engar is in danger, I want to be the one who delivers it to his nest!'

'Tomar does not need you as an instrument of vengeance. But if your thirst for revenge is based upon guilt for not coming to our aid before, then make amends now. Come with me back to Tanglewood. Tomar needs your help, and Birddom needs your strength.'

'Pagen,' Merion said. 'Will you help us in your father's stead?'

'My place is with the flock,' he replied, matter-of-factly. 'I have not long been chief gull, and it has taken a considerable effort to establish myself. There are always subordinates looking for the main chance, who would jump at the opportunity of replacing me. Were I to go with you, I cannot be sure that I would still be chief gull on my return.'

Merion stamped his claws angrily on the rocks. 'What is the point in being chief gull if the flock no longer exists? If what Tomar believes is true, then Birddom is finished, and that includes these waters and these rocks that you deem so precious. Finding a way into Avia is our only chance, and, as leader of the seagulls, it is your duty to do all that you can to save your flock!'

'I do not need to be reminded of my duty,' Pagen said, stone-faced. 'I did not want this responsibility but, now that I have it, I understand well enough what it means. My place is here. I am sorry that you have had a wasted journey, Merion.'

The robin was on the point of continuing the argument, in the forlorn hope that he might yet persuade the seagull to change his mind. But wisdom prevailed. The very set of Pagen's beak told him that he would only be forcing the gull into a more entrenched position. So Merion took his leave, and flew off to find a place to shelter for the remainder of the day. He was emotionally drained, as well as exhausted from the long flight to the coast, and decided that he would delay his return journey until the morning.

The robin sat slumped on the bough of the copper beech, his spirits at a very low ebb. How could he go back to Tomar and report yet another failure? His sister, he was sure, would succeed in persuading Storne, and surely Darreal would not reject the call for help. It was different with Pagen. He was not one of the triumvirate. He had no specific loyalty towards Tomar, and no interest, it seemed, in the wider world that existed beyond the spray-soaked rocks that were his home. Merion cheeped loudly in frustration, 'Oh, why is it that some birds just can't see beyond the end of their beaks?'

It had taken several hours for all the owls to pluck up the necessary courage to confront their leader. Though their voices had remained silent at the Council meeting, muted largely by the sudden desertion by their friend, Faron, there was a great deal of unease among them. Pellar, Cerca and Steele had met first to discuss the implications of the events at the Council meeting, and each felt that things were happening that could easily escalate out of their control. These three sought out Creer,

Wensus and Janvar, and, finding them of a like mind, decided that they would all raise their fears to Engar.

Standing aloof before their verbal onslaught, Engar was certainly taken aback by their vehemence. His face remained a mask of unconcern, betraying none of his surprise. But his mind was racing, as he pretended to listen sympathetically to their worries. When each owl had had their say, Engar thanked them for bringing the issue to his attention.

'My friends,' he said. 'You have acted in the highest traditions of the Council, according to your own interpretation of the perceived threat that you say the corvidae pose. But I must ask you a question. How long is it since they were our mortal enemies? Do any of you here even remember the Great Battle?'

He paused, and smiled in satisfaction at their uncertainty. 'We are a new generation, as the corvidae who now join us are a new generation.'

He held up his wing to silence Pellar's incipient protest. 'Yes, I am well aware that Traska doesn't come into that category. But you all heard him speak. You all witnessed his mercy and charity towards Faron. Having done so, can you doubt his sincere intentions to undo the wrongs of the past? Must a bird be persecuted with unjust suspicion for misdeeds committed so long ago, and so evidently regretted? Traska is a bird reborn, and an example to us all. For, in taking a place among us on the Council, he has shown that he is prepared to forgive and forget.

'But let us address your concerns about the new structure of the Council. We have been bold, I cannot argue with that. But we have not acted foolishly, or without caution. We still hold the majority on the Council. We are seven, while the corvids will have only five members. So long as we retain our unity and friendship, Birddom will always be wisely led. You are good owls, one and all, the finest in the land. We are the law-makers, and will steer a true course for our beloved Birddom while we have the strength of body and mind to continue to do so. And when we move on, other owls will replace us, and will carry on our legacy with honour and distinction. They will work primary in primary with our corvid brothers and, who knows, maybe with birds of every shape and size. Perhaps the Council will grow. Perhaps it will change. But that can only be a healthy thing, as we are proving by our current courageous choices for the future. Now, go back to your nest-holes, and exercise your minds more positively. Forget your fears, and trust that your Great Owl would never lead you astray.'

The eagle and the robin made an unusual and somewhat comic picture as they flew side by side. Storne's mighty wings flapped in leisurely fashion, as slowly as he dared for continued flight. By contrast, Olivia's beat at an exhausting tempo, in order to keep up with her companion. The golden eagle had to resort to periods of gliding so as not to tire his friend on their journey. Their conversation while they flew was necessarily staccato and broken, with the eagle doing most of the talking, while Olivia saved her breath for flying. Storne told the robin of Engar's visit, how the barn owl had allayed his fears and convinced him that there was no danger or threat to Tomar. The regret was evident in the great eagle's voice, and Olivia answered him kindly.

'Even my brother was taken in by Engar for a while, and then only the incontrovertible evidence of his own ears and eyes convinced him of his error. Don't be too hard on yourself, Storne. Your eyes are open now, and that is all that matters.'

'The eyes of an eagle see very far, when they are not blinded by delusion. And now, I promise, I will put them to good use. If I can see into the future, maybe I can help to solve this puzzle of yours. Tell me those lines from the rhyme again, Olivia.'

'"Avia is a state of mind, which few if any bird can find,"' she dutifully replied.

'Well, I know one thing. If Tomar is going to so much trouble, sending you all this way to fetch me, then he must believe that Avia is a real place. So, how is it that it can be real, and also only "a state of mind"? Perhaps the reality of Avia can only be reached by adopting a certain state of mind. That would fit, wouldn't it?'

Olivia's eyes flashed with excitement, and she suggested that they should immediately alight and continue the discussion. Coming to rest on the sturdy bough of a horse-chestnut tree, the eagle and robin eagerly pursued Storne's train of thought.

'What state of mind could Septimus mean?' Olivia asked. 'We can be positive or we can be confused. At the moment, my mind feels more like the latter. But, if a positive frame of mind is required for us to enter Avia, what do we need to be positive about?'

'Being positive is being determined,' the eagle answered. 'We must be determined that we will succeed.'

'But what use is determination when we don't have the key? How can we be positive when we don't know the way?'

'We must have faith,' Storne replied. 'We must trust that the way will be revealed to us.'

'But that implies doing nothing, and waiting for the answer to be handed to us, without any effort on our part. What sort of state of mind is that?'

'It is acceptance,' Storne said, simply. 'Acceptance that we do not always control our destiny, and that sometimes we must have faith in a higher power. A power that knows, far better than we do, the way that is right for Birddom, and for every bird in it.'

'Merion, wake up!'

The robin started at the loud screech near his ear, and swivelled round to see who was making such a racket. He had slept for several hours, and the gloom announced the onset of evening. In spite of the rest, he felt heavy-headed and disorientated.

'I'm sorry,' Pagen said. 'You look as if you still need your sleep, but I had to talk to you.'

'It's all right,' Merion replied, still groggy with tiredness. 'How can I help you, Pagen?'

'I've been thinking over what you said to me earlier. I was very rude to you, I'm afraid, but the truth is that I was frightened by what you told me. The very idea that Birddom could come to an end...'

Merion understood only too well the emotions that Pagen had been going through.

'We're all frightened, my friend. Even Tomar. But there is always hope. If we can find the key, then Avia awaits us. And it will be paradise, Pagen – for all birds!'

'I know it will, Merion, and I know that my duty, as you pointed out so strongly, is to get my flock there by any means that I can.'

'I apologise if I spoke so vehemently, but I wanted you to see...'

This time it was Pagen's turn to interrupt. 'I do see, my friend, but it comes to something when I am scolded by a bird no bigger than my claw!'

'What changed your mind?' Merion asked, to hide his relief.

'It took a long while, wrestling with my own conscience like that. I knew that you wouldn't have come if the situation wasn't extremely grave, but I didn't want to face the truth that I wasn't ready for another challenge, so soon after taking over the leadership of the flock.

However, in the end, it all came down to one thing – what would Kraken have done? Once I asked that question I knew that I had no other choice. I will go with you, Merion, as soon as I have made arrangements for the care of my father. Will Avia come soon enough for him, I wonder?'

'Maybe in that final hour,' Merion answered softly, 'Kraken will see the way more clearly than any of us.'

From the east and from the west they flew; disparate pairs journeying together with a common goal: to come to the aid of their friend, Tomar. And the old owl awaited their arrival, like the thought of sunshine after a long, dark winter. He had tried to focus his mind solely on the problem of solving Septimus' riddle but, all too often, his thoughts had strayed to his friends. Would they be successful in persuading his old allies once again to leave the comfort of their nests and journey so far? After all, he no longer had any authority in Birddom. And Storne had not responded to Portia and Olivia when they had asked for his help the last time. Could Meldra convince Darreal that Birddom really was finished?

It was a difficult concept to grasp, when the sun still shone and the wind still blew. Externally, there was no sign of impending doom. Man's nets had been a part of normal life for some time now, and birds had adapted in order to survive, as they always did. And the threat of retribution from the insects, which Tomar feared so greatly, had not materialised. Although he was sure that it was only a matter of time before the insects rose as a single organism and crushed the life out of Birddom, how could he be so certain that he was right?

'Because Septimus has confirmed my fears,' he said aloud. 'He has given us the date. We must leave Birddom for ever on the anniversary of the Great Battle, when the eye of the moon is at its largest. There is so little time, and so much that we still do not know. Hurry, my friends. I have never been in such need of counsel.'

Tomar shook his head, as if to rid himself of his uncertainty. He must get his mind back upon the problem. If he had not known at the outset, when he sent Olivia and Merion on their mission to consult with Septimus, Tomar knew now that Avia was real and unreal, at the same time. It was a different reality, that was all. But it did not exist in the way that his beloved crooked fir existed. It had no physical reality in the world that Birddom occupied. But then, he supposed that, in Avia, Birddom was a dream also. He had not expressed this concept to his friends. They had a difficult enough task to perform without clouding their minds with doubts. To them, Avia was as real a place as Wingland. The robins' mother had journeyed there, and had confirmed its existence, whereas before only the word of migrant birds had provided information about the land across the sea. But no migrant had ever come from Avia, and Tomar knew that, when they travelled there, no one would return to Birddom to report back that it was real.

Engar faced his six fellow Council members with a great deal more confidence and self-assurance than when they had confronted him with their doubts about the corvids. For surely they could hold no such fears now? The latest gesture from Traska re-enforced the authority and the esteem in which the owls on the Council were so obviously held. The magpies had asked for their help in reassuring the local community in the vicinity of Cra Wyd that corvids were allies and not enemies.

'They place their trust in us completely, and we should reward their faith in us by staunch support. We must move the Council for the next meeting. We will hold it in Cra Wyd, so sending out a signal to the birds in that area, and indeed to the whole of Birddom, that the days when owl and corvid faced each other in conflict are long over.'

Six heads nodded at his words, whilst the four magpies kept a respectful silence. Only Retch, the jay chosen by Engar to replace Faron on the Council, voiced his noisy acclaim for the Great Owl.

'What wisdom you show in this decision, Engar! What leadership, to demonstrate the courage of your convictions in such a way! I will fly at once, northwards to Cra Wyd, and inform them of your decision, for I am sure that they will want to prepare a suitable welcome!'

At this point, Traska intervened. 'Do not be too hasty, my young friend. I am sure that you have only the very best of intentions, but you exceed your authority at this Council. Such decisions must be left to the Great Owl. You will take your leave only at Engar's bidding.'

The barn owl puffed out his chest feathers at this show of obsequiousness towards him, and pride radiated in his voice as he responded to Traska's words.

'My friend, we are all equals here. And Retch, although our newest member, has a voice on this Council. His idea is a good one. We will make this a momentous occasion. When the Council meet at Cra Wyd, let it be a new beginning. A signal to every bird that we are not remote from Birddom's needs and wants, worries and fears. Let us return from there, proud of our achievements and stronger in the knowledge that our future, and the future of Birddom itself, is assured!'

Chapter Eighteen

"'Don't fear the tunnel, black as night, for darkness comes before the light.'"

Pagen repeated the lines over and over as he flew. They frightened him more than he cared to admit. He was a big bird, and never happier than when in flight, stretching out his wings to soar and dip. Flying was a skill over which he had supreme mastery. But he was terrified of being confined. The very thought of a tunnel made him quake uncontrollably. He had even been unable to visit his own father because of this, sending others in his stead to feed and clean the older bird. In his mind, a seagull had no place underground. Flight was useless there, and Pagen felt that he would be a lesser bird in such restricted places. The idea of blackness brought fear bubbling up from his guts, too. Kraken, his father, knew only blackness, but Pagen had never experienced it, and did not relish the prospect. On the coast at night there was always some light, whether provided by Nature, in the form of stars, or by Man, with his twinkling ships' lights and the far-seeing beam of the lighthouse. No, the gull had never known true night.

But it seemed that he would be asked, required rather, to face his fear of the dark in order to gain entry into Avia. If only he could just have stayed where he was, safe and sure on his webbed feet, his future as solid as the rocks beneath his nest. But it was all a delusion, he realised that now. Birddom was no longer built on a solid foundation. The rocks were crumbling into the water, and would soon disappear entirely beneath the waves.

Merion heard his companion muttering to himself, and recognised the part of the rhyme that Pagen was repeating.

'I've been into that tunnel. It is a beautiful place,' he called across to the seagull.

Pagen faltered in flight, and turned his head sharply to stare at the robin in astonishment. 'How?' was all that he could manage to utter.

'Oh, in a dream,' Merion replied. 'It was when Septimus told me that part of the rhyme. I dreamt that I was in a dark tunnel, but I wasn't frightened. It felt warm and comforting. It felt right, as if it was the place where I was meant to be. And I knew the way. Even before I could see it, I had no doubts that I would find the light.'

'But didn't it frighten you – going underground?' Pagen was amazed at the robin's apparent calm.

'It was only a dream. But no, I didn't feel frightened, and in many ways I am looking forward to the real experience. Anyway, it is difficult to explain but it wasn't like entering a solid place at all. It didn't feel confined, yet, at the same time, it felt like being inside a living, breathing being, not cold rock and earth. I'm probably not making a lot of sense, am I? But I know that I will not be afraid when the time comes.'

Cra Wyd was heaving with black bodies. Every branch was laden with rooks and crows. Magpies proliferated. Jackdaws sat around in huge groups. Even the usually-reticent ravens had left the fastness of their mountain homes and joined the throng. It seemed that every coven, across the length and breadth of Birddom, had sent a delegation, and that some had emptied themselves completely in an exodus to witness the arrival of the owls. A huge clamour of raucous cheering greeted their flight into Cra Wyd, and each owl felt a deep inner glow of pride at this spectacular reception, which allayed any doubts about coming to this corvidae heartland.

Alighting in a ring of trees, especially chosen to represent the Council ring itself, Engar and his fellow Council members looked about them, nodding and smiling, acknowledging their welcome. The noise went on for several minutes before finally dying down. Engar's gaze once more swept the ring and beyond, and he could see nothing but black heads and beaks, as far as the eye could see. They were perched in concentric rings, and the depth of their ranks gave him just the slightest feeling of trepidation.

'Thank the Creator that they are on our side!' he breathed to himself. Then he began to address the vast crowd.

'My friends. We are overwhelmed by your welcome. Thank you for the invitation to come to this beautiful part of the world. Cra Wyd was well-chosen as the stronghold for the corvidae. It is a magnificent place, and populated, may I say, by magnificent birds. As I look around me now, at your multitude, I see the future for this land of ours reflected in your eager eyes. A future of co-operation and co-existence between all birds. A bright future, where the wise heads of your leaders will contribute to the decisions made by this Council for many years to come. Indeed, five of your own kind are already very much an integral part of this Council, and play a full role in deciding the destiny of Birddom. I speak, of course, of Traska, Drag, Smew, Chak and Retch.'

Each name was greeted by deafening caws of approval, and Engar smiled patronisingly at the named birds perched in the ring around him.

'All of them have earned the right to sit on the Council, and I am sure that they will all serve Birddom with distinction. They form one wing of our new leadership, and I would like to introduce you now to the fine birds who make up the other wing. As we go round the ring you can see Pellar, Creer, Steele, Janvar, Wensus and Cerca. I think that I can safely say that you will not find six finer owls anywhere in the land. And I am Engar.'

He paused at this point, and was slightly put out by the muted adulation that emanated from the crowd. But he brushed it from his mind, like dust from his wing-tips, and continued, 'I have the honour to be your Great Owl, and leader, by right, of this Council. We are your servants as well as your leaders, and it is our role to guide Birddom in the right way. We shall not be found wanting, you can be sure of that. We relish any challenge, and will rise up to meet it. But we do not look for your thanks. It is sufficient to serve and, in so doing, to build, with you and for you, a stronger, better Birddom.'

Engar was well into his rhetoric now, delighted with his own performance, and oblivious to the subtle change of mood in the gathering. Feathers ruffled and rustled as the watching birds hopped from foot to foot on their perches. Engar went on with his speech, mistaking their impatience for eagerness to hear his words.

'We come to your fine home, at your invitation, to help our brothers and partners. Traska has made us aware of the local hostility towards you, and I can see, from this meeting here today, that it surely stems from misunderstanding. The small-bird population obviously has nothing to fear from your strength, and everything to gain from your friendship. I can promise you all that, when we leave here, we will go among the local birds, and reassure them that Cra Wyd is a place of honour. A neighbour that can be nothing but beneficial. They will learn, from our beaks, that this corner of Birddom is safe in your wings, my friends!'

*

'There's one part that I simply can't get my head around,' Darreal groaned, as they went over the rhyme once more. 'Septimus told the robins that, "The path where you would choose to go is one that only a wolf might know." Well, I can understand that. Septimus himself knows the way into Avia, and he is a wolf. But Avia is for birds, isn't it? Tomar believes Avia to be a paradise for birds alone, doesn't he? A place free from predators, where every bird can live in peace and ever-lasting happiness. Well, I am not sure that I could spend the rest of my days in a state of bliss with great big wolves roaming around the place. There is very little that frightens a bird of my size, but I retain a healthy respect for wolves, and would choose to keep them at a reasonable distance.'

Meldra laughed. She felt at ease in the red kite's company, and his positivity had energised her, allaying her doubts about the wisdom of Tomar's plan. Of course he was right to seek the aid of such fine birds. And if Storne and Kraken were anything like a match for Darreal, their contributions would be invaluable.

She and Darreal had spent hours pouring over the lines of the rhyme, and had retained an enthusiasm for the task that had lifted her spirits, even if they could not make head nor tail of much of it. Success was surely only a matter of time. Once they got back to Tanglewood, and put their great heads together, there was nothing that they could not achieve.

'You really are a bit of a windbag!' Traska exclaimed, raising a massive laugh from the corvid audience around the ring.

Engar blinked in utter disbelief at this unexpected attack from his friend. 'But, but...' he spluttered.

'Oh, shut up!' the magpie snapped. 'You are far too fond of the sound of your own voice. But, fortunately for the rest of us, we won't have to put up with it for very much longer. None of us came here to listen to you droning on and on about honour and friendship. Look around you, and ask yourself where your friends are.'

'I don't understand,' Engar muttered, in a bewildered voice.

'No, you don't, do you? But they do. Each of your fellow owls has more brain in a single talon than you hold in your great empty head. But I fooled them too, didn't I? They are too trusting to deserve to be our leaders, and their trust in you was misplaced. That is becoming clear to them now. You thought that you and I were partners. Equals in a venture to take Birddom into a glorious future. But you *have* no future, for one very simple reason – your presumptuousness at considering yourself my equal. For that, you must pay the ultimate price, and your friends also, I'm afraid.

'We no longer need you anyway. Yours is a redundant species. We corvids can rule Birddom more effectively than you ever could. Because we are not soft-hearted like them, or soft-headed like you, Engar. We will make the tough choices, and we will do so without regard for the feelings of lesser birds. Slyekin was right about that, at least. His dream of a Birddom ruled by magpie and crow, raven and rook is rekindled here today. He betrayed that dream in pursuit of personal glory. But I will not. The corvidae will rule the world, and nothing will stop us. Once we have disposed of the seven of you, no one will dare to stand against us.

'And, speaking of Slyekin reminds me that there is unfinished business to be dealt with. His plans for the Great Feast included a splendid mass-execution of owls. Unfortunately, he did not live to see this dream become a reality. But what was denied us then will be re-enacted before us here today, with my humble self as Master of Ceremonies. Don't look so shocked, Engar, my friend. You have always loved being the centre of attention, haven't you? All eyes will be upon you, I can assure you of that. I am going to save you until last, so that you can witness the full extent of your folly!'

Tears of self-pity welled up in Engar's eyes, and Traska looked at the barn owl with a sneer of total contempt.

'Pull yourself together, and take what is coming to you like an owl. You have enjoyed the suffering of others. Now permit others to enjoy *your* suffering, my friend. I promise you that it will be exquisite for us – and excruciating for you. Surprise me, and face death with something approaching dignity. I watched Lostri die. And Claudia, too. They met their end as owls should. But will you be brave, Engar, or will you squeal and plead for your life? I think I know the answer to that question.'

Engar's body slumped against the bough of the tree in which he sat, as deflated as a popped balloon. He had no words with which to answer Traska's cruelty. He could not even find it in himself to speak to the owls whom he had led into peril. No apology passed his beak. No words of comfort for his frightened colleagues. The bag of wind was finally empty, and Traska turned his back on him dismissively.

'My friends and fellow corvidae, we are approaching the anniversary of the Great Feast. This is something to celebrate. And, of course, it will be the anniversary of the Great Battle too, which is not. But it is something to avenge, and we have it in our power to do so. We will not wait. The moon is but a sliver in the sky, and pleasures such as this should not be delayed. Her silver eye does not look fully upon us, but casts instead a sly and knowing glance in our direction. Let the deed be done tonight.'

He rounded on Engar and the other owls once again. 'Prepare yourselves,' he warned. 'This is going to hurt you a great deal more than it will hurt us! But pain doesn't last, unfortunately. Soon you won't be able to feel a thing – ever again!'

*

There had been a great deal of meeting and greeting. Pagen and Merion had arrived at Tanglewood first, and the robin introduced his companion to Tomar with formality and respect. 'Tomar, this is Pagen, son of Kraken and leader of the Great Flock.'

'Welcome, Pagen,' Tomar responded, allowing himself a small smile at Merion's overt show of courtesy. 'Thank you for coming to our aid. I cannot tell you how grateful I am that you decided to help us.'

'I come in my father's stead, because he is no longer able to make such a journey. Blindness has robbed him of his majesty, and so you will have to make do with a poor substitute.'

'Not so,' said the owl. 'I know your father very well. We have had adventures together, and I am sure that none of his majesty has been lost. Kraken was always a formidable bird, and may yet have a part to play. I can see so much of him reflected in your eyes, Pagen. You are no substitute, so far as I am concerned. You will bring fresh ideas, and a younger mind to our rather ancient council.'

Merion closed his beak hard on a retort. He was far from ancient! Instead, he proceeded to acquaint Tomar with the discussions that he and Pagen had had, concerning Septimus' riddle.

The seagull joined in, eagerly. 'So much of what Septimus has told us is not as it seems. His rhymes are like tiny fish. Just when you think that you have hold of them, they slip away again. It is very frustrating.'

Tomar nodded his head, in agreement. 'Yes, I have been wracking my brain on their meaning ever since Merion and his sister returned home, and told me the rhyme. At times I think that I understand, but then the significance of a line eludes me, and I begin to doubt that I really grasp any of it. But you must forgive my manners. You must both be tired and hungry after your long journey. Merion, what can we offer our esteemed friend from our meagre larder here in Tanglewood?'

'Do not worry yourself about that,' Pagen replied. 'I stuffed my craw with sand-eels before we began our journey. I have more than enough to keep me satisfied for a good while yet.'

And, as if to demonstrate, the seagull opened his yellow beak wide, and regurgitated a small parcel of fish onto the ground in front of him. He began to peck at it, with deep satisfaction, saying, between mouthfuls, 'If I run out, I am sure that I can find fine fishing in your beautiful forest, Tomar. And, if not, then we seagulls are nothing if not adaptable. I am sure that you would be quite shocked if you knew what has found its way into my belly in the past!'

The following morning saw the arrival of Meldra and Darreal. Again there was much hugging and exchanges of greeting. Merion had not seen Darreal since the time when, as a young fledgling, he had hidden behind his mother's wing and had stared, open-beaked in awe, at the magnificent falcon who sat so proud and fierce in his place at the Council of the Owls. Time had done nothing to diminish the red kite's glory. His curved beak and wickedly sharp talons proclaimed that here was a bird equipped to tackle the world. And yet the warmth and humour in his black and amber eyes told of a depth of character to match his physical splendour.

Once more, the necessity of finding food delayed serious discussion among the gathering, but it was not long before both owls, one robin, a black-backed gull and a kite were putting their heads together over the knotty problem of Avia.

'From all of the rhyme, we have only managed to solve a solitary couplet, with any certainty, and that was entirely due to Merion here.'

Tomar patted the robin on the back with his wing.

'"When all is lost and hope is gone, think back to former battles won." I am confident that Septimus was telling us when we need to be ready for our entry into Avia. He was referring to the Great Battle, when he spoke of "former battles won". That was a victory that saved Birddom, and its anniversary at the time of the harvest moon is very near. We have less than a single passage of the moon from dark to light in which to solve the remainder of Septimus' puzzles, and to prepare every bird in the land for the journey into Avia, when the time comes.'

'Merion seems to be by far the most productive among us,' interrupted Pagen. 'He seems to have some knowledge of the tunnel that Septimus spoke of.'

All heads turned to look at the little robin who bashfully demurred, and said that, while he had no definite answer to that part of the rhyme, he was sure that it had something to do with what he had felt in his dream. Tomar had heard of this before, of course, but Merion explained to the remainder of the gathering.

'It is nothing definite,' he said. 'But I feel that the tunnel, referred to in the wolf's rhyme, was the one that I dreamt about. He says not to "fear the tunnel, black as night", and I certainly experienced no feeling of fear. It might be different in reality, of course.'

'Fear of the unknown is a most natural reaction,' Darreal replied. 'But the very purpose of Septimus' rhyme was to forewarn us, and to enable Birddom to prepare. When the time comes, every bird will know that the tunnel is not to be feared, and will undertake the journey with a glad heart, knowing it to be but a passage to a better place.'

'To some that will be easier than to others,' Pagen mumbled, shame-faced. 'I just hope that the journey will be worth it, and that Avia's seas are filled with the fattest fish that I can swallow!'

*

In the end, the Council of the Owls faced their deaths with honour, in a manner befitting the last of a long and proud lineage. Hopelessly outnumbered, the owls formed themselves into a defensive ring, and raised their beaks in defiance as the black hordes closed in. Hundreds of rooks and crows had taken to the air, forming as they did so an impenetrable dark barrier above and around. There would be no escaping their fate. Those corvids in the front ranks seemed intent on having the pleasure of the kill, while others had to content themselves with watching the slaughter.

Traska's voice rang out urgently. 'Remember what I said. I want Engar to witness the death of his friends. He must be the last to die, and anyone who disobeys me, and kills him before I am ready, will face my displeasure!'

It was a relatively easy task to separate Engar from the rest of the owls, in spite of their valiant efforts to protect a leader who had proved so false and had done so little to deserve any show of loyalty. Engar sat abjectly, and only removed his wings from over his eyes when the mob pecked him repeatedly. His shame was now complete. A tiny part of him wished that he had the courage to fight his way back to the side of the other owls, so that he could die with them. But it was too late for that, and his monumental folly in trusting Traska denied him the right of a dignified death in their company.

He could only look on, in open-beaked admiration as the other owls fought for their lives with magnificent bravery. They endured far longer than their Great Owl would have thought possible, and even Traska was impressed enough for him to berate his fellow corvids, urging them on with withering contempt.

'What are you waiting for, you miserable cowards! Tear them to pieces. There are only six of them! Kill them. Kill them!'

*

Traska couldn't help but feel that he was acquiring a taste for owl. Even though he had not been particularly hungry, he had used his dominant position to purloin the tastiest morsels from Engar's carcass, and was enjoying a fine feast. The tongue of the ex-Great Owl had been a delicacy, for Traska had ordered it to be removed while Engar was alive, and had consumed it with the nerve-ends still twitching. The magpie thought that it was most appropriate – the damned thing had never been still.

The tongue devoured, and washed down with a draught of owl's blood, he turned his attention to the eye-balls, which still held the look of absolute agony, mixed with shame, and the horrific realisation of imminent death. Traska had ordered that they be torn out of the barn owl's skull, and now he gazed at them almost lovingly for a few moments before swallowing them. As an appetiser for the main course, they were exquisite. The magpie looked down at Engar's heart, clutched tightly in his talons, slick with gore, and then stared around for any challenge to his prize. But his authority, and his right to this meal, was unquestioned.

Two more days passed, and Tomar had begun to fret, when he heard an unmistakable sound.

'Twee-oo, twee-oo,' Storne called out in greeting, and his loud screech was complemented by Olivia's more melodious warble.

'Hello, Tomar. We made it, as you can see.'

'Well done,' the owl hooted back, and each bird there joined in with their own call of welcome.

When the golden eagle had settled himself on a sturdy bough near to ground level, and Olivia had flown to her brother's side, nuzzling up to him in pure joy at their reunion, Tomar spoke.

'Now we are complete. We have an onerous task ahead of us, my friends. But it is one that I believe we can accomplish. Indeed, nothing is beyond us, if we work together for the good of Birddom. I place that responsibility upon our backs and wings because I believe that, under the leadership of Engar and influenced by Traska, the present Council of the Owls is not at all concerned with the best interests of this land of ours. No, it will be up to us, as the new guardians, to put the needs of Birddom to the forefront. But I do not wish us to be called a council. We need no title, for we are a gathering of equals, large and small. We have no need for a leader either, for none outranks another in wisdom and goodness of heart.'

Storne cut in, voicing the unanimous feelings of the whole group. 'Tomar, you do yourself an injustice. Remember that you were Great Owl, and so leader of us all. And if it were not for a trick you would be our leader still. We know that you have no vanity, but to me, and to everyone here, you remain our best hope of salvation.'

'That was kindly said,' Tomar replied, deeply touched. 'I deem it an honour to count you all as my friends. But such glad-winging will not find any solutions to our problems. Let us hear the rhyme in full, as Septimus told it to our colleagues here. Merion, please repeat the words for us, just as you heard them from the great wolf's mouth. I think that it is best this way, as I would probably imbue the rhyme with inflections and accents, according to my own interpretation of its meaning. Speak up, my friend, so that everyone can hear you.'

Merion cleared his throat, and began, slowly at first and then with increasing confidence and reverence, to recite the poem.

'Avia's neither far nor near,
Not over there, but not quite here,

The path where you would choose to go
Is one that only a wolf might know.
Avia is a state of mind
Which few if any bird can find.
Avia lives within your heart,
You'll find the end is but the start.
But peril lies at Avia's doors
If you're not true to Birddom's cause.
Choose any but the common good
And ever you'll be bathed in blood.
When all is lost, and hope is gone,
Think back to former battles won.
Make ready all who chance the gate,
For courage will decide their fate.
Don't fear the tunnel, black as night,
For darkness comes before the light.'

For several seconds afterwards no one spoke, each bird digesting the rhyme anew.

Finally, Tomar broke the silence. 'Thank you, Merion,' he said. 'Well, my friends. You have all heard the words of Septimus. Within them lie the clues that will enable us to discover the key to Avia. Let us begin.'

Chapter Nineteen

The insects were angry. Theirs was a slow-burning fuse, but the time of detonation was fast approaching. Attacked on two fronts, by Man and birds, they had failed to maintain their discipline, and thereby their strength. That strength lay in the insects' unity. But that had been fractured by the concentrated fury of Man's onslaught against them. From day one, the insects had been under siege, and all thought of collective action was scattered to the four winds. And so they faced decimation at the hands of an infinitely numerically-inferior enemy.

Many insects had fled from Birddom, with great clouds of swarming creatures taking their chances with the sea crossing, and heading for Wingland. Billions stayed, of course, and lived their lives in constant fear of an agonising death. But as this became the norm, the feelings uppermost in their mind were not those of fear, but of frustration and increasing anger. The insects felt impotent, and they did not like it one bit.

And so, the collective psyche that was always the source of their power began slowly to reform. Unity gave the insects a strength that had been missing for so long. And it gave a focus to their anger. They had two enemies – birds and Man. Even amidst the terrible onslaught inflicted upon them by Man's murderous rage, they had registered their betrayal by the birds. The pact that had so fundamentally changed their lives, and their very outlook on how life *could* be, had been broken in two, and insects were prey once more. But prey could become predator, if it were strong enough. And the insects were incredibly strong.

Somehow, they would rebuild their armies, and devour their enemies. Man and bird. But Man first. The sheer ferocity of his unprovoked aggression demanded revenge. Birds would not be forgotten or forgiven, but they would have to wait their turn. Man would be first. This message spread like brush-fire and, all over Birddom, a low hum of rage began to build and build. Insects that crawled; insects that slithered; insects that flew. Each began a gathering. And as they gathered, they talked of the coming war, and of total victory.

The clock had ticked inexorably onward. Everything was now ready. The evacuation was irreversible, now that the time had come for the lowering of the nets. Normal life ceased to exist across the country. Traffic came to a stand-still, as commuting no longer became necessary. Every hand was turned to the huge task of dismantling the huge structures that had provided protection from the insect enemy.

There was no great method involved. The nets would hopefully never be needed again. Discussions had been held, where some voices in government had been in favour of a structured and disciplined operation. But the consensus was that they would let the people enjoy themselves. Nothing is quite as satisfying as unfettered destruction. Across the country, men and women, boys and girls tore down the nets. Young and old stood side by side, a look of elation on their faces as they strove to outdo each other. The nets came down at an astonishing rate, and were largely left where they fell. Their removal and disposal had already been factored in as part of the clear-up, following the evacuation and the magnetic massacre. The nets might even be useful in collecting up all the bodies of insect, bird and animal dead.

So, working together to a common goal, the human population completed their task in a single day. That night, huge parties were held all over the land, and the evening sky was lit by fires of celebration.

Perhaps it was eating so much of the flesh of his fellow birds that triggered what others would certainly have seen as Traska's apparent descent from reason. Or maybe they would have surmised that his belief in his own invincibility had triumphed over his usual cold and calculating logic. But Traska brimmed with self-confidence. After all, hadn't everything gone exactly as he had planned from the beginning? This was merely the next step.

However, in choosing this course of action – whatever lay behind the decision – the evil magpie was seemingly taking a crazy risk. He had flown back from Cra Wyd, and had decided, after sufficient rest, that he needed another ace before he went ahead with his schemes. The killing of the Council had only been the beginning. Ultimately, he wanted absolute power for himself alone. This would take time, and compromises would have to be made in the short term. But he would only succeed by making use of those resources that could, with audacity, be at his disposal.

Traska headed towards one of the urban waste-dumps, that was situated a couple of miles from the town whose rubbish it took in and accommodated. The dump stood outside the perimeter netting, and had become a habitat for scavenging cats and dogs – so much so that sanitary workers carried guns when they drove through the gates to dispose of their noxious loads. The magpie kept a careful eye on the proximity of the netting and supporting wires. He had no intention of falling foul of them and sharing Kopa's fate. But he needed a high, safe place to alight. He chose a stanchion pole, and flew down to land on the top of it. As he did so, several pairs of eyes watched his approach, and several tongues licked their lips in anticipation of a meal, then snarled and spat in frustration on seeing the magpie well out of the reach of their claws.

'Greetings. My name is Traska. I am the leader of all of the birds in this land. Is there any among you who can understand what I am saying?'

A large ginger tom-cat hissed in reply, 'We can understand you well enough. Now what do you want? Come down and talk to us.'

'I don't want to feed your bellies, so I'll stay where I am, if it's all the same to you. I need to talk to your leader. I have an important proposition to put to him.'

'Her, actually. Queenie is the chief around here, but I doubt whether she will waste her time over the likes of you.'

'You might be wise to let her decide that for herself,' Traska snapped back, angrily. 'Now bring her to me!'

The ginger cat was shaken by Traska's imperious commands, but did as he was bid, and soon the magpie watched the slinky approach of the cat called Queenie. She looked sleek and well-fed, and her coat was very clean, considering the environment in which she had made her home. Queenie gazed up at Traska with amber eyes, and spoke with a seductive purr.

'Welcome to my domain. Chester here tells me that you are a bird of some importance. We tend not to get too many avian guests dropping in for a chat. Won't you come a little closer? I'll get a crick in my neck looking at you way up there.'

'I am quite comfortable where I am, thank you. And I hope that you will consider it worth a little discomfort when you have heard what I have in mind!'

*

Although their infrastructure was not yet rebuilt, the speed with which the insects reacted to Man's decision to remove the nets was as astonishing as it was ill-advised. Now, finally able to get at their enemy, their frustrations spilled over before they had the time to prepare a proper and co-ordinated attack. Clouds of insects swarmed and boiled, then fell upon their unprotected victims. Man was taken aback by the suddenness and savagery of the assault. But some thought had been given as to this possibility. Although inadequate to the eventual needs of the population, handouts of protective clothing had been organised. Beyond that, Man improvised, even to the extent of cutting the fallen nets and turning them into cumbersome but effective body-suits.

Man did not strike back, however. The discipline imposed by the tight time-scales allowed no freedom to retaliate. There was still much to be done, to prepare for the total evacuation of the country, now less than two weeks away. The insects might bite and sting, but they wouldn't undermine Man's single-mindedness and determination. Anyway, their life-spans, naturally brief, would be cut short, irrevocably and en-masse, in a fortnight. That was consolation enough for the need to endure without response.

However, it was a massive surprise and relief when the insects withdrew. The angry buzz of noise, which had risen to a crescendo in the days following the downing of the nets, had disappeared overnight, as had the insects themselves. The collective will had finally prevailed, and a message went among the multitude – a hum of promise, soft and low, but with a singular menace. 'We will kill them. We will kill them all,' it said. 'But we cannot do it this way. We are many, and they are few. We have them at our mercy. Let us gather, and build our strength. Let us construct a huge mandible to encircle and crush them. If we are patient, nothing can stand in our way. It will take but a few days to unite our battalions, to consolidate our armies. And then we will strike with an irresistible force, and destroy our enemy utterly. We will feast on man-flesh, my brothers!'

Traska relished this moment as an expression of his absolute contempt for the law-givers of Birddom. He looked around the circle of mighty oak trees that formed the sacred ring, and smiled malevolently, seeing that atop of each was a black and white body. His magpies now formed the Council that ruled the land. At last he had ultimate power in Birddom! He had swept aside all opposition, and was now king of the world! *His* Council was a perversion of all that the original Council of the Owls had stood for, a deliberate mockery of all their efforts over the generations. Birddom could look forward to a very different future. A much darker future.

'Brethren,' he called out to the assembled membership, 'today we begin to rebuild Birddom in our own image. For too long, the corvidae have been reviled by the rest of Birddom. Well, it is our turn now. We are the new lords of this land. Each coven will now have the freedom to strengthen its resources, and to rule over the lesser birds within its dominion. Rook and crow will hold the power of life and death over them, and it may well be that they will choose the latter. So be it. We have waited a long time for this moment, and we deserve to reap the rewards of our success. The corvidae will reign supreme in Birddom, and we, the magpies, will be the rulers over the corvids.

'For we are the finest of the fine. Our minds are superior, and we are stronger and more cunning. We are braver in battle. We have always been able to dominate and manipulate even those far larger than ourselves. Ravens may have the bulk, but we have the brains. Hooded crows might have enormous individual strength, but their pea-size intellect limits its effective use. Yes, only magpies are fit to rule in this new Birddom of ours.

'I would like formally to welcome our new Council members, who join Smew, Chak, Drag and I as the highest leaders in the land. Sad to say that Retch, fine jay though he was, won't be joining us. He met with an unfortunate, but timely and terminal accident. Perhaps it is as well. We do not wish to dilute the purity of the Council. We are the true race; the ultimate expression of everything that a bird should be. Look around you and marvel, my friends. Where in all of Birddom, past and present, has there ever been a gathering as fine as this? Be proud of *who* you are, and *what* you are. Your ancestors are watching you this day. The dead look upon us, and their chests heave once more with life, hearts beating with pride, that magpies have at last found their rightful place as leaders of Birddom!'

To the small bird population, it was as if they were reliving their worst nightmare. At first it had seemed so promising. The removal of the netting across Birddom was greeted with elation. More food was instantly available and every bird took his fill. It was timely too, for the disappearance of the insects shortly afterwards had withdrawn a vital food-source from their beaks. But this scarcely mattered when they could feed on an abundant supply of grain and fruit. The spraying had stopped, too. It was a time for celebration. But then rumours began to spread about an atrocity in the north.

Disbelief was the common reaction. Surely the magpies wouldn't dare to take such murderous action? But then their own corvidae began to flex their muscles, and every bird feared for his life. It was like living under the tyranny of Slyekin, all over again. And this time, there were no owls to stop them. Only now did the small birds bother to ask the question: where was Tomar? What had happened to their old Great Owl? Inside they knew the answers only too well. They had rejected, humiliated and ousted him, for the sake of a full belly. Besides, could they look to him again to save them? He was too old and too feeble to stand alone against the magpies. No, there was no hope. It was every bird for himself, and survival was once again the only game in town.

'Fellow magpies,' Traska began, imperiously, at the next Council meeting. 'What a success we have made in our first few days in power. We have transformed Birddom. It has become a place where the proper order now prevails. The corvidae are dominant and all other bird-life subservient. They exist only at our pleasure. But now we have a different and infinitely more exciting task ahead of us. For if we want utter supremacy over our land, we need to defeat our mortal enemy, Man. And he has never been more vulnerable, or more ripe for the plucking. He has removed his only means of protection against us.

'We all know that the nets were his shield, erected in the sure knowledge of our supremacy, and his weakness. Now his neck is bare to our sharp beaks, and we *will* strike. How can we not succeed? We have defeated the high-and-mighty owls. None stands against us in Birddom. Even the insects fear us, and have run away to hide. We are invincible and we will prove it. Birddom will love and respect us when we destroy her greatest enemy.

'We must prepare for battle, and the timing will be of the greatest significance. Some of you might have thought that I denied the importance of our heritage when I chose not to honour our dead, by slaughtering those fool owls from the old Council well in advance of the anniversaries that so dominate our minds and hearts. But I had planned all along for a more impressive way of celebrating the time of the Great

Feast and the Great Battle. When the moon is full, we will wage war on Man. He will not be ready, and our triumph is inevitable. Man will be vanquished, or will flee like the coward he undoubtedly is!'

'Let us not give up hope!' Merion exhorted his companions. 'We have worked so hard, and come so far.'

'I am afraid that it is hopeless,' Tomar replied, a note of despair in his voice. 'We have laboured over the meaning of Septimus' riddles for five full days together, in addition to all of the time that we have each invested individually in solving the problem. It is enough. We have understood much of what the old wolf has told us, and everyone should be proud of their efforts. We know that we need to prepare the rest of Birddom as best we can for something – we do not know what – that will happen on the anniversary of the Great Battle, now only a matter of days away.

'We comprehend that Avia is very different to our own blessed homeland, and that getting there is far from straightforward. We know that each bird must achieve a state of mind that will prepare him or her for whatever test comes. And test there will be. We do not know the "peril" at "Avia's gate", but we understand that only the courageous will be able to face it, and still go on. We also realise that those who lack that courage, or are false to the needs of Birddom, will not pass the gateway, and will, in all probability, die a horrible death. We have some ideas about the tunnel that Septimus speaks about, but we do not know of its whereabouts. It is frustrating!

'I cannot see how we can achieve our aim of saving every good bird in Birddom if we do not know *where* to find this tunnel, which Merion has described as a living, breathing thing. And even if we succeed in locating it, it is simply impossible to gather all of Birddom together in one place. So the talk of the tunnel must be nonsense, or must have a different sense and meaning altogether. But I am at a total loss as to what it might be.

'So we are left with this. We have failed our land and our brothers and sisters in their hour of need. But we must do the best that we can. We must go out among them, and make them ready for a journey that we cannot describe, prepare them for a peril that we cannot name. It seems hopeless, but it is the best that we can do.

'Oh Septimus, in my vanity I thought myself wise. But you have taught me a great deal about my limitations. I am but a single bird, and age has revealed less to me than I believed. Your path – no, our path – is still "one that only a wolf might know."'

'I have been brilliant!' Traska cawed, at the top of his voice. The remaining eleven magpies sat silent, awaiting the revelation that was surely to follow this pronouncement. When it came, they were shocked to the core.

'We are preparing for our greatest battle. I have no doubt that we will succeed. Man, however, is a fearsome enemy, and has weapons at his disposal which could severely deplete our armies. But why should we fight him at all?'

The question seemed an extraordinary one to every single bird there. Only Traska seemed to know what on earth he was talking about.

'We have our own weapons, or soon will have,' he continued grandly, to the utter bewilderment of his colleagues. 'Man has delivered them into our wings, and we will turn them back upon him with devastating effect. For those that once loved him are now his deadliest enemies. Man rejected them and threw them out of his homes, to survive or to starve. And, in doing so, Man unleashed one more threat to the survival of Birddom.

'But survive we did, and prospered, too. And now the time has come to ally ourselves to those outcasts. Cats and dogs will become our instruments to strike a massive blow against our greatest enemy. They will submit to our superior intellect, and we will train them for battle. I have already prepared the ground in this, by speaking to these fine beasts myself. They are as eager as we are to rid Birddom of our mutual enemy. I am sure that revenge against Man is uppermost in their minds – whatever limited minds they possess. It will not be hard to persuade them to serve us.

'And that will be your task, my friends and loyal followers. Each of you is to go out, and gather up a battalion of strays for war. You will talk to their leaders. Promise them power, if you have to. When this is all over, and the battle is won, we will renege on those promises. I will not share Birddom with a pack of wild brutes. No, we will deal with them in their turn. But not before we have made use of them, for our own purposes. Do not delay. Go now, and bring me back the weapons that I need for total victory!'

Smew and Zelda were very worried magpies. They had chosen so secret a meeting place for fear that their discussion might be overheard and reported back to Traska. That would indeed be fatal for both of them. But that fear paled against their deep unease about the state of mind of their leader. Oh, they knew that he had achieved a great deal, and had given them Birddom on a plate – just as he had promised. But these latest plans stretched their loyalty and belief in his abilities to the limit. To wage a war on Man, and to use cats and dogs in the process, was a monumental task, and one that they were not sure Traska could pull off – brilliant though he had always been in the past. It was as if his recent successes had stripped away any fear of the possibility of failure, and had left their leader dangerously over-confident.

'But what can we do about it?' Zelda asked. She, being so new to the Council, was looking for reassurance from her more-experienced colleague. But none was forthcoming.

'I'm not sure that there is anything that we can do. If we challenge Traska in his present mood he will just have us killed and replaced with two others who will carry out his orders. And, anyway, who's to say that he isn't right? He has never failed us yet. Perhaps we really can defeat Man. It seems impossible, but then so did a Council made up entirely of magpies. Using the cats and dogs is a brilliant idea, in theory. Maybe we can do this. We have no choice, anyway, but to go along with Traska's wishes. Let's just hope that he really is as invincible as he thinks he is – and that some of it rubs off onto us!'

The logistics of emptying a whole country of its population were quite staggering, and yet every man, woman and child in the land co-operated without complaint. They began at dawn, packing whatever final belongings had not already been stowed into the waiting vehicles during the preceding days. Every form of transport was put to its fullest use. Trains overflowed with passengers and their luggage. Buses and coaches heaved with bodies, and yet the highest of spirits prevailed. Singing and jollity buoyed everyone enormously. After all, they knew that it was only temporary. They told themselves that it was like going on an extended holiday. The government had promised them that it would only be a matter of a few months, and then they would be able to return home to a safer, cleaner, insect-free country.

So the roads began to fill with overburdened cars, all travelling in the same direction – towards the coast, and the embarkation ports.

Never had there been such a migration of people. In excess of fifty million individuals were on the move, and all the preparation and organisation in the world could not lessen that astonishing reality. But, to a man, the entire population were models of patience and self-discipline, and the country's leaders congratulated themselves, and spoke with pride of how no other nation in the world would have been able to achieve this momentous undertaking.

Temporary refreshment stations kept the people fed and watered. Huge, makeshift latrines, erected specifically for this event, provided for Man's more basic needs. In all of the coastal towns and villages, every room in every hotel or guest-house was filled with exhausted travellers. But no one made a profit. Altruism prevailed in the national interest. Every private residence also accommodated as many people as they could hold. And those who could not find a room or a bed slept in their cars, or by the road-side, and waited for their turn to climb wearily aboard one of the myriad of boats and ships which chugged ceaselessly back and forth across the sea, ferrying this endless stream of human cargo to a new land, and a new, albeit temporary, home.

Chak felt somewhat nervous as he landed on the open expanse of scrub-land, and saw the three cats roaming restlessly a little way off to his left.

'Get a grip on yourself!' he chided. 'Traska has already spoken to some of their kind, and he came to no harm. You must just keep telling yourself that yours is the superior intellect. These creatures will do anything that you say, as long as you don't show any fear.'

But, as he walked towards the cats, the magpie quailed a little inside, covering his anxiety with a swagger. Six yellow eyes watched him approach, and the cats smiled a welcome to their visitor. Only the twitching and swishing of their tails indicated anything other than friendliness. Chak paused when he was about ten feet from them, and began his rehearsed speech, in a rather shaky voice.

'My name is Chak, and I am a member of the Council. We are the rulers of Birddom, and serve Traska, who is both my ruler and yours too. He has parlayed with some of your kind, and has discussed a plan which will be to our mutual benefit.'

The three cats seemed more than content to listen to what he had to say, and the magpie relaxed for the first time since he had landed. Why had he ever doubted Traska? This was going to work. The Master was a genius – there could be no doubt about it. Continuing more confidently, Chak outlined Traska's plans for a co-ordinated attack on Man.

'You must hate him for the cruel way that he treated you when he turned you out of your comfortable homes into the cold and wet. Wouldn't you like to get your own back? You can, you know. Traska has thought it all out. An army of cats and dogs... you don't mind the dogs joining us, do you?'

The cats continued to wear their innocent smiles, and even sat on their haunches, as if happy merely to be in his company.

'Good, because the dogs are vital. They will add greatly to our overall strength. They are stupid creatures of course, not like us. But they will understand enough of the plan to do our bidding when the time comes.'

A soft hiss from behind his ear told Chak that he would never live to see that time – if it ever came. He reacted fast, but not fast enough. A massive weight drove his body forward and down, pinning him to the ground. And there the fourth cat held him with her paws, while the others rose eagerly and stalked over to share the meal.

*

News of the mass exodus of Man sent a seismic shock-wave throughout Birddom. Man does nothing quietly, and the enormous upheaval terrified the whole of the natural world. Every creature – bird, animal or insect – feared for their life. Initially it was seen as Man launching a massive and unprecedented attack. But, apart from the noisome and almost overwhelming stench of petrol fumes created by the river of cars which poured out their filth into the already polluted air, no attack came. This was not an act of aggression. Instead, the unbelievable was happening: Man was leaving!

Word spread rapidly across the land. Bird whispered to bird, breathless with the excitement of such news. Fox barked a message of hope, and his words were carried on by every tongue, delivering the thrilling new reality to every part of Birddom. Man was going away.

Then Nature gave voice to its pleasure and the cheering began, creating the sweetest cacophony ever heard in the land since Man first emerged to make his mischief. A song of triumph rang out, mingling with a buzz of excitement, and a roar of disbelief and immense relief. The enemy was removing himself from their home. Not a single creature questioned why. The news itself was sufficient for now. Nature united in its celebration. Innate enmity was suspended as natural foes joined together in a dance of joy, laughing and rejoicing, singing out their uncontrollable happiness and thanking the Creator for their great good-fortune.

Tomar received the news with somewhat less enthusiasm than had been expected by the thrush who delivered it. She had been careering wildly through the treetops in Tanglewood, shouting out excitedly to every creature that she met. 'Isn't it wonderful?' she called. 'Man is leaving. Birddom is ours once more. Man is leaving!'

Flying nearby the crooked fir, the thrush spotted Tomar on the ground beneath its stout trunk, and flitted down to join him. 'Have you heard the news?' she asked, bubbling with joy.

'No, what news?' Tomar enquired, and was quite taken aback when she burst out with her tale about Man's evacuation from Birddom.

'Well, can you believe it? Have you ever heard of anything so marvellous?'

Tomar chuckled at her excitement. 'It seems very good news indeed, on the face of it, and I thank you for bringing it to me. But I need to think this through. There may be implications that we do not yet realise.'

Seeing a cloud of uncertainty cross his companion's beak, Tomar laughed and patted her softly with his wing. 'Forgive an old fool. It is wonderful, wonderful news, and you must tell it to the world. Go now, and spread the word. What a great day for Birddom! What a future now lies ahead of us!'

And, when the thrush had gone, Tomar added, though only the trees could hear, 'If you only knew. Our future will be very different from anything that you could possibly envisage in this moment of triumph. Nothing has been changed by this. I am certain that these events, staggering though they seem to me now, are but part of our pre-planned destiny. It is ironic. When we are finally set on our course, with no alternative but to depart from Birddom, Man leaves before us!'

The old owl sat in quiet meditation for a long time. As he had said to the thrush, he needed to think things through. His failure to unravel fully the mysteries of Septimus' rhyme had left him a little unsure of what he personally could do in these last hours before the answer was revealed to him. The others all had a vital task to perform, but age and infirmity had given him no choice but to remain behind, alone. Surely it shouldn't be this way? His mind – for so long his strength and the strength of Birddom – was now virtually useless in his current situation. Action was needed. But what action was he even capable of? Age and infirmity had robbed him of so much. But he knew that he must do something to feel worthy of his place in Avia.

Chapter Twenty

The news that the rook brought to Traska cheered him up immensely. He had been feeling rather deflated, and, although he would never admit it to anyone else, not a little foolish. For previously, he had been told of the fate of his magpie lieutenants. Faithful to his vision, they had sought out the roving bands of semi-wild cats and dogs, and had asked for their aid in the battle against Man. The response was unanimous and unequivocal. To a bird, they were eaten. Traska's folly had cost him eleven of his best cohorts, and, as the word had spread, the corvidae began to seriously question whether this really was the best bird to lead them, and Birddom as a whole.

But now, the more that he thought about it, the more Traska realised that the outcome wasn't so bad, after all. He hadn't intended for his councillors to meet such a grisly fate, and the response of the cats and dogs should have been a setback to his plans. However, the Council was really a bit of an impediment to his own desire for ultimate power. So maybe their deaths had just killed two birds with one stone, so to speak.

For the rook's news had changed everything. The unbelievable message about Man's evacuation of the country was a godsend to the evil magpie, and the need for the cats and dogs was suddenly irrelevant. He could brag that Man was fleeing before his majesty, not from fear of attack by their erstwhile pets. He could announce to the world that, somehow, humans had got wind of his plan for a magpie-led attack against them, and had crept cravenly away rather than be destroyed by the corvid armies.

Traska roved around the country, preaching this new gospel to the covens and shoring up support. Maybe, in the privacy of their own nests, an occasional crow or jackdaw might question the sanity of their leader. But, in his presence, none dared to let any doubt show. Indeed, the sheer magnetism of the bird's personality was compelling evidence that what he said must be true. So, they cheered him, and acclaimed him a genius. Traska lapped it up, of course, as his due, and it fed his delusions until he believed himself both infallible and immortal.

'We need no Council to rule this land of ours!' he trumpeted to a large gathering of supporters. 'That has always been Birddom's mistake. Government by consensus? By committee? It is transparent nonsense. You only need to find the right bird, and then one is enough. A ruler with real power. One you can trust to lead you wisely. One who you can leave to take all of the decisions that will help to make your lives easier. Birddom needs a *king*, not a Council.'

Traska paused at this point, and looked around the crowd for the plant. Catching the young magpie's eye, he nodded once.

'We want you to be our king!'

The call rang out above the heads of the gathering, and was immediately taken up by a rising crescendo of voices.

'Yes, yes. Lead us, Traska. Be our king!'

The pair of robins, the two mighty raptors, the youthful leader of the seagulls, and the last remaining member of the final Council of the Owls flew out of Tanglewood with a common purpose, but with heavy hearts. Failure sat on their wings and backs. But it was matched by a determination to carry out Tomar's instructions.

'Take the message to the populus,' he had instructed. 'Prepare every bird for our day of reckoning. The most difficult part of your task will be convincing your audience of the seriousness of your message. It will be hard for them to believe that Birddom is finished. But you must succeed in persuading them to believe you. We have to try for Avia, even if we do not know the way.

'The seven of us must act as the catalyst for spreading the word across the land. I am sure that you have all realised that we cannot accomplish this alone, in the time available to us. It will be up to each of you to organise every grouping that you talk to. Normal life in Birddom *must* cease to exist. Nothing matters but the message. Every bird must journey, as you are doing, and take the news to his or her neighbour. We have only a few days to prepare, and, although it is inadequate in the extreme, if you can succeed in the task that I set you, at least all of Birddom will know that there is an opportunity – to be saved, and to attain a higher place.'

And so, the messengers took Tomar's word to the wider world. But they were immediately met by almost universal disbelief and scorn. It did not help that, even as they had begun their journey, the news of Man's exodus from Birddom had created such an atmosphere of joy and celebration. The whole of Birddom was in festival mood, and Merion, Olivia, Storne, Darreal, Pagen and Meldra were spoiling the party.

Lesser birds would have given up in the face of such a rebuff. But the messengers stuck to their task, and the sheer force of their will convinced one or two birds to take them seriously. Those birds went back to their nests, impressed, and discussed it with their mates. And like a ripple spreading out from a pebble thrown into a pool, the truth began to take hold.

'After all,' they started to ask. 'Why would Man leave, if Birddom itself were not doomed? He has abandoned the land because he knows that there is no future here. Tomar must be right. He was ever the wisest of birds, and led us in peace and happiness for many years – something that we certainly do not enjoy now. Avia is our only chance, and every bird must know about it.'

It was as if he were an infant once again, and another, bigger bird had snatched a juicy worm from out of his beak. Traska had revelled in his triumph. He had become what he had dreamed of so long ago, when Slyekin had imprisoned him in his dungeons: king of the world! The ultimate ruler of Birddom. Nothing could now stand in his way. All birds would kow-tow to his every edict. More – they would worship him. Adore him, and bow down in obeisance wherever he went. Traska let his mind wander luxuriously over mental pictures of subservience and obsequiousness towards him.

But then his reverie was broken by the word that reached his ear. What was this about Avia? He had never even heard of the place. But, suddenly, every bird was talking about going there. They couldn't do that! They were his subjects, only there to do his bidding. What was the point of being king of the world if there was no one left to rule? Traska's reactions moved swiftly from bemusement to annoyance, then anger and, finally, to an overwhelming rage when he heard who was behind it all.

'Damn that bloody owl!' he stormed. 'I will not let him get the better of me again!'

But, all around him, his support melted away, as even the corvidae realised their desperate plight if they continued to follow the path of evil. They would surely "bathe in blood", as the now-famous rhyme foretold. But it wasn't too late, was it? What could they do to attain salvation? Turn their backs upon that bastard Traska, for one thing. It was all his fault that they were now in such a perilous position. There was a little time left for repentance. They would go to their neighbours, and beg for forgiveness. Wouldn't the Creator recognise a contrite heart, and spare them from the peril to come?

Traska exhausted himself, flying here and there, ranting and railing in a desperate attempt to contradict the growing belief that there was salvation to be found in Avia.

'We have a paradise right here. I have given you everything that you could possibly need. I have made Man's nets disappear so that it is safe for you to fly unhindered across the land. I have even driven Man from Birddom. A tyrant, who has oppressed our kind for generations, is now gone, and we have no more enemies. No crow will ever be shot again, thanks to my selfless and unstinting efforts. Everything that I have done has been for you. How can you think of abandoning me? Now, in the hour of our greatest glory?'

The many enclaves of the insect hordes were buzzing with the news. But the withdrawal of Man was met with mixed feelings. Mingled with the joy and sheer relief, after such a prolonged and persistent assault against them, was an under-current of annoyance. Having finally regrouped to gather their strength for a war with the humans, the insects felt thwarted by their enemy's disappearance. Man had no stomach for a fight. He could dish it out, but he could not take it.

'But we want revenge,' was the word in every insect community. 'We want to kill!'

A large consensus was in favour of following Man and driving him before them, never allowing him to find a place to settle, never giving him a moment of peace. But this was met with opposition from the majority who felt that it was illogical to pursue Man, if it meant abandoning the very land that they had won by dint of his disappearance.

'We have a victory without the losses that we would have incurred in battle. Moreover, we will suffer no more depletion of our numbers from Man's attacks upon us. We are free, brothers and sisters, from his webs of oppression. The nets are down, and we can feed on pollen once more. Nectar will again be our drink, and the rain that falls upon us will be clean and free of poisons. Never again will Man pour death upon our heads. Never will he deny our mandibles the right to feed where they choose. Our antennae will no longer quiver in fear. We can walk where we wish, fly where the fancy takes us. We are free, and the land is ours.'

'But what of the birds?' The question raised its head, and a bright flame of anger blazed once more through the multitude. 'The birds! They are our enemy now. An enemy who we thought of as our friend. We trusted them, even helped them in their hour of need. But they betrayed us, and now eat us in our thousands every day. We insects are proud, controllers of our own destiny, not fodder for our avian enemies. We have been thwarted in our revenge against Man. We will have that revenge, however – against the birds! We will kill them instead. We will kill them all!'

The realisation came slowly to Tomar. He had not understood the implications immediately, on hearing the news of Man's departure. And then, the turmoil generated in his brain by the enormity of it all had precluded serious consideration as to the impact that Man's evacuation process itself might have. Man was leaving Birddom, that much was obvious. But how was he doing it? He was heading en masse for the coasts of Birddom. All of his number would be concentrated in a thin band encircling the land, while the embarkation took place.

But what would it be like for those who lived in such places? Birds whose natural habitat was that same coastline. Wouldn't it be terrifying? Devastating for the environment in their home region? And what would those birds do, when faced with such a huge threat? Fly away, of course. They would have no alternative, once the invasion began. But Tomar knew of one who would not be able to fly away, who would inevitably be abandoned by those whose support he needed to stay alive. Kraken would be helpless and vulnerable, and Tomar had sent his son, Pagen, out on a mission, and could not recall him.

At last the Creator had given him something that he could do. He remembered his first meeting with Pagen. At the time he had known, somehow, that Kraken might have some part to play, and now only he could help the seagull play that part. Tomar realised that he alone could and should save his friend. But how could he possibly make such a journey?

'Easier for me than for Kraken,' he told himself. 'I still have both my wings attached, don't I? Even if they have been under-used of late. At least I can see the way I have to go, and, in this way, I will be able to play my part, rather than sitting here helplessly, waiting for judgement day.'

Having made the decision, Tomar allowed himself no time to change his mind, or to make excuses about his age and infirmity. Flapping his great wings, slowly at first, to get them used to the idea of once more carrying his body where it wanted to go, he began a slow and lumbering run across the ground, and increased the speed of his wing-beats. He gained an inch or two of height, but then collapsed, exhausted, in a heap of tangled feathers.

'It's no use. I am too old!' he cried in his pain, but then rallied his spirits for a second try. And, when the outcome was the same, he summoned every reserve of his strength and sheer bloody-mindedness to launch himself into the air once more.

But gravity prevailed over lift, and he sank back to earth, having accomplished only a few feet of flight.

'I might not make it there in time to warn him!' Tomar thought, laughing at his own absurd efforts. The old owl lifted his head to the sky, as if exhorting his Creator for help. And, in a strange way, his prayers were heard. Heard, and answered. For Tomar's gaze fixed upon the bough of the crooked fir adjacent to his nest-hole. The very bough that had been his launch pad for every morning and evening flight, when he had hunted for food. From where he had flown to the sacred site, to fulfil his role as Birddom's leader.

'If only I can climb up there,' he thought. 'I could use the height to get my wings going before I crashed to the ground. I can feel that they will carry me. They just need enough air beneath them.'

So saying, Tomar struggled to his feet, and hopped slowly over to the base of the fir tree. Then, summoning every ounce of inner reserve, he reached up with his powerful beak and took a grip of one of the lower branches that swept the floor of the forest with its needles. Digging his massive talons into the trunk, he hauled his body away from the ground. Supporting himself on his toes, he reached higher with his beak and gained another purchase. And so, slowly and painfully, he began to climb.

He could not believe how high the bough was, now that he had set himself the task of reaching it. Inch by inch, Tomar hauled himself up the crooked fir. Eventually he came to the point where he dared not look down. Now there was no going back. If his strength failed him, or his grip could not support his weight, he would tumble and crack his skull like an egg on the hard ground and tree roots below. He would die, for sure. He could feel gravity wrapping its fingers around him, pulling him down. But he persevered and climbed ever higher, and now his bough was within reach. He could make it! Tomar's strength was leeching away fast. But he was so close! He had to do it. He couldn't fail now.

'One more inch,' he repeated, encouraging himself onward and upward. All he had to do was stretch his neck a bit further – and bite. Bite hard, and hold on for dear life, while his feet scrabbled against the trunk of the crooked fir tree, anxious for purchase. And then he felt the ridge of bark, and clutched at it with his toes. This gave him a brief respite, while his chest heaved and he gulped in great breaths past the wood clamped between his jaws.

'One last effort, you old fool, and you need never do this again!' Tomar almost laughed, but resisted the urge for fear that his grip would slacken, and all of his efforts would have been for nothing. 'Either way,' he told himself. 'Either way, I need never do this again!'

Traska was filled with an impotent fury. Tomar had done this to him. It seemed that the whole of his life was one continuous showdown with that dratted owl, and that he had been bested time and again. No, Tomar had been lucky, that was all, ever since his first attempted confrontation with the old owl, once he had worked out Tomar's plan for combating Slyekin's schemes. Hadn't he flown to Tanglewood, ready to do battle with the owl, only to find that Tomar had already been captured by Slyekin's hench-birds? And then, when he, Traska – the most brilliant bird who had ever drawn breath – had devised his cunning plan to lure that damned owl into his clutches by kidnapping Kirrick's two offspring, it had only been Katya's astonishing revelation that he had been guilty of raping her, which had distracted the evil magpie from his purpose in finishing Tomar, once and for all. Perhaps the fates were against him? Traska shook his head in self-disgust, at even thinking such things.

'I have no time for this!' he admonished himself. 'I *will* finally have my revenge on Tomar. He is at my mercy now. I have broken his spirit, and stolen from him that which he deemed most precious. He is humiliated, feeble and alone. He will not get lucky again. This time I will take his life – and nothing will stop me!'

Tomar had never been happier to crawl inside his comfortable and familiar nest-hole. It was cool from lack of use, but that itself was welcome after the old owl's massive exertions in reaching it.

'I must rest,' Tomar told himself. 'Even if my journey is urgent, I need to regain some of my strength. The flight will be long and arduous, and will probably be the last that I ever undertake. But I am not daunted. The Creator will fly with me, and will keep me aloft if I falter. I *will* not fail at the eleventh hour. But, for now, my nest is calling me.'

He woke, refreshed, several hours later. Darkness had descended, and the heat of the day had given way to a cool and fresh evening. 'Perfect weather,' he told himself. 'This was always my favourite time of day for a flight.'

Tomar emerged from his nest-hole, and stood gingerly on the bough that had been his goal when he essayed that tortuous climb. 'This was what you went through all that for. Do not let your courage fail you now. You can do this.'

With such words of self-encouragement Tomar sought to stiffen his resolve. He knew that he had, at best, only a fifty-fifty chance of managing to fly at all, and that, if Fate was against him, he would be dead brief seconds after he launched himself into the air. 'Oh well,' he chuckled, nervously. 'We all have to die sometime.'

Without further ado, Tomar opened his wings to their fullest extent, and flapped them slowly to get out all of the kinks in his feathers, and to ensure a good circulation of blood. Then, pushing off with his feet, the old owl flung himself into the night air.

Chapter Twenty One

Tired, covered in dust and weary to the bone, Merion and Olivia flew back to Tanglewood. Over the last few days their efforts had been unstinting, but now, on the eve of the anniversary of the Great Battle, they had reunited and had agreed at once to return to be at Tomar's side when the time came. Avia was so close. Tomorrow they would know the answer, as would every true bird in Birddom. Excitement countered their exhaustion, and gave them the strength to fly back to their mentor and friend.

The pair of robins were astonished to find that Tomar was nowhere to be found. They searched high and low, checking the bushes and undergrowth around the crooked fir, to see if the old owl had hidden there in the face of some danger. But Tomar had gone. What should they do now? There was no time to begin a wider search for their old friend. Besides, they needed to rest. Tomorrow was full of uncertainties, but both of them wanted to be fresh and ready to face whatever trial lay ahead.

'We can no longer worry about Tomar. Something tells me that it was meant to be this way. We must ensure that we are prepared to enter into Avia.'

Olivia's voice betrayed her disquiet, which tempered the excitement that she felt now that the time was so near. Her brother looked at her lovingly. She had changed a great deal since they had returned home, and still carried the hurt of their mother's loss. That wound would never heal. But she had not let it overwhelm her, and her resilience and strength – needed so desperately in these final hours – left him open-beaked with admiration. Merion went to his sister, and wrapped her in his wings. They sat together like that for a long time, drawing comfort from each other. Then Merion asked his sister a question. 'What would Father and Mother do now? If they were in our position, facing what we have to face? Where would they go to find the gateway into Avia?'

Olivia's reply surprised her brother. 'We should go to the Council ring.'

She said it with a certainty that brooked no denial, but Merion could not help himself. 'Why, sis?'

'Because it is the holiest place in all of Birddom. It is also the place where everything began. So it will be a fitting place to be when it all ends.'

'Do you really believe that Birddom will come to an end, Olivia?' Merion asked, in a subdued voice.

'I do not know *how* it will happen,' she replied. 'But I trust Tomar. He has said that Birddom is finished, and the timing of our planned entry into Avia was very specific. Septimus ensured that we understood that, at least. Why would we need to adhere to a particular date for leaving if some catastrophe were not imminent? We could wait here, and see if Tomar comes back, but I feel strongly that the Council ring is the right place.'

'Then we will go without delay,' Merion confirmed, kissing his sister tenderly. 'Come on, sis. One final journey. One more adventure.'

'Not so, brother. Tomorrow we will take our last journey – in Birddom, at least. And that will be our greatest adventure.'

*

Every wing-beat was agony for the old owl, but sheer persistence kept him in the air. He faced a dilemma when thirst began to parch the roof of his beak. It had taken such a huge effort to get airborne in the first place that Tomar was loath to land, lest he would be unable to take wing once more. So he tried as best he could to ignore the dryness in his throat, and flew on.

To travel from Tanglewood to the eastern coast of Birddom was always going to be a huge task, even for the fittest and most able-bodied bird. Tomar's years weighed heavily upon him, and by the early hours of the morning his ancient body had suffered enough. The owl began to scan ahead for a suitable perch, where he could rest for a couple of hours. An elder provided him with the answer. Its trunk was great in girth, indicating its age, and even its uppermost branches were sturdy enough to support the old owl's weight. More importantly, they were well-leafed to provide both shelter and concealment, and bore a late crop of berries, whose sweet juice helped Tomar to slake his thirst and fill his belly. In the morning light, he found that he had chosen wisely, for he had perched at sufficient height to enable a safe launch. Moreover, his flight-path was clear, as the tree stood some way apart from a copse of its own species.

The slow flap of his wings gradually ate up the miles, and he eventually spied the sparkle of sunlight on water that announced that he was close to his destination. Looking down, Tomar was both amazed and disgusted by the casual damage that Man had wrought. For many miles inland from the coast, he had abandoned his vehicles in every available field or patch of wild scrub-land. The roads were completely clogged, and it seemed that the late-comers would have had to walk for several miles from the point where they were forced to park.

Any with a view to the future would have blanched at the logistical nightmare of reclaiming their cars, when finally Man returned to his homeland. No one doubted that their car would be exactly where they had left it. After all, who could possibly steal it, when the country would be devoid of all human presence? But the immediate priority of evacuation had clearly overridden any innate caution. Time did not allow for any undue precautions. These were problems for the future. The pressing need was to leave – and to leave quickly.

And it seemed to Tomar that this particular aim had been achieved, far more quickly than he would have expected. Why had Man acted with such urgency? Why had he left Birddom in such a hurry?

Traska's flight back to Tanglewood had brought him to Tomar's crooked fir scant minutes after Merion and Olivia had left it. Only sheer good-fortune had meant that the robins had avoided a potentially-deadly confrontation with their oldest enemy. The evil magpie roared with anger as he found that his travels were fruitless. Where had that bloody owl gone? Had he been killed by a predator? He was weak and old, and probably unable to fly away from any attacker. But there were no signs of blood in the vicinity to support such a theory. No owl bones either.

He couldn't be sure that Tomar had been taken, and, with nothing left but his revenge, Traska's only option was to cast about for clues as to what had happened to his foe. It took a while for him to focus his search at its most central point, but finally the magpie noticed the damage done to the trunk and lower branches of Tomar's own tree. Sap still bled from the wounds that the old owl's claws had inflicted during his desperate climb.

Traska chose a simpler and quicker route in reaching the owl's nest-hole, and, having flown there, found a residue of warmth that told him that Tomar had slept there, and not long ago.

'The old fool must have flown. I didn't think that he still had it in him,' he said aloud. 'But then, I've underestimated him before. I will not be thwarted. Someone must have seen him go, and they will know the direction that he took. So, I will do what I do best: torture someone, until they tell me what I need to know!'

The aura of calm and peace still radiated from the sacred ring, as the two robins crested the brink of the hollow and flew in, between the mighty oaks. It seemed that not even the sacrilege of Traska's attempts to defile and debase it had adversely affected the holiness of that place.

Merion spoke in a hushed and reverential tone. 'You were right, Olivia. This is the place. If Avia is as Tomar has described it, then this Council ring must be as close to it as Birddom gets.'

The robins landed on the springy, flower-strewn carpet of lush grass that occupied the space encircled by the dozen oaks. Its softness provided a cushion for their weary bodies, and they rested awhile where they landed.

Merion broke the comfortable silence. 'What do we do now, sis?'

'We wait. What else can we do? I suppose it will all be about preparing mentally, now that we are here and the time is almost upon us. Remember Septimus' words: "Avia is a state of mind, which few if any bird can find."'

'Well, I'm going to be one of the few. I've not been through so much just to fall at the final hurdle,' Merion said, belligerently. 'And anyway, we should have a better chance than any, as we've had the longest to prepare. We were the first to know, sis! Doesn't that make you feel special?'

'In a way, yes. But we were very much only messengers. And we haven't made too good a claw of solving the riddle, have we? Besides, by being the first to know, we have had the longest to become confused and defeated by the old wolf's subtleties.'

'Don't start getting negative, Olivia,' Merion scolded, fondly. 'That certainly *isn't* the right frame of mind. We need to be positive, yet ready and willing to accept the will of someone far greater than ourselves. It will be hard though, sis. Knowing me as you do, can you see me accepting without question whatever will befall us?'

'Maybe it will be so marvellous and wonderful that it will silence even you, Merion!'

Tomar wasn't entirely sure where to look when he finally arrived at the cliff-side dwelling where Kraken had ruled his sea-bird colony in his prime. As the owl had suspected, the place was utterly deserted and seemingly devoid of life. But Tomar knew that this could not be so. Kraken must be here somewhere. It would not have been possible for the great black-backed gull to have left, whatever threat had assailed his community.

Evidence was everywhere of recent human invasion, although this place was only a point of passage en route to the more accessible harbour areas, where the embarkation would have lately taken place. The very height of these cliffs meant that Man had not remained here long in his impatience to be gone from Birddom. But the devastation that he had caused in his brief sojourn was sickening. Litter of every possible form covered the grass, and was wedged among the rocks. Bottles, whole and smashed, reflected the sunlight into Tomar's eyes, and the old owl had to choose a place to alight with considerable care.

Well, he had arrived. But what was he to do now? Tomar was exhausted, and somewhat annoyed with himself that he had not thought things through very well.

'How could I have done anything differently? The journey had to be made. Well, I made it. I am here now, and that's half the problem solved anyway.'

Tomar hopped hither and thither, not sure what he was looking for, but largely to keep himself busy so that he would not have to consider that he might have come on a wasted journey. But Lady Luck smiled down upon him once more when the bright sun overhead flashed off an empty coke bottle. Tomar shielded his eyes with his wing against the sudden glare. He was about to turn away when he noticed a frantic movement inside the bottle. A tiny mouse had crawled into it and was now trapped and desperate, as the fierce heat generated by the sun was magnified by the glass of her prison.

Tomar shuffled over to where the coke bottle lay, and, without ceremony, upended it and began to shake. Within a few seconds, the mouse fell out of the neck of the bottle and landed on the ground below. Instantly, she bunched her muscles, preparing for a speedy escape. After what she had been through, she was not going to be a snack for a hungry owl, that was for sure. But as she began to run away, Tomar called out to her.

'Wait, my friend. I mean you no harm. How could I? I saved your life, didn't I? You owe me a few seconds of your time for that, don't you?'

The small mouse hesitated, and then squeaked back at him. 'Thank you for freeing me. It was an unexpected kindness from one whom I would normally call my mortal enemy. What can I do to help you?'

'Courteously said. My name is Tomar, and I am looking for a seagull friend of mine.'

'They are all gone,' she replied. 'They were the lucky ones. They had their wings to carry them far from here. We could only hide when Man came in his multitudes. And then, when he had gone, we emerged to find all this.' The mouse gestured expressively at the devastation all around. 'Our homeland is ruined. I do not think that the seagulls will return here. Their homes too have been destroyed.'

'My friend would not have left. Indeed, he could not. He is blind, and quite unable to fly.'

'Do you mean old Kraken?' asked the mouse.

Tomar heaved a huge sigh of relief. 'Why, yes, do you know him?'

'Everyone around here knows Kraken. For years he was the biggest villain in the region. A real killer. I can tell you that he didn't receive much sympathy from my kind when he lost his sight. But perhaps I do not really mean that. I would not wish such a plight upon any living thing. I do not know if he is still there, but he was housed in a hole halfway down the cliff-side. You may look askance, but it is the truth. There is a tunnel, not far from here, that leads down to a chamber, which also has an exit on the cliff-face. That is how they feed him. I will show you the entrance, but I'll not come down with you, if you don't mind. I'd rather not push my luck too far!'

Tomar smiled down at the tiny creature at his feet. 'You have been a great help. Thank you, my little friend. Lead on.'

Dusk was falling, and the light inside the Council ring dimmed as the sun began to sink behind the rim of the natural dish. The robins sat in silence, each lost in their own private thoughts. Besides, there was no more need for talk, only preparation. However, their voices were reawakened involuntarily when they saw a familiar shape appear over the horizon, silhouetted against the setting sun.

'Storne!' they cried, in unison, and the great golden eagle, hearing their greeting, circled once before alighting by their side.

'I wondered if I might find anyone else here,' he said. 'I thought that it would be the best place to be, and, if even I could work that out, I'm surprised that there aren't more here.'

'It is good to see you,' Olivia replied. 'I can't think of a finer companion for our journey into Avia.'

'Do you think that there might be room for a couple more?' Darreal called out, as he flew in fast over the top of the Great Owl's oak. At his side flew Pagen, and the two majestic birds swooped down without further ado, and joined the three already there.

There was much joy in their mutual greetings, and any individual nervousness about the morrow was lessened by the fact of their number.

'Peril is much easier to face when you're in good company,' Pagen said.

Storne nodded in agreement. 'The best,' he screeched loudly. 'The very best.'

Darreal joined in the good-humoured banter. 'Five of us. That's almost enough to hold a Council of our own. But then, maybe it's not such a good idea, after all. Whoever heard of a Council without any owls?'

'Who indeed?' A familiar hoot answered the falcon's jesting question, and, in seconds, Meldra had flapped down from her perch on her own oak tree, and joined them.

'How long have you been there?' Merion asked, intrigued by the owl's sudden appearance.

'I arrived this morning,' Meldra replied. 'I've been asleep since then, I'm afraid. You see, that was my tree when the Council meetings were held here, and there is such a comfortable nest-hole.'

Laughter drowned out the rest of her explanations, and another round of back-slapping and welcome started.

Finally, however, darkness took hold of the scene, and the birds settled into a comfortable, companionable silence, and waited for the dawn.

The governments of both countries met in celebration, and, all across the Continent, parties of welcome were held. Hosts and guests united in recognising the magnificent achievement. After a few drinks, language barriers magically disappeared, and bonhomie reigned supreme.

A somewhat more subdued celebration took place on an off-shore rig, fifteen miles from the coast of the now-empty island. The scientists there had every reason to be pleased with themselves. It had been their idea in the first place, and it was most gratifying to them that the nation had responded. Now the country was empty and their job could begin. Maybe the odd vagrant might have been left behind, but that could not be helped. To all intents and purposes, the task of evacuation had been achieved.

Now, at midnight, the clock could be set to countdown. The magnets would require twelve hours to reach full power – an inordinate length of time for producing a pulse that would last for scarcely more than a single second. But it would be enough. Every indication from their experiments confirmed this. Anything longer would be overkill, and a massive waste of expensive energy. As it was, the population would be paying for this for years to come. But what a benefit. No more insects to buzz and annoy; bite and sting.

The senior scientist cleared his throat. 'Ladies and gentlemen, this is an historic moment for our great country. The national sacrifice must be honoured and justified by our actions. We must not shirk from our duty. Killing is no pleasure for any of us, but we are being as merciful as we can possibly be. Remember why we are doing this: for the betterment of life for all of our people. Man has always battled with Nature, from pre-historic times, when he marked his achievements with daily survival in the face of terrifying predators, to the time when Man reached into space, defying gravity in his thirst for exploration and knowledge.

'It is in that spirit that today we join those great pioneers of human achievement. It is my particular honour, and privilege, to begin the countdown by pressing this switch. A countdown to an unforgettable moment in Man's history.'

Tomar found that the entrance to the tunnel was scarcely large enough to allow him passage, but he turned and thanked the tiny mouse, who smiled briefly and then scuttled off into the safety of the undergrowth.

'How on earth did they ever get Kraken down here?' he mused, then, shrugging his wings, entered the hole head-first and plunged into its gloom, noticing the coolness inside the tunnel, after the warmth of the mid-morning sun on his back. He was also immediately assailed by the smell. Acrid and fishy, it reeked of seagull, and nearly made the old owl retch. He persevered, however, and soon heard a plaintive whimpering coming from the darkness ahead. Kraken was calling out, but in a broken voice, dispirited and forlorn: 'Where is everybody? Help me. I need some food. I must stretch my wings. Is anybody there?'

Tomar called back, telling the great gull that he was coming, and that everything would be all right. Kraken's response was almost pathetic in its gratitude, and Tomar winced at how far the leader of the Great Flock had fallen. Turning a bend in the tunnel, Tomar could make out a light, presumably coming from the other entrance, and could see a large central chamber where Kraken slumped in a debris of fish-heads and faecal sacks. Tomar gulped, then forced a smile for the benefit of his old friend – realising the foolishness of this a second later.

'He can't see you, you fool,' he scolded himself softly, before calling out once more to the seagull. 'Kraken, my friend. It is Tomar. Do you remember me?'

'I'm blind, not senile!' Kraken snapped back immediately, before continuing apologetically. 'I am sorry, Tomar. Of course I remember my Great Owl. It has been many years, my friend. How have you been?'

'The years have not been kind to either of us, Kraken,' Tomar replied. 'But we are still here. Old and cranky we may be, but still very much alive. Now, let's get you out of here.'

Kraken's horrified reaction surprised Tomar. But then he realised that the events of the last couple of days must have given the seagull a severe fright. It would have been bad enough for any bird incarcerated in what was virtually a cell, but for one that was blind? Tomar could not begin to imagine what his friend must have felt. He knew that he would not be able to rush Kraken. He would need to take it slowly, and help his old friend rebuild his courage.

He sat quietly next to the seagull and, ignoring the noxious smell as best he could, chatted to him about old times and former glories. He could feel Kraken gradually relaxing, but it took a long time before he dared broach the subject of departure again. A look of concern flickered across the seagull's face, and he smiled bravely but nervously. Tomar reached forward, and touched the seagull's outstretched primaries with his own wing-tips.

'Don't let go!' Kraken's voice was a mixture of hope and despair.

'I haven't made this journey purely for the exercise, my friend. I will not let go. Now, can you stand?'

'Barely. The chamber gives me enough room but the tunnel is very narrow. I will try, though, but please keep talking. I can follow the sound of your voice if I lose contact with you.'

Tomar realised, with some shock, that Kraken was terrified of his solitude, but did as the great black-backed gull asked. 'It is much more difficult to get an owl to stop talking. Especially one who is so fond of his own voice. Oh, by the way, I met your son the other day. Pagen is a fine bird. You must be very proud of him.'

'Yes, I am,' Kraken answered, following his friend slowly up the long underground run. 'He has taken over the leadership of the flock in a most satisfactory manner.'

At this point, Kraken's voice betrayed his bitterness at the wing that Fate had dealt to him, and Tomar intervened swiftly.

'There were some other birds there that you might well remember: Storne and Darreal.'

Kraken's mood brightened at the mention of these names. 'A pair of scoundrels if ever any flew in Birddom!' he said, laughing deep in his craw.

'They send their greetings – to the biggest scoundrel of them all!' Tomar replied, matching the seagull's improved mood.

Their upward progress was slowed by the narrowness of the tunnel, and Tomar's awkwardness in trying to walk backwards, while keeping hold of one of Kraken's wings. Eventually, however, the old owl could feel the first stirrings of a breeze on his tail, and the air pushing past him became welcomingly fresh after the stench of the chamber. Wriggling free of the ground, Tomar backed out of the tunnel entrance, and, turning, came face to face with Traska.

'Look what the earth just spat out!' the magpie sneered, derisively. 'Not that I am surprised. I can't stomach you myself!'

Chapter Twenty Two

A low hum that resonated throughout the whole of Birddom commenced at first light. It was a natural sound, part of everyday life, but pitched at an unnatural intensity. It spoke of injustice and deep, deep anger. Billions of insects were communicating, gaining strength from the unity of their rage.

'Kill!' some said. 'Kill every bird in the land!'

'It will be done, but we must have patience for a few short hours more,' others replied, and their cautiousness prevailed. 'We have waited so long for our revenge, and have planned it so carefully. With the full height of the sun, we will be at our most active. Its warmth will give us the power to kill. We must wait until noon.'

'We will wait, because it will be worth waiting for. Not a single bird will sing for their supper tonight. Instead they will provide a great feast for all of us. We will dine on bird-flesh, my friends.'

This message buzzed through the enclaves, heightening the excitement of the billions that waited, and intensifying still further the wall of sound that echoed across the land. Every bird heard it and trembled, without knowing the cause. Not a single insect could be seen, but the noise confirmed that they had not chosen Man's path in abandoning the land. They could not be seen, but they could be heard.

The gathering of heroes in the Council ring could hear the hum of the insects, and it caused them great disquiet. They had stood together, some hours earlier, facing the rising sun at dawn with a mutual feeling of exhilaration. The day had finally come. Today they would enter into

Avia. But what had this eerie sound to do with the mystery? Did the insects somehow have a part to play? No. It was inconceivable that they were bound up in every bird's destiny. The sound was altogether wrong. There was immense anger in its music, which jarred with their notion of the joyous experience to come.

The six companions all started talking at once, as if, by so occupying themselves, they could stifle their individual fears, for each was clearly unnerved by the sounds that they heard.

'Will everywhere in Avia be as beautiful as this?' Merion asked, to no one in particular.

'More beautiful,' his sister replied. 'Birddom is a wonderful place, but Avia will be magical. Remember, it is a place where Man has never been, and so it will bear no trace of his blight, as Birddom does.'

'The water will be clean and pure,' Darreal promised.

'And don't forget, teeming with fish!' Pagen added.

'More than even you can eat!' said Storne. 'And there will be no disease. No bird will ever be sick again, and no predator will take advantage of one weakened by illness.'

'There will *be* no predators,' Meldra assured them. 'You cannot have a paradise with such enemies within its bounds, can you?'

'No,' Olivia replied. 'If Avia is as perfect a place as Tomar says it is, we will finally be free from all danger, and will live out our lives in perfect peace and contentment.'

'The perfect peace part would do for me right now,' Storne said, reluctantly acknowledging the continual hum of noise that pervaded even this quietest of places. And, as he spoke the words, each of the heroes' minds was refocused on that dreadful sound. What could the insects be doing? And would it interfere in any way with their journey into Avia?

*

Tomar's body blocked Traska's view of the entrance into Kraken's tunnel, and, alerted by the tensing of the owl's wing muscles when Tomar had registered the presence of the evil magpie, the seagull sat silently inside the tunnel and listened, with horror, to the voice of his old enemy.

'You have led me a merry dance, that is for sure. But look at you, you ragged old fool. You're covered in dust and cobwebs. What have you been up to? And you smell to high heaven. Have you been scavenging for rubbish like your friends, the gulls? Is that what you are forced to resort to now? What a long and wasted journey you must have had, and you supposed to be so clever. Any fool could have worked out that the seagulls would have been long gone, with Man trampling all over this place. I mean, just look at it. Whatever possessed you to come all this way in the first place?'

'What are you doing here?' Tomar asked, in an attempt to distract the magpie from his train of thought.

'Oh, that's simple. I followed you, my oldest and dearest friend, because I have decided that the time has come for me to end your life. You have plagued me for far too long, and enough is enough. I am going to kill you, Tomar, ex-Great Owl of Birddom. Oh, by the way, I am king now. Had you heard?'

'I have no time for the prattle of idiots,' the owl replied.

Anger flared in his opponent's eyes. 'I won't be looking so idiotic to you in a minute!' Traska screeched indignantly, and made as if to lunge forward at his adversary. Tomar forestalled him by taking several steps sideways, drawing the magpie's attention away from the entrance-hole.

'Have you the courage?' the owl taunted. 'You talk a great deal, but, if my memory serves, you have always found others to do your dirty work for you.'

'Don't forget Kirrick!' Traska snarled.

'No. I will never forget my friend. But that was an uneven contest and a sneak attack. You have never had the guts for a fair fight.'

'Well, here I am now, and ours will be a fair fight, right enough.'

As he spoke, the magpie hopped a little to his right, forcing Tomar to emerge from the shade of a rock into the bright sunlight. The sun was almost overhead, and there were few shadows to offer protection from its glare – a factor which would count against the usually-nocturnal owl. Tomar realised the evil magpie's intentions, and yet saw at once how they might be used to his own advantage. He continued to circle around the magpie, until Traska now stood where he had a minute before.

Inside the mouth of the tunnel, Kraken seethed with anger. He had unfinished business with this bird. This cruel and wicked magpie, who had stolen the life of his daughter all those years ago. Robbed of his sight, the seagull's other senses had sharpened remarkably. Now that the fresh air had cleared the stench out of his nostrils, Kraken could smell his adversary. And his keen hearing could pinpoint the magpie's position. So long as Tomar could keep Traska talking...

The stored energy in the vast array of magnets that totally encircled Birddom was reaching its maximum. Each huge metal structure vibrated with a deep musical hum, which acted as a bass counterpoint to the buzz of the insects. The latter rose and intensified as the excitement level increased. Acting now as one massive organism, the insect nation prepared itself for battle. Barely able to contain the mounting thrill of anger within its ranks, the beast screamed out its warning to the world: 'Soon. Very soon!'

The sun was a mere degree or two away from its zenith, but

Nature's own clock was not sufficiently precise for Man's needs. His countdown was ordered by the latest technology, and the very finest of precision instrumentation. On the other hand, short of an event that would signal the end of the universe, the sun had no parts that could break down. The electronic timer did, however. At exactly five minutes before noon, the clock stopped.

This went unnoticed for thirty seconds only, before a junior technician on the oil-rig spotted the problem. After jumping several feet in the air with shock, he reported the failure to his superior. A back-up system had been provided, of course, for such an eventuality, but, upon inspection, this was found to be lacking an ordinary cell battery. The irony of this, when so much stored energy had been pumped into the magnets onshore, was lost on the man in charge, who proceeded, with quiet anger, to unclip his wrist-watch ostentatiously from his left arm, and to order that control be switched to manual-override.

'At what point did the countdown stop?' he demanded.

'Five minutes to go, sir,' the young man answered, nervously.

'Right then. We are at D minus five and counting from... now.'

The scientist ignored the questioning look in his subordinate's eyes. So, they would be a couple of minutes late. What of it? What possible difference could a couple of minutes make?

Nothing seemed to be happening. The group of heroes stared at each other, uncomprehending. Oh, nothing had ever been said about the precise timing of any possible event that would lead to the gateway being revealed, but every bird there had assumed that noon was a logical point in the day for such a revelation. But, now that it had all but been reached, they were at a loss as to what to do next. Should they simply continue to wait? After all, the day still had twelve hours to go.

Or had they somehow got it horribly wrong? Had they misunderstood Septimus' urgent message about the timing? Had Tomar jumped to conclusions and, if so, how could they know when the gateway to Avia would appear?

Nothing was happening, except for the constant and menacing hum that filled their heads and drove them to distraction. A sound that rose with each passing minute, becoming more strident and more urgent. But what did it mean? All they had were questions, and the heroes, large and small, felt their failure keenly.

'We have made fools of ourselves,' thought Storne. 'Everyone in Birddom will laugh at us when this day is over.'

'We've made a mistake,' Olivia told herself. 'It doesn't seem possible that there can be any other explanation. Tomar must have been wrong, after all. Perhaps he really is too old?'

Darreal's thoughts took him on a more resentful track. 'Waste of bloody time!' he grumbled, and then checked himself at the change of sound. The insect hum had altered pitch and timbre, as if a trap-door had been opened, and the tight expression of rage had finally been given its freedom. Was this the signal? Did the insects hold the key to Avia after all?

Merion noticed the new sound before the others. Initially it was very low and soft, almost entirely drowned out by the buzz of the approaching insects. But it grew louder, like a rushing wind. A mournful sound, that built and built until they could hear nothing else.

All across Birddom, birds gathered together in their thousands. Each massive crowd was an exotic mix of species, and every bird there drew strength from the multitude – reassuring themselves and quelling their doubts. Each looked at their neighbour and thought, 'Well, he believes in Tomar's Avia, or he wouldn't be here. It must be true. We will be saved!'

The need for reassurance was great indeed. For Birddom seemed suddenly full of menace. Tomar's messengers had warned that their land, as they knew it, was finished, and now the dreadful sounds all around seemed to confirm this. The terrible and ever-increasing noise of the stirring insects, that had begun shortly after dawn, had been compounded in the last hour by an ominous unnatural hum, which unnerved all in the gathering and made them huddle closer together for comfort.

Was this the sound of the apocalypse? And would their salvation come in time? They had been promised a gateway into a better world, but their fear of the present peril ate away at their faith in that glorious future. They had been told of the need to find a state of mind – a tranquil acceptance – that would help them to face the trials to come. But, now, as their ears registered a new sound and their eyes told them what they could scarcely believe, the collective state of mind was one of pure terror.

'Come on then, get it over with.'

Tomar faced his enemy without fear. He had lived long enough in this world, and had tried to serve it as best he could. If he was now to die, so be it. He would have liked to have seen Avia before he died, but maybe that was not the Creator's will.

'A pleasure like this should not be rushed,' the magpie answered, and his taunting comment gave the old owl an idea. Screaming suddenly, more for Kraken's benefit than for himself, Tomar launched himself at the evil magpie, forcing Traska to retreat a few steps to avoid the thrust. It was enough. Kraken's heightened senses served him well. Judging, with pinpoint accuracy, the position of his enemy, the seagull flung himself forward out of the mouth of the tunnel, and wrapped his wings tightly around Traska. To the magpie's utter astonishment, he was now pinned to the ground by an adversary who had taken him completely by surprise. Squirming desperately to free himself, and, at the same time, to avoid the seagull's deadly beak, Traska fought for his life.

Tomar was mesmerised by the effectiveness of his friend's attack, and paused for a vital second before rushing to Kraken's aid. But, at that moment, all three birds froze, stricken by the sound that assailed their ears. It couldn't be happening! Such a thing was not possible! Not in Birddom. But there could be no mistaking that sound. A baying, throaty roar that swept towards them at astonishing speed: the howling of wolves.

Tomar jerked around to face the source of that sound, and instantaneously the fear etched upon his face was replaced by a beatific smile. Of course! How could it be otherwise? There had been so many clues. Tomar stood erect, and began to walk slowly toward the approaching pack.

It was left to Traska to voice his astonishment. 'I don't believe it!' he gasped. 'There must be hundreds of them!'

And, as he said this, it seemed that he, too, realised some of the significance of what was happening. The evil magpie renewed his struggles to free himself from Kraken's clutches, but the seagull held on desperately.

'Let me go!' Traska screamed. 'I will *not* be denied again. Tomar will never make it into Avia, not while I have any breath in my body!'

But Kraken held on fast, and the evil magpie could only watch, in impotent rage, as Tomar walked towards his destiny.

*

They came at the speed of the wind, their paws devouring the ground beneath them as they ran. Their soft, grey fur streamed out along their flanks, and their golden eyes gleamed with zeal at their mission. As robin and owl, falcon, eagle and seagull watched, transfixed, a mighty wave of wolves swept over the rim of the Council ring, and raced towards the clearing. Hundreds of tongues lolled from salivating jaws. Hundreds of pairs of ears rejoiced in their triumphal howl, as they thundered towards the small band of Birddom's heroes. Not one of them thought for a moment about attempting to escape. Not that it would have been possible. The wolves came on at an astonishing speed, covering the distance between them in the twinkling of an eye.

Merion called out to his friends, trying to be heard above the all-encompassing song of the wolves, 'Do not be afraid. The time is come. Make yourselves ready, my friends.'

Turning to Olivia, he reached out to her with his wing. 'I love you, my dear sister. And I will see you again in Avia.'

She returned his touch, and looked at him with eyes that shone with ecstatic fervour.

'We are saved, Merion!' she cried, and launched herself towards the nearest wolf, with a song of joy that thrilled all who heard it.

Merion watched her with a full heart, and then turned placidly to face the creature who had singled him out. He closed his eyes, and then opened them in realisation, staring into the gape of the wolf's jaws – blood-red and black beyond. A living, breathing thing.

'The tunnel!' he sighed, and then was gone.

Many birds throughout the land managed to find that courage within themselves. Faced with onrushing death and without hope, they acquiesced at the last and accepted their fate with stoic hearts and calm minds. The packs of ravening wolves swept through them, taking their fill to left and to right. But no blood was spilled, wherever the huge creatures perceived goodness. The false alone suffered an agonising end, perishing at the very gates to paradise.

Some corvids survived, for the Creator is not vengeful and recognises a contrite heart. But most paid the full price for their wickedness in elevating an evil idol in his place. Their folly in believing in Traska, and in his promises which fuelled their baser instincts, now cost them dear. Their bodies were rent asunder, and their life-blood stained the land across the length and breadth of Birddom. And still the wolves moved swiftly and inexorably onward, in accordance with their given role, saving or damning as they raced across the land.

Desire for his own salvation made Kraken falter in his task. His wings slackened their grip on the magpie, and, instantly, Traska sprang from his grasp. The evil bird raced forward to thwart Tomar in reaching his goal, but he was too late. The wolves had descended upon the old owl, and left no trace of him in their wake.

Traska suddenly realised the peril that he had placed himself in, for now the eyes of the pack were fixed upon him. Turning on his tail, he fled back towards Kraken. But the seagull was not his objective. Kraken, disorientated by the rush and swirl of sounds, felt something brush past him, and tried to grab a hold of the fleeing magpie. But his wings folded onto empty air. Traska raced for the safety of the seagull's tunnel, and dived into its rank depth a split-second before the wolves flowed, in an inexorable tide, over the entrance and onward, over the cliff itself.

But no wolf fell to its death upon the jagged rocks below. They vanished into the air, as if they were as insubstantial as mist. They had done their work, taking the seagull last of all, and now responded to the call of their leader, and returned to their homes. Septimus' howl rang out across the land, and Birddom emptied of its ghostly horde, the wolves disappearing as swiftly as they had come.

Traska emerged, blinking, into the noon sunlight. He was dishevelled and dirty, and his body felt bruised and battered all over, both from Kraken's unwelcome attentions, and from his incautious flight into the depths of the narrow tunnel. Guano smeared his black and white feathers, and cobwebs hung limply from his long tail. However, he could not help but feel happy. He was alive. He, probably alone in all of Birddom, had cheated Fate. The others, the goody-goodies, may have gone to Avia, or they may, just as likely, have simply been eaten, in their foolish quest for salvation.

He, Traska, was alive. He had defied the Creator – and had won. Here he was, the king of all Birddom. The whole land was his, and nothing could mar his intense feeling of pleasure. It was almost a sensual thing. So what if there were no birds left to rule over. Birds weren't the only creatures who made up the natural population. Now that Man was gone, there was nothing to stop him. He would rule over the animals. Sure, many of them might be bigger than him, but none of them had his brains. His genius!

Traska revelled in the tranquillity of his domain. 'What a beautiful place!' he crowed aloud, ignoring the carpet of litter all around him. 'So resplendent in its autumn glory. My land. My kingdom. So quiet and peaceful.'

But all was not quiet, and, if Traska believed it to be so, he was deluding himself. An angry hum cut through the silence, and a deep, mechanical throbbing underscored it, both sounds delivering a promise of impending retribution. Traska shivered, and looked skyward. One minute the warmth of the sun beat down upon his back from directly overhead. The next, a cloud appeared. A cloud that moved impossibly fast, given the prevailing wind. A cloud that increased in size, until it stretched from horizon to horizon, blocking out the sun as it approached.

Traska yelled at it, angrily. 'Go back! I command you. For I am king of the world, and ruler over all of Nature. Go back, I say!'

It seemed at first as if Nature did not recognise its new ruler. For the cloud descended upon him with frightening swiftness, and this time there was no time, and nowhere to flee to.

Traska waved his wing futilely at the huge swarm of insects. 'Be gone!' he screamed.

And the insects fell at his feet. Not that Traska bore witness to his own triumph. He too lay dead where he had stood. For it was two minutes past midday, and time had finally run out for Birddom.

Epilogue

The light blinded the old owl. Everything shone with a crystalline brilliance. Tomar hopped slowly and uncertainly into a landscape that resonated with health and vitality. The colours seemed more defined, and everything pulsed with an inner glow. And everywhere there were birds. Birds of every colour, size and shape. They cavorted and played, rejoicing in their beautiful new home. The old owl shared in that joy, for he knew that this was Avia, and that many of his flock had made the journey into paradise.

'Welcome!'

The voice seemed to come from inside his own head, and yet it was everywhere, all around him. And he looked into the eyes of a rabbit. A rabbit who was just as Merion had described him, but who was so much more, as Tomar had guessed. The rabbit smiled, and Tomar bathed in the warmth of his Creator's love, feeling renewed and reborn. The cares and worries of Birddom, which he had carried for so long upon his great back, fell away, and his heart sang with joy.

'What kept you so long?'

The tawny owl's head turned rapidly at the sound. He remembered that voice. And there he was, as large as life, although, in reality, tiny in comparison to the owl himself.

'Kirrick!' Tomar cried out, in joy and disbelief.

'How good it is to see you again, my dear friend,' the robin responded, flying up to embrace the amazed owl.

Tomar's gaze moved from point to point, as he recognised another voice, another face. He let his huge eyes graze happily upon the scene, devouring each sight that met them. They were all there.

Portia flitted over to join her husband. And Merion and Olivia danced in circles, a spontaneous expression of their delight. Storne and Darreal waved their great wings, and screeched out a welcome. A little to one side, father and son embraced warmly, as Kraken held on to Pagen's face, staring deeply into the young gull's eyes with purest joy. Everywhere, there were scenes of greeting and celebration, as all the birds revelled in their wonderful new surroundings. Portia had turned momentarily from her husband's embrace to call out a welcome to Mickey, and the bullfinch looked up from his jovial banter with Kopa and Cian, and responded with a cheerful cheep of his own.

The owls were all there, too. Every Council member, past and present. So many heroes and heroines of Birddom. So many dear, dear friends. Tomar wept openly on seeing Cerival, and went immediately to meet his mentor.

'Well done, Tomar,' Cerival said. 'Only you could have achieved this. For you have not only saved every good bird in Birddom, but you have also made Avia itself whole. It was ever meant to be a paradise for the living as well as the dead and, for those of us who dwelt here, it fell just short of perfection, although we could not have told you why. But it is perfect now, Tomar. Welcome home, my friend!'

ACKNOWLEDGMENTS

To my two sons, Chris and Dave – the creators of Birddom

To Mum and Dad – for starting me off, boy, man and writer

To Franc, publisher and friend – for taking the chance,
and so much more

To Sam – for the first review, and the hard work that followed

To Dotti and Ruth – for lifting me out of the ordinary

To Geoff and Jim – for giving me wings

To Liz and Barrie – for seeing something and doing something

To Eilish and John – for encouragement